# The Princess Match

## by Clare Lydon

custard books

First Edition March 2025
Published by Custard Books
Copyright © 2025 Clare Lydon
ISBN: 978-1-912019-30-4

Cover Design: Sharn Hutton
Editor: Cheyenne Blue
Typesetting: Adrian McLaughlin

Find out more at: www.clarelydon.co.uk
Buy direct at: clarelydon.shop
Facebook: www.facebook.com/clare.lydon
Instagram: @clarefic

# Also By Clare Lydon

## Other Novels
A Taste Of Love
Before You Say I Do
Change Of Heart
Christmas In Mistletoe
Don't Marry Me At Christmas
Hotshot
It Started With A Kiss
Just Kiss Her
Nothing To Lose: A Lesbian Romance
Once Upon A Princess
One Golden Summer
The Christmas Catch
The Long Weekend
Twice In A Lifetime
You're My Kind

## London Romance Series
London Calling (Book One)
This London Love (Book Two)
A Girl Called London (Book Three)
The London Of Us (Book Four)
London, Actually (Book Five)
Made In London (Book Six)
Hot London Nights (Book Seven)
Big London Dreams (Book Eight)
London Ever After (Book Nine)

## All I Want Series
Two novels and four novellas chart the course
of one relationship over two years.

Get great bundle deals and other offers when you
buy direct at clarelydon.shop!

# Acknowledgements

The inspiration for this book struck in the year after the Euros, when a steady stream of triumphant Lionesses visited Windsor Palace to receive their MBEs. Seeing them receiving their medals from Prince William sparked a thought: "What if the heir to the throne was a woman, and she fell for a footballer?" Thus, *The Princess Match* was born. These 'what if?' moments often lead to my favourite stories, and I hope this becomes one of yours. And since practically every London-based female footballer seems to live in St Albans, it felt natural for Ash to call it home, too!

My deepest gratitude goes to my brilliant bunch of early readers, whose enthusiastic praise gave me the confidence to share this story with the world. Their sharp eyes caught countless inconsistencies, typos, and missing words (my speciality, unfortunately!). Their encouragement means everything: I couldn't ask for better champions.

As always, I'm indebted to the professionals who polished this book to perfection: Cheyenne for her brilliant editing, Sharn for creating such a stunning debut cover, and Adrian for his impeccable typesetting. Publishing truly takes a village, and my village continues to amaze me.

All my love to my beautiful wife, Yvonne. This year has

been fraught with stress (hello renovation!), but she is my constant voice of reason, and calms me down when I feel like it's all about to tip over the edge. Having someone who believes in me unconditionally is the best gift.

Finally, thank you, dear reader. In these challenging political and economic times, I'm grateful for every purchase and every message. Without you, I'd be writing into the void. This marks my 27th novel, a number that still astonishes me. I might need to plan something extraordinary when I reach the big 3-0! Until then, keep smiling, keep hoping, and keep believing in happy endings. I promise to keep writing them.

If you fancy getting in touch, you can do so using one of the methods below. I'm most active on Instagram.

Contact: mail@clarelydon.co.uk
Facebook: www.facebook.com/clare.lydon
Instagram: @clarefic
TikTok: @clarelydonauthor
Find out more at: www.clarelydon.co.uk

**Thank you so much for reading!**

*I hope this book serves as a reminder
that you deserve your own queen.*

*Crown optional, feelings mandatory.*

# Chapter One

Ashleigh Woods had faced down a penalty shootout in the European Cup final, but nothing had prepared her for the challenge of walking in heels across the polished floors of Buckingham Palace. If she face-planted in front of Prince Michael when he was about to award her MBE, she might have to leave this planet and never return. Maybe life on Mars wouldn't be so bad. Who knew what kind of football league they had? Maybe she could be a standout creative midfielder there, too. Captain of her country. One of the best on a whole new planet.

"Your Royal Highness," she whispered under her breath for approximately the 37th time that morning. "I am *deeply* honoured. Or is it 'I am *most deeply* honoured'?" She frowned. Her agent, Marianne, had been specific about which one sounded posher, but could Ash recall which one they'd landed on?

She could not.

Marianne had spent 20 minutes last night drilling her on protocol. "Don't worry," she'd told Ash as she shoved a pair of murder-weapon heels into her reluctant hands. "He's easy-going. I've met him before at functions. Just don't lean into the football angle. Apparently, he's more of a rugby man."

"I know zero about rugby, except that they pass the

ball backwards, which is all sorts of weird." Ash paused. "I shouldn't ask about his recent bout of falling out of nightclubs in the early hours of the morning, either?"

"Please don't," Marianne had replied. "And for god's sake, remember it's 'Your Royal Highness' the first time he addresses you, then it's 'Sir'. Under no circumstances should you switch to Mike or Mickey."

"No Prince Mickey, got it."

Ash had met Prime Minister Angela Fallon last month at a function, and accidentally called her Ange when she said goodbye. To her credit, the Prime Minister had simply laughed. Marianne and Ash's mum had gone a deathly shade of green when she told them. It was one of Ash's strengths but also a curse. She chatted to anybody. She cut to the chase, as her dad always pointed out. Apparently, she should steer clear of that with a prince.

"Your Royal Highness," Ash muttered again as she carefully navigated the corridor. "I am most deeply honoured... then 'Sir'... then something about it being a team game, steering clear of too much footy chat. Then shut up before I say anything ridiculous."

Another aristocratic-looking woman glided past with enviable grace, shooting Ash a concerned look as she continued her whispered rehearsal. Ash wriggled her toes inside her heels and wished for the umpteenth time she'd worn flat shoes. However, both her stylist, Luke, and Marianne, had been insistent she wore heels. She'd joked she should have worn her lucky football boots, but they'd make far too much noise. Just imagining her studs click-clacking on the polished wooden floors made her smile.

Plus, like most ballers, Ash was superstitious. She only wore her lucky boots on a serious matchday. Sure, today was important, but it wasn't as big as that day last year when she'd scored the winning goal in the European Cup final. The day football had come home. It was part of the reason she was here at Buckingham Palace, receiving this prestigious award.

She'd YouTubed previous MBE ceremonies obsessively: 30 seconds of walking, a brief chat, then a handshake from a (possibly balding) royal. Simple. Straightforward. She had it all planned out, right down to the acceptable number of seconds to hold eye contact. (Three to five, according to the internet, although Marianne said the upper end sounded a bit serial killer-ish.)

"Right this way, Ms Woods," a uniformed attendant gestured, and Ash managed what she hoped was a dignified nod. The Palace corridor stretched before her, its walls lined with portraits of stern-faced monarchs whose eyes all seemed to follow her. Ash smiled back at them as if they had a hotline to her agent and might be taking notes. Wherever her excited parents were, she hoped they weren't chewing the ears off the friends and family of the other honourees. Debra and Mark loved to chat about their daughter, captain of the England Women's Football team. Ash secretly loved it, too.

"Your Royal Highness," she whispered, practising one final time.

A throaty, arresting laugh echoed from around the corner, stopping Ash in her tracks. Whatever the joke, the recipient found it hilarious. She carried on walking, and through an open doorway ahead, she caught a glimpse of emerald-green silk, and dark hair that fell in waves past elegant shoulders, a profile that definitely didn't belong to Prince Michael. A woman leaned against an ornate desk, head thrown back in genuine amusement at something someone had said.

Ash blinked. If she wasn't mistaken, that was Princess Victoria. Heir to the throne. Also, women's football fan.

She gulped. Princess Victoria had attended a couple of England games last year, but Ash hadn't met her, having been sidelined with an MCL injury. Victoria hadn't made it to the European Cup final in Sweden either, as she had to attend a world summit in a far-flung place. No matter, the King had turned up to shake hands and show support. Was Princess Victoria handing out the medals today instead of her brother? Was Ash finally going to meet the elusive princess?

If so, that was a whole different ballgame.

Ash was skilled at those.

She smoothed down the lapel on her Gucci black-and-white chequered suit and cleared her throat.

It was nearly time for kick-off.

\* \* \*

Someone promptly shut the door to the room where Princess Victoria was, and Ash was shown upstairs to the Picture Gallery, which hummed with nervous energy. Again, she was surrounded by elite artworks and gilt-framed mirrors, their ornate frames catching the sunlight that streamed through the overhead skylights. Ash stood among clusters of other recipients, all of them trying very hard not to look out of place, which was sort of impossible. The only people who looked normal in these surroundings were royals. She sniffed the air. Somebody had flashed a can of Pledge nearby recently.

"Esteemed guests, can I have your attention please?" A uniformed attendant with an authoritative voice got the attention he desired.

"There's been a slight change of plan this morning. Prince Michael is unable to attend the ceremony due to illness. Filling in for him is his sister, Princess Victoria, the Princess Royal. Twenty minutes until the ceremony begins. Please see Ruth on the left to double-check the running order. Many thanks, and this is a day to celebrate your achievements. Remember to smile."

A frisson of excitement rushed around the room. This was an upgrade, everyone knew that. Princess Victoria was the future Queen, next in line to the throne. The tips of Ash's ears tingled with warmth. She was about to meet Princess Victoria, who'd just been announced as the new patron of the Women's Football Association. One thing was certain: Ash was going to have to up her chat game.

Ash's best friend and England goalie Cam Holloway had a particular soft spot for Princess Victoria: "She's got these deep-blue eyes you could very easily get lost in." Ash was determined that wasn't going to happen today. Even if her throat had gone that bit drier in the past few seconds since the news.

Where was Cam to bat some ideas around when she needed her? Let her know what Victoria liked and didn't? Somewhere in the back of Ash's mind, she seemed to recall Cam telling her the princess was a fan of cold-water swimming. However, to casually drop that into conversation while Victoria was pinning her MBE to her lapel would be a little weird.

Ash walked towards Ruth, a no-nonsense woman with a

clipboard who Ash was sure had a range of sturdy waterproofs at home for the long hikes she took with her wife. Sure enough, when it was Ash's turn to be name-checked, Ruth glanced up, then promptly blushed bright purple.

"You need to stand in the MBE group, to the right of the ante-chamber door. The door staff there will confirm your ceremony number and tell you when to walk out." She leaned in. "Could I get a selfie with you when I've finished the checks?" Ruth glanced down at the floor before addressing Ash in a low whisper. "I'm a huge fan. Still buzzing about the Euros a year on!"

Ash grinned. Her gaydar never failed. She could spot a queer from 20 paces. It was a special skill of hers. "Of course." She gestured to Ruth's right. "I'll stand here until you're done."

Five minutes later, she'd taken no less than seven selfies with other fans, which she was glad to do, because it took her mind off what was about to happen. She was about to be awarded an MBE. Ashleigh Woods, the girl from St Albans. She still couldn't quite believe it.

She checked her phone: she had a message from her best mate and Lioness goalkeeper, Cam.

> No falling over in front of Prince Michael. Falling at the feet of a man is a very bad look for a lesbian.

> Change of plan, it's Princess Victoria giving out the awards.

Cam was typing her return message almost before Ash had finished her own.

> In that case, remember to be extra charming to our new FA Women's Patron. And tell her hi from me.

Ash sent back a salute emoji, then grinned. Trust Cam to break her steadily building tension. She could always rely on her best friend for that. She'd been a particular rock last summer, after Ash's break-up with her ex, Danielle, who'd cheated on her. When Danielle transferred to a new team, Ash had been grateful. However, when Danielle then plastered her new romance all over her socials, it had stung, making Ash feel like their three years together meant nothing.

The past year, she'd had to cope with Danielle's new romance playing out to fevered online speculation about how she felt about it. She'd taken herself off her socials over the past few months, letting her PR team post whenever she had something to promote. Having lived a romance publicly, she was keen to do her next one in private. It made life a lot simpler.

Ash clicked to the *Mail Online*: they were speculating about Princess Victoria and her boyfriend, Dexter Matthews, who was seen ring shopping at the weekend. Could an engagement be on the cards? Ash made a mental note that it wasn't appropriate to ask that question, either.

Instead, she leaned against the wall and googled 'cold-water swimming'. She did ice baths for recovery, and that was bad enough. She couldn't imagine doing it for fun. Where did princesses do it, though? Did Victoria have a special private pond? Just her and three bodyguards watching her dodgy front crawl?

Half an hour later, she was beckoned forward, and told to be ready in three minutes. Ash was used to pressured situations in front of large crowds, but somehow, this was worse. Maybe because she was on her own, without the backup of her teammates? Ash was very much a team player. Individual accolades for a team sport made her uncomfortable. But she wasn't going to turn down an MBE.

The three minutes soon evaporated, and she stood on the precipice.

"Miss Ashleigh Woods, Member of the Most Excellent Order of the British Empire."

The announcement rang clear through the Throne Room. Ash scanned the heads twisting to see her, then blocked out the crowd. Just as in a game, she had to focus on what was in front of her. Red patterned carpet. A distant gold throne, and a princess.

Twenty steps. That's all it was. Twenty steps up to where the Princess Royal stood, sunlight from the tall windows catching the subtle gleam of her expensive necklace. Ash focused on keeping her pace steady, the way she did when taking a penalty: not too fast, not too slow. Around her, the ballroom held its breath, hundreds of eyes following her progress.

Seventeen steps. The Princess's posture was perfect, of course, the green silk Ash had caught a glimpse of earlier encasing her body perfectly.

Thirteen steps. Their eyes met. The Princess's were dark, intelligent, holding Ash's gaze with startling directness.

The front of Ash's shoe caught on something, but she corrected. Thank goodness for her core strength. If she fell, she would *never* hear the end of it.

Eleven steps. The princess's lips curved slightly, not quite a smile, more like she'd noticed Ash's momentary stumble and found it amusing.

Heat crept up Ash's neck.

Nine steps. Focus, Woods. Just like Marianne said. Step, breathe, don't trip.

But with each step closer, the air seemed to grow thicker. The princess's gaze hadn't wavered.

Seven steps. The princess shifted her weight slightly, and her fingers tightened around Ash's medal.

Five steps. Ash was close enough now to see the precise arch of her dark eyebrows, the subtle perfume with a hint of musk, the way the princess's throat moved as she swallowed.

Three steps. The princess's composed expression flickered for just a moment, as something unreadable passed behind her eyes.

Two steps. Ash's heart was doing the same thing it did before crucial matches, hammering against her ribs like it was trying to escape. She gritted her teeth, but then remembered to smile.

One step. Should she curtsy? Even the word made her cringe. She couldn't curtsy. It went against every lesbian bone in her body. Instead, she briefly bowed her head, then looked up into the bluest eyes possible.

Cam was right. Ash could very much see herself drowning in them.

Princess Victoria held out a hand. The press of her fingers was warm, and her touch sent static through Ash's bones. Her eyes widened, while the princess's neutral expression softened into something more genuine, more surprised.

"Miss Woods." Her voice was low, musical, the same as the throaty laugh from earlier. "Congratulations on your award, and it's lovely to finally meet you in person. You've been absent when I visited the Lionesses. But I have to tell you, I watched your European Cup final performance and your penalty. Extraordinary composure under pressure. You've more than earned this award."

Ash's carefully memorised response evaporated. The princess hadn't just said the usual congratulations followed by a stock line. She'd actually watched her play.

"Thank you, Your Highness." Did she forget to say Royal? Shit. She winced, then stopped. It was okay. She hadn't muttered the words Princess Vicky, and that was a win. As was the fact her voice remained steady, even though the princess's intense gaze was almost like a physical touch. "Though meeting you is considerably more nerve-wracking."

The princess's smile reached her eyes. "No need to be nervous. You've done the hard bit by not falling over. All you have to do now is smile for your photographs." Victoria leaned in and pinned the medal to the hook on Ash's lapel with perfectly steady hands.

Their eyes met once more as Ash straightened, and for a moment, the vast ballroom with all its hundreds of witnesses seemed to fade away. Giddiness popped inside her like a fresh bottle of champagne.

"By the way, I love your outfit. It really suits you. Gucci?"

Ash nodded.

"You wear it well."

Ash blinked, still processing the princess's words as she gave her a small nod.

A dismissal.

Ash backed away the required three steps before turning.

She was still blinking, her mind a blank white slate as she sat down next to the woman who'd been before her. Beryl, who'd devoted her life to helping the homeless. A far greater feat than kicking a ball around a pitch for a few years. Beryl smiled at her, and touched her own medal.

Ash looked down at hers, and did the same. The princess's fingers had just been on it, too.

She also wasn't sure if she was going mad, but she could swear her gaydar went off in Princess Victoria's presence. But even as the thought passed through her brain, she dismissed it. Ash was being ridiculous.

Princess Victoria had been in a long-term relationship with her boyfriend, Dexter Matthews, for years. Everybody knew that. She was the furthest from gay Ash could imagine. Posturing otherwise was just wishful thinking on her part.

Then again, her gaydar rarely malfunctioned.

# Chapter Two

It was gone 3pm when the last guests left, and Victoria could finally take off her carefully manufactured royal smile. Her brother, Michael, said she was born with it in place, whereas he had to work far harder to achieve it. Victoria wished she had some of Michael's arrogance and bluster sometimes. However, as her younger brother, his actions didn't matter as much to her parents.

Whereas Victoria was next in line to the throne. *Everything* she did mattered. Including how she looked, how she smiled, how she pretended every day to be something she wasn't. Michael could afford to smile on his own terms. Whereas for Victoria, that right had been taken away at birth. But she wore the pressure well, because she knew it came with great privilege. As her mother always told her, "Never complain about the opportunities the Crown affords you. Make it fun, and what you want it to be."

However, making it what she wanted did not include being the first queer monarch, apparently.

Victoria headed down the back stairs, into the courtyard and out past the pool. She poked her head in the door, but her brother wasn't there. He often went for a swim to get rid of a hangover. She hadn't seen him so far today, apart from a sheepish text that thanked her for saving his life. She'd messaged back to let him know he owed her one.

In reality, he owed her at least 50 by now.

Her phone buzzed in her pocket. Recently, she'd found a designer who could make her dresses with pockets. It made the world of difference. Having a pocket made her feel like she could be at least ten per cent herself, and ten per cent was better than nothing.

When Victoria saw who was calling, she grinned, then swiped.

"You survived then?" Dexter's warm voice crackled through the phone. No matter what, Dex could always make her smile. It was the reason they worked so well, and had been so successful at their public charade for so long. "No international incidents? Nobody tried to overthrow the monarchy?"

Victoria kept walking, her heels sinking slightly into the immaculate lawn. She waved at Amelia, the head gardener, hard at work in a rose bush.

"I managed to award 53 medals without starting a constitutional crisis," she told him. "Though your lack of faith in my abilities is touching."

"Careful, someone might think you're actually getting good at this princess business."

She should laugh. This was their usual rhythm; him teasing, her playing along with the joke. The perfect friendship masquerading as a perfect romance for the papers. But all she could think about was the way Ashleigh Woods' eyes had widened when they met hers, that flash of startled recognition that had nothing to do with Victoria's title and everything to do with something else entirely.

Could she tell? Victoria would be lying if she said she wasn't rattled.

But also, intrigued.

"Vic?" Dexter's voice softened. "You've gone quiet. Is everything actually okay?"

He cared. She knew that. You couldn't have the bond they had, and have been through what they had, without a huge dollop of mutual respect and love.

She shoved her free hand into her dress pocket. "Of course. I'm always fine, you know me. I'm the reliable princess."

"Have you seen Michael yet and given him what for?"

"He's hiding."

Victoria approached the stone summer house her mother and father, Queen Cassandra and King Oliver, had authorised last summer. Previously, there had only been a far smaller, white summer house with an open front held up by statuesque pillars. It was still there, but the Queen had built a modern structure further along the perimeter wall with a sturdy roof, windows and doors. It was watertight, which was far more appropriate for the British weather.

Crucially, it was that rare thing in Buckingham Palace: a space away from prying eyes, with a kettle, a comfy sofa, and, amusingly, a pool table. Her mother had asked what she most wanted in there, and that had been Victoria's answer. She'd always wanted to learn. She dreamed of going out on London's queer scene, of playing a game of pool as a lesbian rite of passage. But if that was never going to happen, she could at least spend the occasional afternoon teaching herself how to play. She'd learned the basics from YouTube. All she needed now was practice.

She fished the key from her pocket, opened the door and walked over to the small kitchen on one side of the room.

"He might turn up when he realises I'm in the summerhouse."

She opened the American-style fridge and surveyed its contents. Wine, champagne, ham, cheese, olives, burrata, hummus, carrot sticks. There were also two rogue cans of some IPA with elaborate artwork on the can that showed Michael had also been here, practising without her. Last time out, she'd beaten him. She was determined her winning streak would continue.

"Not after the way you demolished him at pool last week. Is everything really okay? You sound a bit weird."

She shook her head even though he couldn't see her. "I'm fine. I got to meet some interesting people for 30 seconds at a time today. Like some weird sort of speed-dating. Including that hot actor who's the villain in the latest James Bond movie. I thought of you."

"Lucky you," Dexter replied. "Whereas I'm stuck in Stockholm for the next couple of nights, working on some deal with Dad. Wish I could have met him, too."

"Probably best you didn't." She gave a wry smile.

"Anybody else famous who might make me drool?"

"That buff diver you like from the Olympics, but he had all his clothes on."

"Blond or dark hair?" Always with the details, her Dexter.

"Dark."

"Shame about the clothes."

"I also got to pin an MBE to Ashleigh Woods. Who was just as striking in the flesh as she looks on TV." Victoria had admired Ash's firm thighs through a TV screen, but up close, it was her mesmeric green eyes that had caught her attention.

"I think I saw her on the BBC website posing with it already. She looked hot in her designer suit. She plays for your team, doesn't she?"

"In what sense?" But even as she said the words, she blushed.

"In every sense, darling."

Victoria couldn't help a grin as she put the kettle on and grabbed some rooibos tea bags from the cupboard above the sink. People didn't think royals made themselves tea, but she did. She couldn't imagine not doing the simple things every day. Whereas Michael needed a little more encouragement.

"I think you might be right."

*Extraordinary composure under pressure*, Victoria had said to Ashleigh, and meant it. She'd watched that European Cup final from Buenos Aires, and held her breath along with the rest of the country as Ash stepped up to take that final penalty.

"And did you say anything to her? Tell her you admire her ball skills almost as much as her shapely legs? Invite her over for a game of pool?"

If she was a normal person, perhaps she would have. But those things didn't happen in Victoria's life. She'd had a string of liaisons with other women in her situation, but nothing that ever stuck. Because she was under strict instructions that nothing could *ever* stick. That was her life. She might not like it, but she was used to it.

But today, when she'd leaned into Ash, she'd felt different. Like Ash looked at her and truly saw her for who she was. Which sounded absolutely ridiculous. But when Ash's gaze had fallen on her, it was as if she saw Victoria as simply a person with thoughts, feelings, and wants.

What would happen if they saw each other again without a room full of people looking on? Without any titles on show? Rather, they could just be two people, meeting, chatting, getting to know each other.

Victoria shook her head. Who was she kidding?

"I did just that. She's currently naked on the pool table, and I'm about to have my wicked way with her."

"That's my girl," Dexter replied. "It sounds like you could use a little time away. Which is perfect, because I met the Swedish royals again last night at my business event, including our favourite couple, Princess Astrid and her wife, Sofia. How is it that Scandinavia is so fucking progressive? Why can't the UK be like that? It's the 21st century, after all."

Victoria snorted. "Because we're British, darling. Stiff upper lip. We can never have too much fun, it's simply not in our makeup. And we certainly can't be anything but straight. Hell, up until three generations ago, we couldn't even choose our spouse. At least my parents got to do that."

"And you?"

That was the million-dollar question, but she always swept it under the carpet.

"You know the rules, boyfriend dearest. I don't make them."

"You know the person who does, though." He cleared his throat. "Anyway, I have a proposal. Or rather, our favourite queer Scandinavian princess does. She and Sofia are going to Marbella this weekend. They've invited us. I said I'd ask you, hence I'm calling. Before you say no, please say yes. I could do with a break, you could do with some sunshine, and if it's with Astrid, she might have a willing friend who could maybe put a smile on your face. It's my best offer, please take it."

Victoria stared at the perfect roses climbing their perfect trellises on the deck outside. Everything in her life was perfect, controlled, exactly as it should be. Ashleigh Woods' life was exciting by her standards. One thing was certain: Ashleigh wouldn't want to get caught up with Victoria. She came with far too many strings attached. But it didn't stop Victoria thinking about those bright green eyes, that hint of a cockney slur, and the way Ash's composure had slipped, just for a second, when their hands touched.

"You still there?"

She got her mind back in the room. "Yes, I'm here." But she'd rather be elsewhere. Wasn't somewhere sunny always better? "And yes, you're on. Let's go to Marbella."

Dexter's gasp was audible. "Just like that? No persuasion needed?"

"Fuck it," Victoria replied. "A summer weekend in Marbella with the girls? Count me in."

"Glad I'm still one of the girls," her fake boyfriend replied.

"Always," she told him.

# Chapter Three

"Here she is, the woman of the hour! We get two Woods for the price of one this morning." Ash's hairdresser, Monique, crushed her in a bear hug because that was what Monique did. "Your mum is already in getting her hair washed."

Monique had been cutting and colouring Ash's hair ever since she turned 16. When Ash was a child, her hair had been the colour of golden sunshine. Now, it needed a little help getting to the same level. Luckily, Monique had the magic touch.

The salon buzzed with Thursday-afternoon energy: hairdryers, gossip, and the rhythmic snip of scissors punctuating every third word. The usual chatter dipped when Ash walked in, curious eyes flicking towards her. She was still getting used to her relatively new-found fame. She'd always been a footballer, but until last year, she could walk around with no cameras in her face. She trained, played, saw her friends and family, no drama.

However, since England won the Euros, and the Women's Super League was now live on Sky Sports every week, it had all changed. People knew who her parents were. Who her nan was. Where she lived. It was hugely unnerving at times. But Ash wasn't one to complain. Fame came with upsides, too.

In the past year, her pay had doubled, she'd been given

a car, and she had lucrative sponsorship deals with premium brands. These days, VIP passes to Grand Prixes, concerts and plush hotels fell into her lap, and they didn't cost her a penny. It was a far cry from all those nights spent as a teenager training on cold, muddy pitches.

"What was she like?" Monique asked, running her fingers through Ash's golden strands as she sat in the chair in front of her. "The princess. Everyone's dying to know after I told them I styled your hair to go to the Palace. I'd have preferred Prince Michael, obviously, but you got to meet the future Queen."

She had, hadn't she? But even though that was true, meeting Princess Victoria hadn't felt starry. Yes, she'd been formal, but also familiar. As if Ash might go for a coffee or a glass of wine with her afterwards. Which was the weirdest thing.

"She was…" Then Ash stopped. What had the princess been? Beautiful, but that was obvious. Beguiling. Shy, but also confident. "She was very… professional," Ash said carefully, watching Monique's reflection in the mirror. "It was a formal ceremony, you know? Quick chat, pin the medal, move on."

"Professional?" Monique's frown told Ash what she thought of that answer. "You promised to not stop spilling the tea now you're famous, but all I get is 'professional'?"

Ash had promised that, but she hadn't meant it. She hadn't changed, but the things she could divulge had.

Ash grinned. "What do you want me to say? That we're best mates now? That she invited me round for cocktails? That she told me all about how the rumours were indeed true, and that she and Dexter Matthews are now engaged?"

"That's exactly what I want to hear!" Monique rolled her

eyes like it was obvious. "Then you could recommend your favourite hairdresser to her, and she could come and get her hair done here, and my bookings would be through the roof."

Ash glanced around the packed salon. "You look like you're doing okay to me."

Monique put her hands on Ash's shoulders and looked at her in the mirror. "That's true."

"And I'll still put a link on my socials for you when you make me look irresistible."

"You're an absolute doll!" Monique kissed the top of her head. "Did Victoria seem happy? I want her to be happy, even though I don't know her. But we've all watched her grow up, haven't we? We want the best for her. Dexter seems to care about her, at least. It doesn't seem like it's one of those forced royal relationships."

Ash had always thought the same, until she met the princess and her gaydar had screeched loud in her ear. Maybe Victoria was bi? Queer? Plenty of Ash's teammates who were in relationships with men identified as such. The same could equally be true of royalty.

"She seemed happy. And nearly engaged, if the papers are to be believed." Ash's arched eyebrow told Monique they absolutely were not.

"I had a lady in here yesterday who'd already bought a Victoria and Dexter mug and tea towel. The merchandise people jump on this sort of thing as soon as the news breaks, don't they?" She held up strands of Ash's hair.

"Usual cut and colour?"

Ash nodded. She hadn't had time before the Palace to get it done properly.

"Any occasion?"

"She's going to Marbella." Her mum walked up beside Monique, a towel wrapped around her head. Debra Woods was wearing her favourite colour: hot pink. She was a walking fluorescent marker, ensuring nobody had a dull day around her. "There's a whole gang of them going, and she won't take me with her." Her mum pouted. "Tell her she's being mean and she should invite me, Monique."

"I love you, Mum, but we've been over this. You go on holiday with Dad, I go with my friends." Ash got up, grasped her mum's shoulders and kissed her cheek.

Her mum laughed. "But in here," she tapped the side of her towel. "I'm still in my 20s. I can still party like a young person."

"Which is doubly the reason why you're not coming."

Ash's parents, in particular her mum, had been instrumental in her success. She wouldn't be the person she was or be anywhere near the Lionesses team without all the support and driving to games her parents had committed to from a young age.

"Spoilsport." Her mum gave her a wink, then wandered off to her stylist at the other end of the salon.

Monique waited for Debra to sit down before she turned back to Ash. "You might have to bring her back a nice present. A straw donkey or something." She stepped back. "Shall we get you to the basin and get your hair washed, ready for my magic?"

Ash followed Monique down the salon, ignoring the head twists from a couple of the younger clientele.

Monique took the opportunity to bump Ash's shoulder.

"I'm really proud of everything you achieve. You're such a great example of hard work and being kind. I just hope the world knows that. I didn't like the abuse you got the last time you played for England."

Ash shrugged. It was all part of being a professional footballer, particularly now that everyone had an opinion on the women's game. But she couldn't deny it stung. Mistakes were a part of the game, and she'd learn from hers. But making them in front of 60,000 people (plus a TV audience) brought its own pressure. But Ash could handle it. She had to. Even though she wanted to scream that it was only to be expected after months out of the game with a serious knee injury.

However, she bet it was nothing compared to what Princess Victoria had to handle on a daily basis.

Monique pointed into the kitchen. "Coffee?"

Ash nodded. "Yes, please."

Monique grabbed the full pot on the side, along with a clean mug. It was only when she offered it to Ash, she saw what it said on it: *Princess of Fucking Everything!*

"Next time you see Princess Victoria, you should take her one of these. It might make her smile."

Ash rolled her eyes, ignoring the way her stomach flipped at the memory of the princess's blue eyes meeting hers. That moment when she got her medal, when the world seemed to pause around them.

"I don't think there's going to be a next time. I'm just some footballer from St Albans. And she's the heir to the throne."

"Some footballer?" Monique scoffed, ushering Ash over to the white basins. "You scored the winning penalty in the European Cup final. You brought football home. I don't think people are going to forget that in a hurry." She put a small towel around Ash's neck before she sat, tucking it in when the top of her back hit the basin. "She'd be lucky to meet you again. When do you go away?"

"Tomorrow. Thought I'd treat myself to a proper cut before my ten days of hedonism."

"You always look gorgeous anyway."

Ash tipped her head back, then closed her eyes as the water hit her head. Was there anything more soothing than someone else washing your hair? She always looked forward to the head massage she got right after her shampoo and condition, too.

"Such gorgeous skin, and hair. You're going to make some woman very happy one day, mark my words."

Ash was glad Monique had faith.

# Chapter Four

"If you put your hand on my arse, I swear, I'll stamp on your foot." Victoria spoke without moving her mouth, a skill she'd acquired growing up. Dexter had touched her bum once before, and they'd only just shaken the tag of being the royal couple who simply couldn't keep their hands off one another.

In response, Dexter squeezed the hand he was holding. "I wouldn't dare touch your royal arse again, Your Highness."

They'd arrived at the airport half an hour ago, but the press had followed them. To satisfy them, the princess's staff had organised a five-minute photo opportunity on the steps of the royal private jet, and now the pair were in the thick of it, pretending to be the golden couple everyone assumed they were.

"Give us a wider smile, Ma'am!" shouted one photographer. "You're flying off to the sun, while the rest of us are staying in this gloomy country!"

There was that. Victoria tried not to glance at the grey June skies, instead giving the press her full set of pearly whites, and one photographer gave her a thumbs-up. Two minutes later, to a cacophony of "Victoria! Dexter! This way!", they escaped into the royal jet, where they both collapsed immediately onto the white leather sofas.

"How was it for you, darling?" Dexter had boy-band good looks. It was a shame they did nothing for Victoria.

"Ridiculous as ever. But I'm public property, and there's nothing I can do about it."

Victoria leaned forward and picked up a copy of *The Sun* from the low-slung table in front of her. She rarely read the tabloids at home. Her parents didn't allow it for the sake of everyone's mental health, and she knew they had a point. However, when she went away, it was her guilty pleasure. On the front cover was a scandal about a Saturday night celebrity dancing show. One of the dancers had run off with their celebrity dance partner, breaking up said celebrity's 15-year marriage.

Victoria stabbed the front page with her index finger and tutted. "Typical, isn't it? This male celebrity does the dirty on his wife, but it's the female dancer's fault." She glanced up at Dexter. "Imagine the uproar if one of them ran off with a same-sex partner. I might do a little whoop."

"Careful." Dexter wagged his finger in her direction. "You don't want to be seen as the royal who actively promotes infidelity." He paused, looking her in the eye, lowering his voice as their staff climbed aboard the plane behind them. "Whatever next, a queer princess?"

They both shared a rueful smile, then Victoria leaned back in her seat, tabloid in hand. She flicked to the gossip pages, to see if there was anything about anyone she knew. Not that she believed a word of what was written in the papers, because they all thought Dexter was about to ask her to marry him.

However, she wasn't quite prepared for what greeted her. Emerging from a shimmering pool in a daring red bikini that left little to the imagination was none other than Ashleigh Woods. The England football captain whose fingers had brushed against Victoria's just days earlier. She also played for the Royal Ravens, Victoria's favourite club team.

She'd had a free Sunday in February, when the Ravens were playing one of their biggest London rivals. Victoria had contemplated getting out her big coat and going to the game. But then she'd thought about what a palaver it would entail to be spontaneous. It wasn't something baked into Victoria's life. She could go to the match, but she'd have to book security and extra staff beforehand.

The cadence of Victoria's heart betrayed her composure as she read the caption beside the photo. *England captain Ashleigh Woods relaxes in the Marbella sunshine with her team-mates after collecting her MBE.*

She was in Marbella? Victoria's pulse quickened as she squinted at the photo. She recognised England goalkeeper Cam Holloway in the pool looking up at Ash. It was rumoured they were a couple, but who knew if that was true? Ash wasn't one to share too much about her private life after her very public breakup the year before.

After the investiture, Victoria disappeared down a social media rabbit hole, intrigued by Ash's life. Just this week, post-MBE, Ash had shared a 'June So Far' montage that captured her spending time with family, sipping coffee, getting a fresh haircut, and proudly receiving her MBE.

Victoria was one of the most photographed women in the world, appearing in countless social media feeds every day. Yet, seeing herself on Ashleigh Woods' profile had unexpectedly brightened her day.

Ash's final photo was from the seat of her plane with the caption 'Holiday mode, activated.' But Victoria had no idea she was in Marbella.

Dexter pulled down the top of the newspaper and peered over it. When he saw the photo, he rolled his eyes.

"I might have known." He got up, then sat next to Victoria, looking closer. "Although, I can definitely see the attraction," he grinned. "The Lionesses are in Marbella? What are the chances? It wouldn't do you any harm to get your photo taken with them. It would definitely boost your profile with the younger demographic. Plus, you have just been made Patron of the Women's Football Association. It would be very on-brand." He nudged her with his elbow. "And if they're all in bikinis, what's a girl to do?"

Victoria took a swig from her water bottle. "Not sure my mother would see it that way. Especially if I was also in a bikini."

The Queen accepted her queerness. To a point. She agreed that love is love. But also, that the monarchy is the monarchy.

Dexter shrugged. "Why not? You've got a smokin' body, and even royals like a swim every now and again." He grabbed his phone, clicked on his Instagram app, then pulled up one of the Lionesses' wilder players. One more likely to share every step of her holiday on Instagram. Within a minute, he'd figured out where they were. "They're at La Corona Azul. I bet they're being treated to it, because I don't think WSL wages are up to that level quite yet."

Victoria nodded. "Or it could just be a day pass. I know a few people who did that when we were there a few years ago." She put a finger to her chest. "I had a day pass."

He knitted his brow. "You? The heir to the British throne had to scan in like everyone else?"

"Yes!" Victoria laughed at the memory. "Tanya was mortified because they weren't aware we were coming. Prince Raul said he'd sorted it out, but I think he got waylaid by a pretty woman somewhere and forgot." The heir to the Spanish throne was more the party boy of the family, just like Victoria's brother, Michael.

"That sounds like Raul," Dexter laughed.

Right at that moment, the flight attendant appeared. "Everyone, please fasten your seat belts, laptops off, everything stowed." The engines roared as the plane turned onto the runway.

Victoria clicked her seatbelt into place and Dexter did the same beside her. He clutched her hand in his and gave her a loving smile. She was going to miss this when it was gone. She squeezed his hand as the plane hurtled down the runway and climbed into the pure blue sky.

"But talking of going partying—"

"—which I won't be," Victoria confirmed.

"I wanted to set the ground rules for this trip. Because it's getting more complex. You know I've started to see a bit more of Sidney." He paused. "And things might be starting to change."

Victoria sat up, and her heart thumped in her chest. She knew this day would come. However, hearing Dex voice it made it more real. Them splitting up would be big news to the outside world.

"Okay." She was thrilled for Dexter, even if it edged her closer to the inevitable showdown with her parents. "Is this your decision or his?"

"Joint." Dex ran a hand through his thick, dark hair, his face contorting as he spoke. "He'll be there this weekend, but he knows the deal. Even when you and I break up, there needs to be some time before Sidney and I can be open. He gets it, even if he's not thrilled."

Victoria could only imagine. "I need to bring it up with my parents, of course, and brief the press. No big announcement, just a little tip-off should do the trick." She looked over her shoulder, where the six staff with them were busy on their phones. Nevertheless, she kept her voice low. "We need to tell everyone here, too. They're all going to be shocked."

Dexter raised an eyebrow.

"They will be," she hissed under her breath. "We've always been discreet when we've brought other people home."

"Tanya knows," Dex reminded her. "Don't you think she's told other people?"

Victoria gripped the top of her nose between her thumb and index finger and pressed. The morning her aide had walked in on her in bed with another woman hadn't been Victoria's finest. It was why she always had a rule that nobody could stay overnight. But that evening with Hermione had felt too good to kick her out. Victoria wanted to wake up with someone by her side. Someone to snuggle up to in the morning. But that was the last time she'd been with Hermione, because Victoria had overreacted and literally thrown her out the door. She understood why Hermione was now in a relationship with a woman where they could go out for dinner, hold hands in public. Who wouldn't want that?

Victoria wanted that more than anything in the whole world.

"No, I don't." Victoria trusted Tanya with her life. She knew more about Victoria than most of her family. "She wouldn't blab." She was sure of that.

"How do you know?" Dexter never trusted anyone.

Victoria understood. His ex had outed him to his family, Dexter had denied it, then gone back in the closet in the most spectacular way by fake-dating his long-time friend, Princess Victoria.

"I just do." Victoria glanced back at her closest aide. "If she had, the rumours would already be out there. But they're not. Not in the wider public." Maybe in some corners of the press who would never speak up, for fear of the royal lawsuit that would be slapped on them. It wasn't the crime of the century, but it required careful handling. Her parents had made it crystal clear: she couldn't be an out monarch.

Just because it hadn't been done before didn't make it wrong, Victoria argued. However, their silence spoke volumes. The conversation remained on her 'circle back' list.

"We're going to need a proper chat when we get back, okay?" Dex stared into her eyes and didn't break contact. He'd brought this up before, but then backtracked. They were friends, so it worked. Plus, Dexter got perks from it, too. It never hurt that people thought he was dating the future Queen. He enjoyed breezing into restaurants, and being famous. Probably because fame was new to him. It was fun. Whereas for Victoria, she longed for a day where she could be anonymous.

"I know, and we will." She squeezed his knee. "But let's enjoy this weekend first, okay?"

His jaw twitched. "You're okay with Sidney coming?"

"Of course. I love Sidney!" She did. She was pretty sure

the feeling wasn't mutual. Seeing him and Dex together, she'd known things would come to a head soon. She wanted someone to look at her the way Sidney looked at Dexter. With eyes that wanted her. Hungry.

Her mind drifted back to the formal ceremony at the palace earlier this week. The memory of Ashleigh Woods before her, looking up with those startling green eyes as Victoria pinned the MBE to her lapel. It had been living rent-free in her mind for days. Maybe she'd get to see her again this weekend. Would it be that far-fetched to run into her? She knew the answer was yes.

She'd only run into Ashleigh Woods if she got Tanya to track her down. She wasn't about to do that. But it didn't stop her mind drifting off to sun-soaked beach clubs and the possibility of them sharing a smile somewhere in the real world. Somewhere she could actually speak to her, maybe even…

"Vic?" Dexter's voice snapped her back to the here and now. "Where did you go just then?"

"Nowhere," she lied, hoping her cheeks weren't blushing as furiously red as it felt they were. She turned her body to him. "If this is going to be one of our last jaunts before we break up, then let's make this one count." Maybe she did want to be braver. "For a few days, I want to live without rules. Maybe I'll even take up Astrid's invitation to go clubbing."

Dexter widened his eyes. "You? Clubbing?"

"I've been before."

"I know, and you always hated it."

Victoria bristled. "Hate is a strong word." She paused. "Plus, people can change. And the club Astrid suggested is somewhere we can be a bit more open."

He blinked rapidly. "If this is where you tell me you're going to get on a podium and do a pole dance, I might need a bit more warning."

That broke the slight tension and made her laugh. "I just want to live a little. Maybe act my age." She often felt older than her 33 years. "I want to have fun and stop worrying. For just one weekend, I don't want to be a royal, and I've got far more chance of doing that abroad."

"You want to be a commoner? You'll hate it. It's over-rated." A smile spread across his handsome face as he snagged her gaze. "But I, your royal subject, am at your command. If you want fun this weekend, then fun we shall have."

# Chapter Five

"You know I hate doing this?" Ash mock-scowled into Cam's phone. The warm evening breeze tickled her nose as they relaxed on their villa's expansive balcony, overlooking the pool. In front of them was a table set for ten, next to the largest barbecue Ash had ever seen. Bigger even than her dad's industrial-sized grill, which was no small feat.

"I had absolutely no idea. Was it the way you constantly huff whenever I try to get you to do any socials? Or the way you bat my phone away whenever it comes close? I'm not sure."

Cam rolled her eyes at her best friend.

Where Ash was blonde and had a resting I-might-fuck-with-you face, Cam had long dreadlocks, and a smile that belonged on sports drink commercials (and frequently was). She was also taller than most trees, which was helpful as she stopped the ball flying into the net for a living. Cam had waited patiently in the wings, but was now England's nailed-on No.1. She was also the person Ash trusted the most in the whole world. Even now, when Cam sported so much mascara, it almost threatened to glue her eyes shut.

"Social media is ridiculous. Fans only want it one way, right? They want a 24/7 window into our lives, and I'm not giving them that. That's when they love you. But when you make a mistake on the pitch, the vibe soon turns. It's why I gave up doing my own."

She'd watched it all unravel after England's Euro triumph. The Royal Ravens stumbled early in their campaign, and suddenly her every move was under the microscope, with social media giving everyone a chance to chip in with their thoughts. Form questioned, performances analysed, private life dissected. The England captain's armband meant there was no hiding from the spotlight. Her MCL injury halfway through the season only complicated matters, and now she was fighting her way back to full strength. With a home World Cup on the horizon next summer, and Ash turning 30 the same month, time was of the essence.

But however bad it was for Ash, it was doubly worse for Cam, being a woman of colour. That's why she advocated careful curation and sharing, in an effort to control the narrative.

Cam kissed her cheek, then reached over to wipe the lipstick off. If that got on her socials, the interest would reach fever pitch.

"You are right about social media. However, if you give them a little, it gets them off your back for a while. Plus, we're all dressed up for a night out. We never look this good in our kit. Now is the time to share. Summer solstice. The longest day and the shortest night. The Celts believed this was the day when the veil between the two worlds was thinnest, so anything was possible." Cam bumped her with her hip. "Ready?"

They spent ten minutes filming, Cam's boundless energy infectious as Ash found herself genuinely laughing at her friend's antics. The two of them were perfect, Cam a natural balance to her own personality, even if tabloids constantly hinted at romance between them. The truth was simpler: they'd grown up playing football since the age of eight, remaining close despite Cam now playing up north for United. It made this holiday precious, a rare chance for the long-time friends to reunite and decompress after a demanding season. Ash had promised Cam she'd let loose and enjoy herself.

"Hey lovebirds, are you decent?"

Ash rolled her eyes as the Royal Ravens' club captain Sasha Goodall appeared on the balcony carrying two bottles of honey-coloured booze, closely followed by their teammates Kyla Thomas and Marissa Marquez. The former carried cutlery, sauces, napkins; the latter a tray of shot glasses. The trio put their wares on the rectangular stone table and sat in three of the chairs.

"You missed us getting it on by at least two minutes." Cam glanced up from her phone. "You need better timing."

"I've never had any complaints."

Sasha was the joker of the pack. The one everyone looked to when the vibe needed lifting. Sometimes, she got on Ash's nerves, but they'd all be lost without her. Sasha was 33, but you'd never tell with her performances for club and country. She was the defensive midfielder that every team in the league would like. Combative. Sweary. Creative. A wall.

"Food is ordered, and it arrives in ten minutes. Burgers and chips all round because it's the off-season and we can. We've also got a few bottles of tequila to get the night revved up, because George Clooney's brand sent us a case as a present for being gorgeous humans." Sasha waved an arm towards Kyla, currently pouring golden liquid into shot glasses. "Two shots before dinner, two after. No exceptions."

The rest of their crew appeared, all looking very different from their sun-drenched, bikini-clad look of a few hours ago. Footballers didn't get a chance to dress up and be glamorous very often. When they did, they embraced it.

Sasha beckoned Ash and Cam to the table. They downed their tequila shots, half the crowd whining they'd have preferred Tequila Rose.

"George Clooney didn't send us that, so stop moaning," Sasha told them.

"Have you seen our new patron is in Marbs at the moment?" Kyla held up her phone with a photo of Princess Victoria and Dexter Matthews getting on their private jet. "We might run into royalty this week as we're booked into some swanky clubs now we're famous, right?"

Ash jolted, her interest piqued.

"If we do, Ash can introduce us seeing as you met this week already," Kyla added.

Ash nodded, like it was a done deal. "I'll message ahead to let her know we're on our way. She'll be stoked."

"Maybe she'll have Tequila Rose," said their pacy Spanish winger, Teresa, who'd been nominated as the group's spokesperson tonight because she spoke the local lingo.

"If she doesn't, she can get it," added Kyla, refilling the shot glasses for round two. "Imagine being a royal. I'm sure she can get whatever her heart desires."

"She's already got that with her fit bloke!" England striker Denise Maloney was definitely on the pull tonight, with her low-cut little black dress that never went out of fashion, and heels the height of townhouses. She'd already kicked them off under the table.

Sasha pulled back her shoulders, reached over and downed her second shot, then slammed the glass down. "I've always thought Princess Victoria might swing both ways. And if she does, maybe she'll want a little something extra before she commits to a life of hetero-sex. A walk on the guaranteed orgasm side." Sasha shimmied her shoulders. "If I can be of any assistance, I would humbly oblige."

Ash laughed. "For Queen and country, Sash?"

"I'm all about duty." Sasha gave an elaborate bow.

The doorbell rang, and Teresa and Kyla disappeared to get the food. When the spread was laid out, Cam shot a video of their spread, with the caption: 'Off-season, carb-loading.'

Ash made sure to keep the burger as far away from her white halter-neck top and trousers as humanly possible. As they ate, she stared out to the wide expanse of pinky-blue ocean that stretched out before them in the still-hot evening. The serenity of this moment was exactly what she craved.

The year had dragged, between her ruptured MCL, the long road to recovery, and the Ravens losing the title on goal difference. It was a wound that still stung, though softened by their FA Cup triumph. Perhaps this escape was the reset her overactive mind needed. For the first time in ages, her mental static began to fade, and her shoulders finally dropped their tension.

"I could get used to this." She ran her fingertips over her knee, knowing her surgery scar was directly below the material.

"You should, because we're here for the next eight days," Cam stretched out her long limbs. "Relax into it. Dinner every night by the pool, looking out over the ocean, hot women to meet, your best mate by your side."

Sasha handed Ash the second shot, which she downed with a shudder. "Tonight, we celebrate us," Ash declared. "We almost clinched the league this season. Next year, it's ours."

"Damn right," Sasha agreed, sparking whoops from the group.

"We're hitting a fancy club tonight, and we're dancing," Ash announced, despite her notorious lack of rhythm.

"Marianne says this club is top-notch," Sasha added. "No photos without permission. Apparently, it's full of famous people seeking privacy."

Their shared agent knew the best spots. Plus, Ash knew that famous people craved anonymity. Fame didn't change the fundamentals: even Princess Victoria put her pants on one leg at a time.

"Line your stomachs, and let's do Marbs right," Sasha rallied. "Cocktails with glitter, partying with movie stars. We're living large, just for a few days. No counting calories, no training sessions. Touch up your lippy, and let's go!"

# Chapter Six

Victoria leaned against the upper level's Perspex balcony, surveying the sprawling club below. Sparkly booths encircled a sunken dance floor, while VIP corners buzzed with A-listers from music, film, and sport. She'd already exchanged pleasantries with Hollywood stars whose names escaped her, though they seemed to know her well enough. A lifetime in the public eye meant constant double-takes, especially in unexpected places like this. Sometimes she played along when asked if she was the real princess; other times, she claimed to be a lookalike just to escape the conversation.

The music thundered through her chest. It wasn't really her scene, but she'd made promises to herself and to Dexter. Her eyes swept the crowd until she spotted him, deep in conversation with Sid, his boyfriend. So much for having some time alone first.

Victoria's attention snapped to whooping from the dancefloor, where a group of women with athletic builds danced to a familiar football anthem. Her eyes fixed on one face: long hair, gangly, but her name hovered just out of reach. She was one of England's veterans, irreplaceable in midfield.

Sally? Sophie? No. Then it clicked: Sasha Goodall, Royal Ravens' and Lionesses' dynamo. *Of course.* They'd met at a children's home where Sasha had made her laugh, a rare gift Victoria never forgot.

Her heart quickened. If Sasha was here, was Ash, too? Victoria gripped the balcony tighter. Had she imagined their moment the other day? Probably. Ash didn't know about Victoria's arrangement with Dexter. Plus, she was likely attached, and certainly didn't see Victoria as girlfriend material.

*Girlfriend material?* Victoria shook her head. She needed a real life beyond her title and duties. Though that was easier said than done.

A hand on her shoulder broke her thoughts. She turned to find Princess Astrid beside her. Sweden's party princess, also an out and proud lesbian. Victoria had always got on with Astrid, always admired her stance on living as her authentic self. It was easier in Sweden, but it still took courage. Her signature platinum-white hair caught the strobing lights, creating a halo effect that matched her reputation for lighting up every room she entered. She carried herself with an effortless swagger, her tailored blazer draped over a jaunty shirt showing her rebellious spirit.

"How's my favourite princess doing?" Astrid leaned over the balcony and scanned the dancefloor. "Have you identified someone down there you'd like to get up close and personal with?"

Victoria blushed at Astrid reading her mind. "Of course not. That's not how royal minds work." But she grinned at Astrid as she spoke.

"I'm on my way to the terrace. Come with me? There's a bottle of Krug on ice with our names on it."

Astrid's fingers were warm around Victoria's as she allowed

herself to be led through a sliding door, and outside onto a balcony not dissimilar in size to the famous one at Buckingham Palace. The one she'd stood and waved on countless times. When Victoria walked onto any balcony, she sometimes had to stop her hand from moving. Muscle memory was a thing.

Astrid's wife Sofia was already in one corner, chatting to a group of three other women. Astrid led Victoria over, then introduced her around the group. There were a couple of wide eyes when the group clocked who she was. Victoria was used to that.

"And this," Astrid said, giving Victoria a pointed smile, "is Lucienne. She's a friend who's big in the music industry. What she doesn't know about pop stars isn't worth knowing, frankly." Astrid leaned in. "Victoria's a huge Swiftie."

Lucienne shook Victoria's hand while fixing her with a strong gaze. "Lovely to meet you. Astrid's told me a lot about you." Her voice was low, silky, her eyes the colour of burnished bronze.

They were not as arresting as Ashleigh Woods' eyes.

"I never think about British royals listening to pop music," Lucienne continued. "In my head, you're more about the proms and classical."

Victoria tried not to wince as she let go of Lucienne's hand. People who didn't think she did normal things pissed her off.

"We like pop music. We also eat food, go to the bathroom and sleep every day, too."

Lucienne's eyes widened at that answer.

Okay, perhaps that was a little much. It was just, Lucienne had touched a nerve.

"Okaaay," Astrid said, steering the conversation back to the group. "Does anyone need champagne?"

Victoria did, but she also didn't want to be here right now. Her mind wandered to the group downstairs. She bet they were having more fun than she was. She put up a finger. "You know what, I do, but just excuse me a minute. Nature calls."

Without letting Astrid respond, Victoria slipped away and down the steps of the club. However, when she got downstairs and spotted the group of footballers, she was overcome with shyness. What was she going to say if she went up to them? She'd been in dressing rooms before and always found them intimidating places. She'd also been on teams when she was in school, and she knew if you weren't a part of those teams, you were an outsider.

Victoria stopped. This was ridiculous. She'd just run off from Astrid who wouldn't set her up with just a random. Lucienne had been stunning, and clearly available if her solid eye contact was anything to go by. What was Victoria doing, chasing a footballer around a club on her first night away, just because they may or may not have had a connection? More to the point, she hadn't even seen her yet.

She closed her eyes, then had a need to get out of there before things got any worse. Before she started to question her own existence, and why she was living a total lie.

She turned, saw a door, slid it across. Another balcony. She'd take a moment to regroup, then go back to Astrid. To Lucienne. Maybe she needed to give her a chance. Victoria closed the door and breathed in the fresh air. It was only when she looked right, she realised there was another person on the balcony.

Ashleigh Woods.

A bottle of beer in each hand.

Dressed in a white outfit that showed off her taut arms and shoulders.

Far more skin on show than five days ago.

Up this close, Ashleigh only confirmed Victoria's initial impression. That she was stupid-gorgeous.

Victoria instructed herself not to stare too hard.

When Ash saw Victoria, her mouth dropped open ever-so-slightly.

"It's you," Ash blurted, then looked like she wanted the world to swallow her up. "I mean, Victoria." Another wince. "I mean, Your Royal Highness."

All of which caused Victoria to choke out a laugh. A genuine laugh. The first she'd managed tonight. One she desperately needed.

"Victoria is just fine."

But Ash shook her head. "I don't think it is. At least, that's what my agent told me. And my mum. I have a terrible habit of being too familiar with people." She paused, fixing Victoria with her warm gaze, just as she had the first time.

Victoria had been right about her eyes: they sparkled like emeralds.

"Should I already have curtsied or something?"

Victoria walked towards her, then stopped, leaving a gap of a few inches. Stay calm. Play this cool. She could totally do that. She breathed in the Mediterranean air, thick with jasmine. The music from inside thumped against the glass doors: some remix of an old dance track she'd heard a thousand times when she was at college in Oxford.

She stared at Ash, feeling that same pull towards her she had the first time. Which was totally stupid. She didn't even know her.

"I seem to recall you didn't curtsy when we met the other day, either."

Ash grimaced. "Not really my jam."

"Nor mine."

"Thank god." Ash slapped a hand over her mouth. "I mean, cool." She nodded. "Cool, cool." Then she held out a bottle of beer. "Would you like this? I assume it's not all caviar and champagne where you live?" She frowned. "Or it might be. If all those movies I've watched about royals prove to be right, then I'm an idiot." She paused. "I haven't drunk any of it. I got it for my friend Cam, but she's on the dance floor getting lost in the music, and I'm out here escaping it."

Victoria accepted the beer. "Thank you. I was offered champagne upstairs, but I fled." Why had she just said that?

"Beer will help. Probably. Or it'll make it worse." Ash paused. "Anyway, the one thing I haven't even thought about until now is: what the hell are you doing in this club? You're not stalking me, are you?"

# Chapter Seven

Why on earth had she said that? Accusing the heir to the throne of stalking her? She really needed to engage her brain before she uttered words sometimes. But it'd been a habit she hadn't mastered in her 29 years of living, so she wasn't convinced she was going to manage it now.

Luckily, Princess Victoria threw back her head and laughed. The same, melodic, throaty sound Ash had heard floating through the corridor in the Palace. She was drawn to it then, and five days on, nothing had changed. The princess's hair framed her face beautifully as she grinned. Those baby-blue eyes crinkled lightly as she assessed Ash. She seemed different tonight. Less on show. More relaxed. Her blue trousers and cream shirt spoke to that. She looked more at ease. More herself.

"You might be the only person in my life ever to accuse *me* of stalking *them*." She shook her head. "That makes you memorable." She snagged Ash's gaze. "Which I should have expected from England's number eight."

Ash blinked, trying hard not to get too overwhelmed. The reality of being alone with the princess again was sinking in. "You know my shirt number?"

"It's hardly a secret, is it?" A hint of pink bloomed on Victoria's cheeks as she spoke. "Plus, I am the new patron of the Women's FA. I like to be up to speed."

"There was me thinking royalty was all about the posher sports like rugby and lacrosse."

Victoria shook her head. "I'm a fan of all sports, especially when they involve women. I watch tennis and rugby, but I also drink beer and love women's football. I was thrilled to be asked to do my new role."

"I stand corrected."

"Would you believe me if I told you I'm learning to play pool?"

Ash's gaydar blared loud in her brain. She'd tried to talk herself out of the possibility of Victoria being queer, but the evidence was stacking up. Then again, a few of her team-mates were straight and also pool sharks. But the majority of straight pool queens she knew were footballers who hung around with a lot of queer women. What was Princess Victoria's excuse? Ash's gaze dropped to Victoria's hands, and her painted fingernails. Styled, but shorter than most.

Heat ran down her spine, then settled somewhere far, far lower.

She had a short but stern word with herself.

Victoria had a boyfriend.

*A nearly-fiancée.*

She was allowed to have short fingernails.

And play pool.

Then again…

"I'm pretty good at pool. Misspent youth. Maybe I can give you some pointers one day."

"I'd very much like that." Victoria flicked out her chestnut hair, then tucked one side behind her ear.

It did something to Ash.

Something dangerous.

"I had a table installed in the Palace summer house. I went to practice after the ceremony the other day, actually. My mother isn't so keen, but I figure I do enough to please her…" She stopped abruptly, and stared at Ash. "And I'm not sure why I'm telling you this when we literally just met this week and I hardly know you."

It surprised Ash, too. But also, thrilled her. "Maybe you think you know me. I'm a vaguely familiar face who you've seen on the TV?" She paused. "Also, I'm a good listener."

Victoria sounded like she needed that. Ash understood. She wanted to put Victoria at ease.

"And can we circle back to the fact you have a pool table at the Palace? I assume you mean Buckingham?"

Victoria laughed.

Again, it made Ash want to lean in.

"I do. We had to smuggle it in. Mother thought it might be a little weird if the press got hold of it. 'A bit common' I believe were her words."

"It's not a pastime I'd associate with a royal."

Victoria licked her lips before she spoke, raising her blue eyes to meet Ash's. "Maybe I'm not your usual type of royal."

Ash was getting that. Her eyes lingered on Victoria's elegant neck, where the scent of her earthy, woody perfume seemed strongest, before she forced her gaze away. She had to get things back on a more even keel, but her mind was blank.

Luckily, Victoria stepped in. "Let's rewind, though. Why

are you escaping your friends? They looked like they were having fun."

Ash shook her head. "They are. I'm a terrible dancer, so I step away for my own sanity sometimes. Plus, they're trying to recreate the FA Cup Final, but with tequila shots instead of penalties." She held up her bottle. "I'm more of a beer girl."

"Thanks for mine." Victoria clinked her bottle to Ash's and they settled beside each other, overlooking the ocean.

Ash tried not to think that she was sharing body heat with the future Queen, but it was hard not to focus on it.

"It's the summer solstice today: longest day of the year. Also, the shortest night." *Thank you, Cam.* "The Celts believed it was when the veil between worlds was thinnest. When anything was possible."

Victoria turned to look at her, eyes widening slightly. A slow, impressed smile spread across her face. "And here I thought I was the only one who knew her solstice lore. You're full of surprises, aren't you? Good with your feet and your mind." She looked Ash up and down, almost undressing her.

Ash gulped.

Victoria looked away.

A few charged seconds passed.

"I was sad I was out of the country when you won the FA Cup. Seems to be a habit of mine. I would have liked to come along." When she turned back, her cheeks were flushed.

*Extraordinary composure under pressure.*

"Did you watch it?"

Victoria shook her head. "Couldn't manage it. But I checked the score when I got back from my official dinner.

I'm quite the fan of the Royal Ravens. Maybe I'll finally make it to a game this season."

"I'd like that."

"So would I."

Ash wasn't making this energy between them up, was she? She breathed it in, then tried not to focus on it, but that was impossible. It hummed in the air between them like a plucked string.

She cleared her throat. "I'm surprised you're here alone. Should you not have a bodyguard? A boyfriend? Anyone?"

The edges of Victoria's mouth turned upwards at that. "Dexter is upstairs, chatting to a friend. I gave my aide the night off and persuaded my bodyguard to wait in the car. I won't tell if he doesn't." She smiled. "I was on the upstairs balcony, but just fancied a change of scene, so here I am. Plus, you all looked like you were having a better time dancing down here. And I thought, it was nice to meet you earlier in the week..." Victoria looked away.

She wanted to dance with the England football team? To speak to Ash?

"I wouldn't advise joining that rabble. Last time they had a few shots, they dared each other to dip their naked tits in a stranger's beer, and we got complaints from the management." Ash gritted her teeth. "And now I'm not sure I should have told you that in case you get me taken to the tower."

"Relax. We stopped chopping people's heads off a while ago." Victoria smiled as she swigged her beer. "How long are you in Marbella?"

"Ten days in all. This is day two. I'm trying not to go too

crazy as I want to stay in shape in the off-season, but not all my teammates are of the same mind."

"We all need a little downtime."

Ash nodded, trying to not focus on the princess's elegant hands. "Is that why you're here?"

"Something like that. Dexter and I are having a long weekend; we're here until Tuesday morning."

*The boyfriend.*

"We're staying with the Swedish royals in their villa."

A flush of happiness sailed through Ash. "Astrid and Sofia?"
Victoria nodded. "The very same."

"I love those two. They're such fantastic role models, living out and proud."

Victoria properly blushed now. "They are. They're pretty amazing people, too." She paused. "What are your plans for the weekend?"

"Tomorrow is a pool day, so a lot of dive-bombing into the water. Don't ask me why, but it's just what happens when you get a load of football girls together. Then Sunday, we've hired a yacht, which looks incredible. We've already nicknamed it the party boat." Even as the words left her lips, they sounded ridiculous. Like someone who didn't often go on yachts, which was true. She imagined Victoria had been on many – and often.

"Sounds like fun. Which is why I'm here this weekend, too. Blow off a little steam. If you fancy a break from the pool tomorrow, Astrid and Sofia are having a barbecue. You'd be welcome to come along, I'm sure they'd be buzzed to have the England football captain there." She paused. "And of course, bring someone special if there is anyone?"

Ash blinked hard, stalling to process the information. She'd stumbled onto this balcony to get a break from dancing, and now she was being invited to a royal barbecue? None of it made sense. The idea of going to a royal party scared the crap out of her, but could she turn it down?

"There's nobody special," she told the princess. "Hasn't been for a while. We're not all as lucky in love as you."

Victoria winced. "I wouldn't say I'm lucky."

What did that mean? "Sorry, that's me believing what I see on the socials. That Dexter is about to propose to you."

"Don't believe everything you read. I'm sure you understand that, being in the public eye."

Ash nodded. "I do." What about the situation wasn't the truth? Ash wanted to ask, but knew she couldn't. "But it's great that you're such an ally, too. The queer community needs them. I read about the youth homeless charity you're heading up, with a focus on queer youth."

Victoria looked her direct in the eye. "Who says I'm an ally?"

Possibility exploded behind Ash's eyes like fireworks. She opened her mouth, closed it, dizzy with implications. She really had no idea what to say to that.

"Anyway." The temperature cooled. Victoria dropped her gaze like a stone. "Put your number in my phone. Speak to whoever you need to speak to, and let me know if you fancy coming along. Even if there's nobody special, feel free to bring a friend." She held out her phone.

Ash took it, a flush of heat crawling up her neck as she tried to focus on the screen rather than the lingering warmth where their skin had touched. Her pulse hammered in her throat, and she cursed her shaking hands that threatened to reveal every ounce of her attraction. The mere glimpse of the numerous famous names in Victoria's contacts was a stark reminder of the world the princess inhabited, one of glamour and influence that felt galaxies away from Ash's reality. Yet here was Victoria, standing close enough to make Ash unsteady on her feet. Giving her a look she'd seen many times before.

One that told Ash she'd like to get to know her better.

*A lot better.*

"If you can come, that'd be great." She bit her lip.

Was Victoria nervous?

"We're going to be working together more this season, so look on it as networking."

Ash had done plenty of that in the past two years. None of those connections had felt like wildfire under her skin.

Victoria's blue eyes appraised her. "I want to hear more about what it takes to be the England captain." She pushed herself off the railing. "However, tonight, I really should get back upstairs. Mingle. Be a bit more princessy."

Her sigh told Ash that was the last thing she wanted to do.

*Who says I'm an ally?*

What did that mean? Was she saying what Ash thought she was saying?

Victoria took another swig from her beer, then put the bottle down. "I'm leaving that here. I know this club has a no-photo rule, but if I get snapped with a bottle of beer in my hand, my mother will have a fit."

Her mother. The Queen. It was nice to know that all mothers worried about the same thing. "Your mother and my mum should get together. They could bond on the same things they don't like their daughters doing. Kissing women where I'm concerned, although I think she's nearly over that. But drinking beer from bottles is definitely another."

"They really should," Victoria agreed, the redness in her cheeks deepening. "I mean, not the first one, obviously." She glanced at the floor. "But definitely the second." She paused. "I should." She pointed to the door. "Hope to see you again soon?"

Ash nodded. "I'd like that."

"So would I."

# Chapter Eight

"What's the deal with this woman, then? Do you like her? Because if so, this is a plot twist I can *so* get behind."

Astrid sat on the edge of Victoria's small sofa and squinted at her. Sunshine blazed into the bedroom, until Astrid got up and dropped the blind. A darkened hush fell over them.

"I like a lot of people." It wasn't a satisfactory answer, and Victoria knew it.

Her friend duly rolled her eyes. "You're avoiding the question. What I'm saying is, you never invite people to our parties. *We* invite people to our parties."

Had Victoria overstepped? Heat rushed up her. "I didn't think you'd mind." She shouldn't have assumed. "I can message her—"

"I didn't say it was wrong. I said it was unusual. Our barbecues are very informal, and we're happy to host your friends, too." Astrid paused. "Plus, this is not just anyone. This is someone you like, who also happens to be the England football captain." She raised an eyebrow. "I can totally see the attraction. The way she wears that uniform—"

"Kit," Victoria corrected.

Astrid waved a hand. "Whatever. She wears it well. I never

really got what you liked about women's sports until I watched the Euros, and then I was like, I get it!"

Victoria shook her head. "I watch women's sports because they're all highly talented athletes at the top of their game. If some of them happen to look pleasing while they do it, that's an added bonus." She rolled her eyes at her friend, who let out a hoot of laughter.

"An added bonus. Got it." She walked over to Victoria and sat beside her on the sofa in the room's bay window. "I think it's a good thing, by the way. A step forward. That you're acting on your feelings. Being out there. You haven't dared to show anything in public since you've been officially with Dexter. What's that been now?"

"Three years." She didn't need to check a calendar or a diary. The amount of time she'd been pretending to be straight and loved up in public because "it was about time she showed an appetite for it" (her mother's words) felt like a lifetime. At least she and Dexter got on. Could hold hands. Understood it was mutually beneficial for them both. But all good things had an end point, and theirs was looming.

Was that why she'd been so bold with Ash? Maybe. Because Astrid was right. She never invited people to these events. Astrid always had a string of available women. Victoria was well aware some of them were dear friends, and Astrid always held out hope that one of them might stick. Thus far, they hadn't.

One of them, Hermione, had nearly worked out. She'd been kind, gorgeous, and so patient. She was Danish, and from a solid background. Her family were open, honest, loving. They'd encouraged Victoria to be the same, but it wasn't as easy when you had years of aristocracy and tradition to contend with. Hermione had stuck it out for nearly six months, but then she'd called it. Victoria had never given herself over fully, because she knew how it was going to end. How it always ended. Badly.

"If you do like her, she lives in the same country at least. That makes it easier."

"Or harder."

Astrid gave her a look. "You have more power over this situation than you think. You're the heir to the throne. Flex your muscles with your mother. She'll have to listen at some point. You've let her get away with what she wants. But what you want has to come into it, too."

Victoria nodded. That was easier said than done.

"Get your father on your side. The King has been far too silent in this for my liking. Doesn't he have any sway?"

She exhaled. "He always tells me that his role is to support her."

"That's true, but he can support you, too."

Victoria knew she was right. She had to stand up for herself at some point. But just the thought of it made her chest contract. Standing up for herself had never been easy with her mother.

Astrid put an arm around Victoria's shoulder and squeezed her tight. "You know my favourite thing about this, though?"

"Tell me."

"You haven't denied you like her, and you normally do. Which tells me everything I need to know."

Victoria closed her eyes. "I don't even know her." But she wanted to. More than she would ever let on to Astrid. It'd been less than 24 hours since their balcony chat, and she was already nervous about seeing Ash again.

"Sometimes, you don't need to. You just feel it here." Astrid pressed her hand to her chest.

There hadn't been a thunderbolt. But as soon as Victoria had laid eyes on Ash, there had been a connection. Victoria couldn't say any more than that, and didn't know why.

It scared her to death.

But also, excited her more than anything had in a very long time.

# Chapter Nine

"Okay, you literally need to stand still and stop spinning out. You're going to have to talk to her when you get there. I can make you look drop-dead gorgeous, but if you're foaming at the mouth with nerves, I can't do anything about that."

Ash's stylist, Luke, was on the other end of her call, saying all the right things. He was the kind of man whose perfectly sculpted eyebrows could start trends, end arguments, and make Ash question every life choice that had led to her own tragically inferior brow game.

"I know, I know." She was on the balls of her feet, willing her brain to stop somersaulting like an Olympic gymnast. She wasn't sure it was working. She closed her eyes, and tried to employ the breathing methods that had helped throughout her career. The reason she could take penalties under pressure. Block out everything else, and just focus on your breath. She sucked in a lung full of air, then exhaled. She repeated it five times.

It helped.

It always did.

She'd try to remember that for later.

"It's a daytime gig? Did you ask if it was casual?"

Ash nodded. "I did. She said it was, and to bring a

swimsuit." She was trying not to think about that. "But are royals ever truly casual?" What did 'casual' mean in royal circles? No tiaras, but still possibly diamonds?

"Yes! This is out of the spotlight. They don't always wear posh gear. Believe me, I know. I've dressed a few people going to more informal affairs with them in my time. Plus, she's told you to bring your swimmers. I say go with the beige tailored shorts, a white vest and a short-sleeved shirt, and pair it with your Gucci loafers. Low-key, but sophisticated. Not trying too hard, but still gorgeous. It's a barbecue, not a state banquet."

Ash nodded. "Okay, that sounds good. What if I get there and everyone's in evening wear?"

"Ashleigh. It's going to be 35 degrees this afternoon. Everyone will be sweating or in the pool. If you want to impress, make sure you pack your skimpiest bikini. I think Princess Victoria will approve."

*Did everyone suspect something?*

"What does that mean?"

"Just that she loves fashion. She's a style icon. As are you. You can icon each other off." He paused. On the other end of the line, she heard shouting, and Luke cleared his throat. "Are we done? Is my favourite client calm? Know what you're wearing?"

"Yes." Factually, she did. But she was going to doubt it until the moment she walked in the door. Was that because it was royalty, or because it was Victoria? Possibly a little of both.

"Remember to wear your chunky chain necklace, too. And your rings. They might be actual royalty, but you go there and slay like the queen you are."

She hung up, and took another deep breath. When she

looked up, Cam walked in the door, sarong on over her bikini. She gave Ash a wink.

"Shouldn't you be getting ready?"

Ash nodded. "I just got off the phone to Luke, so I will now."

Cam stood in front of her. "Your makeup looks good." She leaned in close. "How you feeling?"

"Like I don't know what I'm doing."

Cam smiled. "It's just a summer barbecue. You've been to them before."

"You sure you don't want to come with me?" Ash had offered, but Cam had turned her down. Her on-off not-girlfriend, Hayley, had said she might stop by today, and that was enough to keep Cam here. Plus, Ash would prefer to do this alone. If it was terrible, she'd have one drink, then leave.

Cam shook her head. "But if you need me to make an emergency call to get you out of there, just message me. I'll have my phone glued to my side."

"Thanks." Ash grabbed the shorts from the wardrobe, and put them on. She discarded her bra, and searched for a new one. Having shared changing rooms and bedrooms with Cam since she was eight, nakedness was nothing new to either of them. When she had her tank top on, she walked over to their window and stared down at the other girls, lounging by the pool, oblivious.

"Nobody's suspicious?" She turned to Cam.

"Why would they be? You said you're going for a drink with a friend. They all think it's a *friend-friend*. But they're not speculating over who it might be. They'd be here for hours and never guess that."

Ash sucked on the inside of her cheek as she tried and failed to find the clasp on her Tiffany necklace, one of her many new sponsors over the past year. "Be honest. Am I stupid to be going over there? Will I be out of my depth?" Yes, she and Victoria had a connection, but did that mean they had enough things in common to talk about for longer than ten minutes?

"I guess you're going to find out." Cam walked over, stood behind Ash and took the ends of the necklace in her hands. She did up the clasp, then turned her friend around until they were face to face. "What you need to remember is that you're Ashleigh Woods. You had to work to get your name known. This lot just got born, and boom! They were famous. You've got as much right to be there as them. Perhaps more. Hold your head up high, work the barbecue, then come home and tell me all about it. And please get a photo with Astrid and Sofia. Put that on your TikTok, imagine how it would blow up!"

* * *

The villa was as grand as she'd expected of a royal property: sweeping crescent driveway, elegant pillars flanking the entrance, vast windows drinking in the Mediterranean sun. In her childhood, she and her mum had always wondered who lived in houses like this. Debra Woods would never believe where her daughter was standing right now.

Ash pressed her palm to her chest, willing her heartbeat to slow. She had a talent for complicating her life, and today was an outstanding example. What had started as a simple sunshine getaway had somehow morphed into royal roulette. She knocked on the gleaming white door and waited, exhaling slowly. When it swung open, it wasn't staff behind it, but rather Dexter Matthews. Princess Victoria's boyfriend, whose face graced the tabloids weekly. He flashed her an easy grin and gestured her inside.

He was not in a tux, which Ash was thrilled about. Rather, he wore pink shorts, a baby blue T-shirt and flip-flops.

"Ashleigh Woods, it's my honour." He shook her hand, his smile genuine. "Absolute pleasure to meet you. I'm not a huge football fan, that's Victoria's department. But whenever we're together and you're playing, it's always on. Lionesses or the Royal Ravens. I even understood the offside rule by the end of the Euros, which I'm particularly proud of, being a gay—" He stopped, eyes wide. Twitched. "Gaaaaymer," he said, almost shouting the word, "who truth be told is not really into sports. But I've kinda turned a corner with women's sports."

Ash stared at Dexter, his cheeks flushing red. Had he just nearly said what she thought he had? Her gaydar blared so loud, it almost deafened her. It would explain Victoria's comments about them last night. Also, her telling Ash she wasn't just an ally.

However, she pushed down those thoughts, because if any of that were true, her brain would scramble.

She was here to have a good time, eat a royal burger, and hang out with queer royalty.

And Princess Victoria.

Or were they one and the same?

Dexter cleared his throat. "You look gorgeous, by the way." He furrowed his brow. "Fit. Athletic."

Was he always this clumsy with words, or was he just flustered?

"You'll fit right in with the garden full of gorgeous women in the back garden. I swear, there's no point going to a lesbian bar right now. All the lesbians within a 20-mile radius are in Astrid's garden." He winced. "And Victoria, obviously."

Ash wasn't sure what to say. Her mind whirled like a Christmas kaleidoscope.

"Follow me."

Dexter guided her down a sunlit hallway and into a sprawling open-plan space where two chefs worked in focused silence, their white toques bobbing as they assembled an array of salads and sides. It was surreal, like walking through a movie set – except the aromas were real, and the marble countertops gleamed under the Spanish sun streaming through floor-to-ceiling windows.

The first thing she saw as she walked into the garden was Princess Astrid, her arm casually draped around her wife, Sofia.

Ash came to an abrupt halt.

She couldn't quite believe she was this close to Astrid and Sofia. One of the only couples who made her override her TikTok ban and watch their videos. She'd seen them shopping at crazy expensive stores for a to-die-for sofa, and then watched them snuggle up on the sofa to watch a movie. She'd gone with them to choose their new puppy from a shelter. Seen them getting dressed for galas. They were royalty, but with a side order of normal.

When he realised she wasn't following him, Dexter turned back. "Everything okay?"

To her left, a group of men clutched flutes of fizz and laughed uproariously. She didn't recognise anyone in that group, but they looked like they had money and status. She could tell by the way they took up space in the world. But then she recalled Cam's words: "You've got as much right to be there as they have."

Ash gave him a tight grin. "Never better."

She'd met royalty before. Mixed with different people at plenty of events since she got the England captaincy. She could do this. Even if her favourite people to mingle with were disadvantaged kids who wanted to play football. Give her those over a corporate function any day.

She followed Dexter to where Victoria stood. At least all the women were in summer dresses, shorts or skirts. No evening wear on show.

*Thank you, Luke.*

"Look who I found on the doorstep?"

A quick smile flashed across Victoria's face when she saw Ash. Quickly followed by something else which Ash couldn't quite place.

"You made it! I'm so glad you came." Victoria reached out and stroked the top of Ash's arm, before quickly pulling her hand away.

It was a weirdly intimate gesture. Over even before it had happened. However, as soon as it was over, Ash wanted it to happen again. She wasn't used to being touched by people she didn't know. In fact, she usually hated it. But with Victoria? Things were different.

"You found us okay?" Victoria clasped her hands in front of her, knuckles white.

She wore a pair of pale-green tailored shorts, a green-and-white-striped short-sleeve shirt, and white deck shoes.

Interestingly, the collar of her shirt was up, and when Ash had walked up, she'd had a hand in her shorts pocket. Classic queer signs. Should Ash believe what she was seeing?

"Found it just fine." She smiled towards Astrid and Sofia. "Gorgeous home you have."

"Thank you, we like it." Astrid held out a hand, and Ash tried not to be too starstruck. "I'm Astrid, and this is my wife, Sofia."

Like she didn't know who they were.

*The whole world knew who they were.*

However, when Ash took Sofia's hand in hers, it was she who swooned. "I cannot tell you how thrilled I am to meet you!"

"We both are," Astrid said, her gravelly voice so familiar, it was like chatting to an old friend. "We were supporting Sweden in the Euros, obviously, but once you knocked us out, we totally cheered you on. We love that you're a fantastic athlete and also a queer role model. When Victoria told me she'd invited you, I was itching to meet you."

"Stop it, you're making Ash squirm," Victoria stepped in. "Dex, can you get her a drink? There's some champagne in the bucket."

"On it," Dexter said.

Ash waved away Victoria's concerns. "It's fine. I'm fans of you both, too. Your TikTok stuff is sensational. I'm addicted, as are most queer women I know."

"You see!" Astrid told Sofia. "We're global, baby! Sofia thinks we sometimes overshare. I told her there's no such thing. We're working royals. We've got brands to promote, and charities to support. Plus, I think it's great that we can show what a healthy, normal, loving relationship we've got. Not everybody with such a platform can or does."

She glanced at Victoria.

Ash saw it.

Something flashed across Victoria's face, and then she stuck both hands in her pockets and stared at the floor. This was not the Victoria she saw every day in the papers in her fitted dresses and tailored jackets. This was the real Victoria. Still not quite relaxed. With friends who knew her enough to make comments like that.

"It's up to us to be the ones at the front," Astrid told Ash. "Not leading, just lighting the way."

Dexter approached, a tray of champagne in his hand. "Are you talking about you being TikTok sluts again?"

"You're just jealous. What you wouldn't give to be a TikTok slut yourself. I know you, Dexter Matthews. Any excuse to put on some glitter and be over the top."

"Now I just have to convince Vicky here to do the same." He stopped at Victoria's side and kissed her cheek. "Isn't that right, darling?"

Victoria rolled her eyes, but smiled all the same. "My glitter days were short, sweet and happened when I was five," she said. "My champagne days, though…"

# Chapter Ten

At the top of the staircase, Victoria led Ash down a cream hallway with massive abstract paintings of women lining the walls. It was Astrid's instructions when she built the house that all the commissioned artwork should be of women, stating she wanted female power flowing through the house. Victoria couldn't imagine any British royal residence following suit.

"I hope you weren't overwhelmed by Astrid and Sofia."

Ash shook her head. "They're interested in my job, and vice versa. Plus, they put on a mean barbecue. That pork belly was to die for. I can't eat that the whole year round, but in the off-season, it's the perfect treat." She patted her flat stomach. "Let's hope I don't look too bloated in my bikini."

Victoria couldn't envision Ash looking anything but perfect. "I'm sure you're going to look stunning."

It was out of her mouth before she could stuff it back in. She was fairly sure a princess wasn't meant to say stuff like that. But hadn't she promised herself she was going to let her hair down this weekend? She'd invited Ash here, after all. Plus, she was telling her the truth.

She came to a stop in front of a pristine white door. "You okay changing in my en suite? I'm not sure which of the other

68

guest bedrooms are taken. I'd hate for you to be half naked and have a Swedish Earl bumble in needing the toilet."

However, when she walked into her bedroom, Victoria remembered her indecisiveness when she was getting ready that morning. How she wanted to make the best impression on Ash, but also not come on too strong. Particularly when Ash still thought she was straight. Three or four tops were still strewn over the bed. Victoria rushed in and collected them up, depositing them on the chaise longue in the corner, and hiding them under two cushions.

Then she turned to Ash, who looked delicious in her shorts. Footballer's legs had always been her downfall. She cleared her throat, then ran a hand through her hair and tucked it behind her ear.

In turn, Ash fiddled with the strap of her Gucci bag.

Now that they were alone, Victoria found herself wishing for the buffer of Astrid and Sofia's chatter.

The silence felt charged, intimate.

Her skin prickled with awareness as Ash watched her.

"Do you come here often?" Ash winced as soon as the words left her mouth. "That was meant to be a genuine question, not a terrible pickup line." Her cheeks flushed. "Not that I'm... you know what, never mind."

The reply, "That's a shame", danced on Victoria's tongue, but she swallowed it back.

"We do. It's a sanctuary of sorts: somewhere we can just be ourselves." She caught herself almost adding more about Dexter, but stopped. "When Astrid and Sofia visit London, they stay with me, so this is their way of returning the favour. You know what it's like, being in the spotlight. Fame is rather like the world's most lavish picnic. Wonderful in theory, but you're still going to get stung by wasps eventually. It comes with the territory."

"I like that analogy."

"Thanks." Victoria gave her a shy smile. "Anyway, sometimes, when I'm here, it feels like a switch-off from being a princess. Which, behind the glitzy title, is really a job you can never leave. I mean, I could, but I never would. But I can come here and have a break for a few days." She had no idea why she'd ended up down this conversational cul-de-sac. "You want to get changed first?"

Ash nodded, and stepped into Victoria's en suite. That was the cue for Victoria to throw all her discarded shirts back into her wardrobe, then plump up her cushions. She didn't want Ash to think she was a slob.

A few minutes later, Ash emerged from the bathroom, and Victoria instantly forgot every lesson in poise she'd ever learnt. The black bikini top and boy shorts showcased Ash's athlete's body: lean muscle and elegant lines that even the loose white cheesecloth shirt she wore on top couldn't fully conceal. Victoria's internal agreement not to stare at Ash's flat stomach was already in tatters. Her eyes traced the subtle definition of Ash's shoulders, the curve where her waist met her hips. Her mouth went dry.

Ash gave her a wobbly smile as she hoisted her bag, and Victoria's heart stumbled in its rhythm.

"Do you need to change?"

"I've got my bikini on already." Victoria's voice came out steadier than she felt, even as her pulse thundered in her ears. Her gaze betrayed her again, drinking in the sight of

Ash's football-toned legs. A lifetime of diplomatic training, of perfect small talk and careful words, and here she was, struck speechless by Ash Woods in beach wear.

She gestured weakly towards the door. "Shall we?"

*  *  *

An hour later, the whole party had decamped to lounge by the pool or soak up the bubbles in one of the two hot tubs. Victoria and Ash were in a very loose game of water volleyball (no net, the object was to keep the ball from hitting the water). Their opponents were Astrid and Sofia, and the Swedish pair were determined to win so they could say they'd beaten the Lionesses' captain. However, Ash was ultra-competitive, as was Victoria. So far, it wasn't going the Swedes' way.

"Fan i helvete!" Astrid exclaimed as Ash slammed another winner into the water.

Victoria was well aware that meant 'fucking hell!' in Swedish.

"I figured it might be easy to beat you at this because it's not to do with your feet. You can't be good at all sports, surely? But apparently, you can. Plus, we already know about Victoria's competitive streak."

Ash grinned at her as they high-fived their latest winning point, and set themselves for the next serve. Victoria was pleased to have something to do to take her mind off the fact that Ash was still in a bikini, and also that Dexter and Sidney were currently on about their tenth glass of champagne, and lying beside each other poolside finding something hilarious.

It wasn't unusual at this particular barbecue. Everywhere

Victoria looked, there were queer couples of all flavours chatting, laughing, arms around shoulders, sharing kisses. She'd asked Dexter to be discreet, but this was his space. *Their* space. A party they both agreed was somewhere they could be themselves. She'd invited outsiders in. It was up to her to deal with that, whether she liked it or not.

But first, they had a game of volleyball to win.

"How many points do we have to get to?" she asked.

"You got some place better to be?" Astrid replied.

"Maybe relaxing with a cocktail?"

"Honestly, British royalty. Always so demanding," Astrid grinned. "It's first to 25. You're two points off. We need to start our streak of 15 points to win. We're ready, aren't we, darling?"

Sofia nodded, pushing her sunglasses off her face.

Ash slammed the next two points beyond them within 30 seconds, and they won with ease. They all high-fived, got out of the pool and Astrid got more drinks. Victoria opted for champagne, Ash for water, then Victoria led her to the vacant hot tub to their left. Victoria hit the button to get bubbles, and they settled beside each other. She was rarely lost for words, but it appeared to happen a lot around Ashleigh Woods.

When she glanced poolside, Dexter leaned over and kissed Sidney. She closed her eyes briefly, then turned to Ash. She was staring the same way. There was no doubt she'd seen it. It was time to address the elephant in the room. She cleared her throat, took a slug of bubbles, then started to speak.

"I think you've probably seen Dexter over there with Sidney. Realised they're actually together." Her voice wobbled as she spoke. This was something she'd never done before outside her circle. But something about Ash made her feel like this was okay. That she wasn't going to betray this confidence.

Hopefully, Ash could join the dots to explain why Victoria had invited her. She summoned up all her courage and ploughed on.

"There are a lot of queer couples here, couples who have very different partners in their public life to keep up appearances. But Astrid's parties are where we can all come to be our true selves. Including me." Deep breath in, as she snagged Ash's gaze.

Damn it, this never got any easier, did it?

"I'm queer. Always have been. As is Dexter." She paused to gauge Ash's response, but her gorgeous face didn't give anything away. "We're good friends, and this arrangement has suited us both. His parents aren't accepting. Mine are, but only so far. As you can imagine, queer royals have existed throughout history, but nobody has ever been out. My mother is not keen on that changing."

Ash's gaze never wavered as she asked. "And you? Do you want to be out?"

Victoria exhaled deeply and stretched out her left arm. It was nice to be listened to. Nice to be asked what she wanted.

"I think I do. I know it won't be easy, but I'd rather be honest than sneak around and lie to everyone. My parents always tell me we have an obligation to the country to be dutiful and serve, but surely our happiness has to come somewhere on the list, too?"

Now it was Ash's turn to exhale. "There was me thinking today was already scoring high on the more surreal afternoons

I've had in my life by coming to a royal barbecue. But now the future Queen has just told me she's queer." But she smiled as she said it.

Victoria frowned. "Is that too much?"

But Ash shook her head. "I picked up something when we met, and today, too. But I would never assume anything. It's what football has taught me: when it comes to sexuality, many people are on a spectrum."

"I'd love to say I'm that interesting, but I'm not. I like girls." Just saying that was freeing. However, it came with an edge of danger, too. Because she was sat half-naked, a little tipsy, in a hot tub with a girl she very much liked. Who, if Victoria wasn't mistaken, was now looking at her with a very different look in her eye.

"Same," Ash replied, raising her glass to Victoria. "It seems then, we have something in common."

Victoria's insides melted. "I'm very much hoping that we do." She was rusty when it came to flirting. The bubbles ran out. Ash leaned over and pressed the buttons. Her muscular arms made the hairs on the back of Victoria's neck stand on end. Ash was ridiculously attractive, and Victoria was about to propose the most ridiculous plan. It had made sense in her head earlier. But now Ash was this close, with flesh on show, she wasn't so sure.

Ash settled back beside her, then stretched her arms out. Her fingertips brushed the top of Victoria's shoulder.

Victoria's breath caught at the ghost of contact, her skin blazing at the site of Ash's touch.

Yep, she was royally screwed.

The water suddenly felt too hot, or maybe that was just her. She fought the urge to lean into the touch, to close the careful inches between them. The jets churned, but Victoria could hear nothing over the throb of her pulse. She had to hold it together; try to forget about the heat radiating between their almost-touching bodies.

"I have to say, you and Dexter play the part well. Until I met you this week, I would never have known."

Victoria nodded. "We're a little *too* good." She glanced across the pool. "But he wants to be with Sidney, and I want my real life to begin. The one where I can hold someone's hand in public."

Talking about it to another woman – another *lesbian* – made her feel positively buoyant. Like she'd just inhaled a ray of sunshine.

Crucially, Ash hadn't jumped out of the hot tub and headed home. That was a good first step. The trouble was, Victoria had no idea what the next step might entail.

"Your parents know you're queer?"

Victoria nodded. "Yes, and they're fine with it in principle. However, they'd be happy for me to have a sham marriage, and just see women on the side. But that's exhausting and ultimately, I know it'll affect my physical and mental health. I'd rather deal with whatever comes with being out than the other way around."

She fixed Ash with her gaze. "If it helps, you're the first woman I've ever invited here myself. The first one I've felt a connection to who I met independently." It was a big deal, Astrid was right. "I wanted you to know. If I kiss someone, start anything with someone, I have to put my cards on the table because of who I am. Am I going mad, or did you feel something between us the moment we met, too?"

Ash licked her lips and swallowed hard. She didn't reply straight away.

Victoria's heart shrivelled to the size of a pea. How quickly could she disappear under the water? Right at that moment, the bubbles ran out again. Dammit, what was wrong with them? The water stilled, echoing Victoria's heart.

But then, Ash shook her head. "You weren't going mad. I felt it, too. I wouldn't be here today otherwise. I had to come and see if what I thought was true. If you were queer. And you are. Also, very attractive. Which makes life that little bit more complicated, doesn't it?"

Her fingertips brushed Victoria's shoulder again, and pinpricks of joy rushed through her. She was hyperaware of everything: the soft lap of water against skin, the afternoon air on her face, but mostly Ash's presence beside her, real and solid and wanting her back.

"I guess you could say that. But you've seen my friends. You didn't run after half an hour." She paused. "Would you like to kiss me?"

Ash narrowed her eyes, blew out a breath, then gave a hesitant nod. "Is that a trick question?"

"No, but I just wanted to check." Victoria dropped her gaze to Ash's lips. Pink, pretty, beyond inviting. "I really want to kiss you, too." Heat swelled in her. Understatement of the year.

"Is it a princess thing to be this forward?"

Victoria smiled, then took a deep breath. "This is not usually me. Nor is what I'm about to say. But because you are who you are and I am who I am, I'm going to suggest something radical."

"Okay?"

"I need time to break up with Dexter, and I don't want to drag you into that. I want you to enjoy the rest of your holiday with your friends, I'll go back to London, and then I go to Australia and New Zealand for four weeks on a state visit." She could see the confusion on Ash's face.

"What I'm saying is, think about if you really want to kiss me. Because it wouldn't end there, I guarantee it." The attraction between them was too strong. It was almost like a magnetic pull, drawing them together. So far, Victoria had fought it all the way, but it was getting harder by the minute.

When she looked up, Ash's heated stare burned her skin.

Victoria shook her head. "What I mean is, I come with a lot of baggage, a lot of conditions." She really wasn't selling this very well. "But I really want to try dating, perhaps a relationship, and give it my all." And now she'd said too much, hadn't she?

Ash sucked on her bottom lip, but then fixed Victoria with her perfect gaze. "And here was me thinking I was just in a hot tub with a gorgeous woman."

Victoria's heart didn't just skip a beat: it detonated. The simplicity of Ash's words stripped away all her careful defences. Every cell in her body screamed want.

"How I wish it was that easy."

A trail of water worked its way down Ash's cheek.

Victoria desperately wanted to reach out and touch it. She sat on her hands to stop it happening.

"First, you need to work on your sales pitch," Ash told her. "Everyone comes with baggage. Even if yours is heavier than normal, it's outweighed by your beautiful face, surely."

Victoria's heart thumped loud. Ash was far better at flirting than she was. Which wasn't hard.

"Second, now you keep talking about kissing, I *really* want to kiss you." Ash did the unthinkable. She shifted closer, until their mouths were centimetres away.

"I understand you want to make a clean break first. I respect that. But I came especially to see you. Plus, he's over there kissing someone else. Aren't you allowed to do the same? What if we just tested the water? Just an exploratory kiss, to see if we're compatible?"

Victoria's lungs forgot how to work as Ash's breath touched her lips.

"Don't make this any harder." The words barely made it past her lips. How she wanted to throw caution to the wind, to taste Ash's lips. But she couldn't. Because she knew herself and she didn't want to fuck this up.

Nothing could happen until the Dexter split was done and dusted. Yes, he was kissing Sidney, but she wanted to start whatever this might be with a clean slate. Because as soon as she kissed Ash, it wouldn't stop there. She was certain of that. She had to sort out her fake relationship before she started a possible real one.

"I've got your number. I promise I'll call you when I'm back." Each word cost her, fighting against every instinct that urged her to pull Ash to her. "Just so you know, I always keep my word."

# Chapter Eleven

"Have you seen the news?" Ash's mum, Debra, walked into the kitchen, phone held aloft. She clutched the top of one of the white wooden chairs. "Your friend has called off her engagement!"

"My friend?" Ash had no idea who her mum was talking about.

"Princess Victoria."

Ash blushed despite herself. She hadn't told anybody but Cam where she went the afternoon of the barbecue. It felt too sensitive to put out there, too dangerous. Even though nothing had happened.

Then again, *everything* had happened.

Ash had known this royal announcement was coming, and that was insanely weird. Victoria told her she was going to break the news by posting her relationship status on her socials to single. By deleting photos of her and Dexter looking coupley. However, Ash hadn't known the exact moment it was going to happen.

She did now.

"I met her once, Mum." A lie. "She's hardly my friend." Also a lie, as Victoria had been messaging her all week telling her how the trip was going.

"She spent at least ten seconds longer with you than she did anyone else at the MBE ceremony. I think there was a connection." Her mum grinned like this was the best joke ever. "Plus, we sat in the royal box at Wimbledon two weeks ago. Who do you think puts in a good word on the invites?"

Ash had taken her mum to the women's semi-final, and she had not stopped raving about sitting in the row behind Bradley Cooper.

Her mum tutted at her phone. "There are crowds forming at the Palace gates. People are holding up Victoria and Dexter tea towels and mugs. Don't get me wrong, I've always liked the royals. Victoria seems lovely, but that Dexter? He always seemed a little too try-hard for me. Too eager. But I hope she's being taken care of in Australia if she's upset."

Ash gave in and opened her phone. Sure enough, her mum wasn't lying. Outside the enormous iron Palace gates, crowds were gathered with candles and flowers, mourning the end of Victoria's relationship. Which is exactly the reason Victoria had done it while she was out of the country.

> Let the media frenzy peak, then die down before I get home, with luck.

That's what Victoria had told Ash this week, via WhatsApp. Who knew that royalty used WhatsApp, too?

Now, watching the interviews on her phone, with reporters and the public speculating wildly on the reasons behind the split, Ash wasn't sure it would die down quickly. People cared about who Victoria was coupled with. But it didn't put Ash off. If anything, it made her *more* interested. Even though she'd said she wanted her next relationship to be low-key. Out of the limelight. Which made this *precisely* what she hadn't ordered.

Sometimes, her choices didn't make sense. But when the future Queen expresses interest in you, you had to see where it went. Even if it meant lying to your mum when you came to see her post-training. A teeny-tiny lie.

Ash had been following Victoria's royal tour with an enthusiasm usually reserved for football stats. The princess's schedule was dazzling, a whirlwind of state dinners, trade meetings, and charity events. Each appearance only made Ash's impression of her grow. She wasn't just beautiful; she was brilliant, commanding rooms full of diplomats as easily as she'd enchanted Ash in that hot tub.

She should probably be asking Victoria for public speaking tips next time they met, but she was pretty sure it wouldn't be top of their agenda. Because every time Victoria appeared on her phone screen or TV, Ash found herself studying her lips, wondering what she was thinking behind that poised smile. Was she ready for today's news? Nervous about tomorrow's appearances, and the inevitable questions about the breakup?

*Focus.* Twice this morning, her drills coach had caught her drifting during training. She couldn't tell him why. She couldn't tell anyone.

There was nothing to tell.

Yet.

"Have you come to see me, or have you come to smirk at your phone at my kitchen table?"

Ash put it down. She'd message Victoria later. She'd be

asleep now, anyway. 2pm here, which meant it was 3am in Australia.

"I'm here to see you, Mother Dearest."

Debra smiled, placated. "How was training today? It's weird having you around during the summer. You're normally off at a tournament, have been forever. World Cup. Euros. Olympics. She Believes. Am I allowed to say I quite like that England didn't qualify for the Olympics?"

"No, you're not." Ash shook her head, smiling all the same. It had stung at the time, but having no competitive games for a month was what her body needed. It was her mind that took more to convince.

"But I like it. You're coming to see us a little more, which is always good." Her mum paused, then nodded towards the counter, where familiar ingredients were laid out on top. "You can help me make some banana bread if you like. You want to do the wet ingredients, and I'll do the dry?"

"Sure."

Ash jumped up, knowing this routine far better than the corner routines they'd been practising this morning. The Ravens lost the league by fine margins last year, and one was their inability to score from set pieces. Their coach, Jo Kendall, had hired a new set-piece coach to try to improve that element of their game. Ash was on corner duty, and had spent a frustrating morning trying to curl the ball to the back post, and failing for a long while. She got the hang of it by the end, but her foot just hadn't wrapped around the ball today.

Set-piece coach, Dwayne, had been nothing but encouraging. However, Ash was her own worst enemy. It was only when she managed to silence her inner critic that her touch started to return. She hoped mashing together two ripe bananas and two eggs, along with some melted butter would prove far less problematic.

Ash had made banana bread with her mum since she was little. It was a staple. Did Victoria do things like this with her mum? She couldn't imagine it.

She whipped the eggs, trying to clear her mind of any princess thoughts.

Her mum put the oven on and assessed her as Ash weighed out the butter.

"Remember to cover it as you melt it. It splattered all over the microwave that one time."

"That was when I was still playing at Crystal Palace. Time to let it go." When she thought about it, she'd always been at teams with royal names. Crystal Palace, then the Royal Ravens. Did that mean something?

Debra grinned. "You never answered my question. How was training? You seem a little distracted."

Ash set the butter to melt at an appropriate temperature. "Fine. We did some gym work, then some corner drills. I was shit at them, but I got better. Then we had delicious salmon in the canteen."

"You don't know you're born, getting your meals cooked at work."

She was well aware. "I'm a peak-condition athlete. They need to make sure I maintain that."

"You're spoilt, that's what you are." But her mum kissed her cheek all the same. "Is there a new woman in the picture? I know the signs, you become all distracted. I remember it well with Danielle. You stop eating as much, and get a little tense, jittery."

"I do not." It was a reflexive response. Ash knew it was true.

"You're not slick. Ever since Marbella, you've been distracted. And don't think I missed that guilty little exchange of glances with Cam at the airport when I asked if you'd met anyone new or interesting." She bumped Ash's hip, grinning. "Trust me, love, I perfected that exact innocent face with my own mum, back in the day."

"I'll have to have a word with Cam about making better faces." Ash was going for making light of it.

It might work.

Or perhaps not, if the raised eyebrow was anything to go by.

"Nothing happened. I didn't kiss anyone." She wasn't lying. "I told you. It was a girls' trip, pure and simple."

Also, a trip where she'd met a girl who she couldn't wait to see again.

\* \* \*

Since the news had broken, they'd started to share regular messages, much to Ash's delight.

> You're all over the news here. I can't pick up my phone without somebody speculating about what went wrong for you and Dexter.

> I know. He's been keeping me up to date.

84

> Can you handle it? Aren't the Australians obsessed, too?

> They are, but it's not anywhere near as bad as it would be in London. I'm still glad my team planned it this way. It means I can avoid the main spotlight glare. Over here, it's more a low-wattage bulb. Plus, I've had three proposals today now that I'm back on the market. You'd think people would leave it at least a day.

She was honest-to-goodness funny. For some reason, Ash hadn't expected that. Perhaps because the royals were fed to us as bland and boring. Beige. Victoria was anything but beige.

> How are you feeling?

> Honestly? Lighter. Happier. Relieved I don't have to pretend anymore. But this is just step one.

The following day, Victoria had flown to Uluru, where she'd gone to visit a lesbian-owned restaurant that did the best steak in the area. It was her third engagement of the day, after visiting a nursery in the morning, along with having lunch with indigenous leaders. However, it was the dinner with the sapphics that Victoria was most nervous about.

> Please don't watch it, because I always blush when I'm around lesbians or queer people in public life. I don't know why. Guilt over not being out?

> Nobody suspects. Just look gorgeous and be nice to the lesbians.

> I'm always nice to lesbians.

> I know.

> I think I'm also nervous because I worry they'll see right through me, and then my deepest secrets will be all over the press tomorrow. Stupid to worry about that. Especially right now.

> The only person with the superpower to see through you is me. We already established that.

Ash loved that it was true.

In response, Victoria sent her back a row of double heart-eyes, along with the Superman logo.

That had been followed by an interminable 20-minute gap where Victoria had been typing, stopped, restarted, stopped.

> Where are you writing these messages?

> Back of my car. I've told my aide, Tanya, that I'm checking in on Dex, but I don't think she believes me. I'm grinning too much at my phone. I love Dex, but now is not the time to grin at any conversation between us. Right now, he's regretting his choices from three years ago. Anyway, both Tanya and I are thrilled to be in the car as it's air-conditioned and away from flies, who attacked us yesterday. They have no regard for royalty.

> Off with their heads.

> Tried that. They were too quick.
> How's your week been?

Victoria, Ash was learning, was always interested in what she was doing.

> Yesterday I made banana bread with my mum and was terrible at corners.
> Plus, it was arm day in the gym.

> I'm a fan of arm day, especially for you.

That text had made Ash sit back on her sofa, then almost fan herself.

> Are you flirting with me, Your Royal Highness?

> Well spotted. No flies on you.

Ash had wondered if this constant messaging at all hours might be a distraction. While the answer was a definite yes, it was also something she'd come to truly look forward to. A highlight of her day. Getting to know a woman she was interested in. Someone she hadn't even kissed yet. It felt like she was courting. Like she was back in the days of her grandmother, or even older.

She'd never done it before. She'd only ever dated footballers, and she'd wanted to change that. Her past girlfriends had always played on the same team or in the same league, so they were usually on the same schedules. With Victoria, there was none of that. Her schedule was the craziest Ash had ever encountered, her downtime non-existent.

> I worked on my biceps, then got them out today for the new Tiffany campaign I'm doing. It's about strength and jewellery. I drive a cool sports car in the ad, I hope you get to see it soon.

> So do I. It sounds right up my ally. Your arms and fast cars are two of my favourite things.

Messaging made Victoria way bolder than in real life. Ash had to up her game. Marianne had sent some initial proof shots already. Ash quickly edited a couple, then messaged them to Victoria. It didn't take long for a row of fire emojis to light up her phone.

> Your football skills drew me in, but your biceps and calves don't hurt. You look incredible.

Ash's heart did a backflip. She could totally get used to being chatted up by royalty.

> I can't wait to get back and run my fingers over your biceps.

Ash blinked. They still hadn't spoken about when they were going to meet up.

> I hope I'm allowed to say that, and you don't feel too objectified.

> On the contrary, I particularly enjoy being objectified by you.

Ash was in so much trouble. She was already skipping her regular sleep patterns to message Victoria in the middle of the night. She didn't care.

It was a slippery slope, she knew that. But somehow, despite knowing it was the wrong thing to do, she couldn't stop herself. She made excuses, saying it was still pre-season. That her sleep didn't matter so much when the games weren't truly high stakes.

But they mattered. After the previous season, every game was a step back to her very best. Past-Ash would never have let anything get in the way of her journey back to peak fitness. Evenings out were routinely turned down. Movie premieres were slipped away from. Alcohol received a shake of the head. But a two-line message with a smiley face from a princess was the catalyst to turn her head.

However, she had it under control. At least, that's what she kept telling herself. If her mum thought she was distracted, and if her coach wondered why her corner kicks kept going awry, they could keep wondering. Right now, it didn't matter. All that mattered to Ash was Victoria's plane landing again and them somehow breathing the same air. Where maybe, just maybe, she might get to kiss her.

> By the way, when I'm back next week, Tanya tells me as FA Women's Patron, I'm slotted in to open a new facility at the National Women's Training Centre in Birmingham. Will you be there, too?

She'd woken up to this message this morning, and then plunged into an ice bath of anxiety. She'd imagined her next meeting with Victoria would be behind closed doors. Just the two of them. Not with the whole world watching, and probably still itching to ask her about what happened with Dexter.

> I will be there. We're in England training camp that week, and that's media day. It's a nice surprise you'll be there, too.

> Not quite the intimate setting I'd hoped for, but beggars can't be choosers. It'll still be lovely to see you.

Ash had stared at her phone as if it were a bomb. Her head throbbed with excitement, but also fear. While the princess was far away, flirting had been easy. Now that she was due back, it was about to get a whole lot more real.

But she was in this now. She was well aware of that. She had to see how this would turn out, good or bad.

Ash's heart wanted Victoria.

There was no turning back.

# Chapter Twelve

With the efficiency that had made her the youngest senior aide in royal history, Tanya checked her tablet and outlined the schedule. "We're going to be here for two hours, Ma'am. You're going to open the centre with the FA Chair, the England Manager, and England Captain beside you," she said, her crisp pink shirt as perfectly pressed as her planning. "I've scheduled you in for an hour afterwards for player interaction and chat. There's also talk of a kickabout for the cameras."

"You packed my jeans and trainers?" Victoria asked.

Tanya nodded. "Of course. Then we're going straight to your tailor for the final fitting of your suit for the upcoming state visit. The burgundy suit. The one you really liked."

Her gran, the Queen Mother, had messaged Victoria earlier, asking how she was after the breakup. It was sweet of her. She and Victoria had always shared a close bond, even if she didn't know all the facts of Victoria's life.

Victoria surveyed her nails, wondering for the millionth time if the pink she'd chosen – Dior's Grace – was a little too garish. She'd agonised over it far too long yesterday. Her indecisiveness wasn't like her at all. As her mother always said, "the country is in good hands with you at the helm.

Thank goodness you were born first, and not Michael." She wouldn't have said that if she'd seen what a basket case Victoria was over a nail colour and her mascara choice.

Today, Victoria was stuck together by hope, Dior, and Charlotte Tilbury.

She sucked on her cheek, trying not to fixate on the fact that in less than an hour, she'd see Ash for the first time in a month. So much had changed between them, yet not enough. They had to take this slow; there was no other option. Though Ash had agreed to meet properly, they hadn't set a date. For now, their reunion would happen here, under the watchful eyes of 50 photographers.

Victoria had managed to survive her lesbian dinner in Australia without outing herself, but Ash hadn't been within touching distance then. Today would require all her self-control not to do something stupid, like kiss Ash in front of everyone. When it came to Ash, it was *all* she wanted to do. Even going cold-water swimming in the royal pond this morning hadn't calmed her down.

She got out her phone and pulled up the messages they'd sent this morning.

> Can't wait to see you today. Will you be rushing off or do you have time for a coffee?

Victoria liked how direct Ash was.

> I'll make it happen if it kills me.

Her tailor could wait if she had to.

I'd prefer you alive, NGL.

I'll try my best.

The car pulled up and Victoria got out, Tanya smiling as she held the door. Creamy sunshine coated them as they walked into the building, Victoria doing her best to ignore the shouts from the waiting press as the cameras snapped.

"How are you, Ma'am? Any truth in the rumour that Dexter is on anti-depressants after the split?"

"Is it true that you found Dexter in bed with two other women, Ma'am?"

"Any truth in the pegging rumour, Your Highness? Was that the straw that broke the camel's back?"

She honestly had no idea where they got their stories from. She kept a straight face as she passed them, only at the end remembering to smile. She still wanted any photos to look good. Not like she'd just swallowed a swarm of bees.

Once inside the building, away from the whir of cameras, her shoulders dropped. Cutting a ribbon was a welcome break from the barrage of interest over Dexter. Her PR team had told her it should die down in a week or two. Until then, she just had to ride it out. Her phone buzzed in her bag, but she couldn't take it out. It wasn't what royals did, even if they wanted to.

Footsteps on the shiny floor snapped her out of her reverie. It was Simon from the FA. They'd had a meeting on Zoom when she agreed to become patron, and Simon had said all the right things about pushing the women's game forward.

Right at this moment, though, Simon was a rabbit in the headlights. She got that a lot when people first met her. It was her job to put them at ease, as her mother always told her. "You serve them, not the other way around."

"Simon, lovely to meet you."

He shook her outstretched hand and bowed so low, his head almost touched his knees. "The pleasure is all mine, your Majesty."

When he looked up, there was sweat on his brow.

"I'm not the Queen just yet, but I like your confidence. Victoria is just fine."

Simon blushed beetroot purple. "Your Highness! Gosh, I'm sorry."

His blushes were spared as more footsteps approached. Victoria's spine straightened as Ash walked towards her, the crisp lines of her England tracksuit making this feel startlingly more real than their late-night messages. She caught the slight hesitation in Ash's step: nearly imperceptible, but there. Was Ash's stomach doing the same pancake flips as hers?

Victoria pressed her thumb against her finger and focused on the solid floor beneath her feet, on England manager Gill Cooper, on anything except how Ash's half-smile made the formal space feel far more alive than it should.

"Victoria, lovely to see you again." Gill shook her hand and gave her a warm smile. Victoria had met Gill a couple of times before, and had always liked her. She wasn't overawed by royalty, which Victoria appreciated.

Then the moment she'd been waiting for. Ash stepped up, so close she could breathe her in.

"Nice to see you again, Your Royal Highness." Ash's

voice was smooth, not betraying an ounce of the messages they'd exchanged for the best part of a month. When their hands touched, an electric current that could have powered Birmingham surged through Victoria, but she kept it together. The centre's frontage was all glass, and photographers' lenses had enormous zooms. She didn't want to give them any reason to speculate.

However, when she looked into the warm embrace of Ash's stare, she couldn't help the slight tremor that ran through her body. The things she couldn't say sat heavy in her chest, but for now, being in the same room was enough. Like the first step of something she couldn't name yet, but wanted to.

"You, too," she told her.

"Okay," Simon said, crashing their intimate moment, completely unaware. "The ribbon cutting is set to take place in ten minutes, but the press are all here, so we could do it now? Get it over with? That would give you more time to meet the team and have a coffee. Would that work, Ma'am?"

Victoria nodded, not risking a glance at Ash. "Lead the way."

\* \* \*

The press pack had behaved and not asked any more about Dexter, which is all Victoria could have asked. She'd cut the ribbon, posed for photos, but now came the part she hadn't prepared for. A kickabout with the team. Their actual training was done, and a select few had been hand-picked to entertain her. Notably, captain Ash, goalkeeper Cam, and the tall one whose name Victoria had again forgotten. She clearly had a mental block when it came to her, but she remembered them all on the dance floor in Marbella.

"Great to see you, and sorry to pull you away from your camp."

"No problem at all." Cam gave a slight bow.

Footballers did not curtsy, Victoria was learning.

Cam held up a finger. "Just know, Your Highness, I'm not going to go easy on you and let you score just because you're a princess. Give it your best shot, okay?"

"I'm not going to go easy on you, either," Victoria fired back, enjoying the look of surprise on Cam's face. "I've scored a penalty before." It was a lie. Her school had frowned on football. But she understood mind games as well as the next person. Yes, this was just a photo opportunity, but Victoria could never let a competitive moment pass her by.

"Pleasure to see you again, Your Highness," the tall player said. "I'm Sasha Goodall."

Did she know Victoria never remembered her name?

"If you've ever watched a game, you'll know that without me, the team would fall apart."

"If you believe that, you'll believe anything, Ma'am," Ash chipped in.

Ma'am. The word dropped from Ash's lips and straight into Victoria's bloodstream. She couldn't meet those eyes, not when her mind was already stripping that formal address down to its bare skin.

She blinked, shook her head, and snapped her gaze to Ash.

Victoria pressed her tongue to the back of her front teeth, and tried not to think about how turned on she was.

"We're going to do three penalties each. Loser carries the coffees after from the free coffee van. Okay?" Ash aimed the question at Victoria.

She cleared her throat and tried not to taste desire. "I hope you've got asbestos hands. You'll need them to carry those coffees." She hadn't quite worked out how she was going to beat the England captain at penalties, but bravado won out before her brain engaged.

"Are you sure you don't want to borrow a pair of football boots, Ma'am?" Sasha asked. "The pitch is a little churned up, and boots might offer you more grip than your trainers."

Victoria glanced at her trainer-clad feet which she'd hastily changed into before taking the field. She shook her head. "I'm sure I'll cope." Her mother would already have a cardiac about her appearing in jeans and trainers.

Victoria's stomach knotted as they approached the penalty spot. The irony wasn't lost on her: trying to impress Ash by displaying her complete lack of football skills. But beyond her personal feelings, this mattered. While her grandfather had widened the gap between crown and public, and her mother walked a cautious middle ground, Victoria had different plans. Every photo op, every awkward penalty kick, was another brick in the bridge she was building. She wanted her legacy to be about lifting people up, not knocking them down.

However, if she ended up as a meme looking like one of those women who'd never kicked a football in her life, she might die. This wasn't just her reputation at stake. This was her reputation as a queer woman, too.

Sasha went first, and hilariously, blasted the ball over the bar. She threw up her hands, then turned to the rest of them. "It was all those photographers putting me off!"

Next up, Ash.

Cameras clicked.

Victoria tried not to focus on Ash's bum, but it wasn't easy.

She stepped up, buried it in the bottom corner, then punched the air.

Now it was Victoria's turn.

"You're going to smash it," Ash told her. "You can achieve anything you put your mind to."

Victoria's gaze dropped to Ash's mouth.

Ash's gaze settled on Victoria.

She knew exactly what she'd like to put her *lips* to. She closed her eyes and willed herself into the here and now.

Ash stepped closer. "Ready to show the waiting press pack you're not just a pretty face?" Her hot whisper in Victoria's ear did nothing to calm her nerves.

Victoria took a deep breath, blocked out the cameras, took a short run-up and blasted the ball down the centre of the goal. Clearly not expecting that, Cam dived left, and the net billowed. Someone nearby let out a yelp. It was only after a couple of moments she realised that person was her.

"Good shot, Ma'am!" shouted Billy, one of Victoria's favourite photographers. He'd never posted a shot of her she didn't like, and that put him on a very small, venerated list. The rest of them wanted to get the worst shot they possibly could and sell it to the highest bidder. A morning like this was liquid gold.

She turned, and Ash gave her a fist bump. "Smart work, Your Highness."

"I got some moves, Woods." She was pleased with that response.

Ash's expression gave nothing away. Was she impressed? Damn it, every single fibre of Victoria hoped so.

Sasha slammed home the next penalty, while Ash skied hers, and put her head in her hands.

Then it was Victoria's turn again. She tried to go full power, but instead her foot got stuck in the mud just before it connected. The ball trickled to Cam.

"All to play for! I hope your lenses are ready for my victory lap," Sasha shouted, working the press pack. The photographers chuckled.

Victoria couldn't let her have the last word. She stepped forward and shouted: "Let's see what you've got, Goodall!"

The laughter this time was louder, and the look on Sasha's face was priceless.

First to go was Sasha. Her run-up was short, and she slammed the ball into the top right corner. Even Cam applauded.

Next was Ash. True to the captain she was, she scored with the perfect penalty, low and sure.

Victoria stepped up. She got some encouraging shouts from the photographers, and Ash gave her a "you got this".

She couldn't fuck this up. Just get it on target and hope for the best.

She drew in a breath and ran forward. But her trainers betrayed her, sliding on treacherous mud. Time slowed. Her body pitched sideways, and she knew with crystal clarity before she even hit the ground that this would be tomorrow's headlines. That's how it worked: her mishaps went viral before she could even process them herself.

Victoria kept her face neutral as gravity took over. Her arse hit the turf with a thud, and mud seeped into her jeans.

Had she even connected with the ball? She wanted to curl up into the foetal position, but that wasn't an option. She could play the tragic princess, sprawled on her back studying the cobalt sky, feeding every tabloid's favourite narrative of her horrible week.

Or she could flip the script.

One quick push and she could be up, already lining up another shot. Let them see this instead: a princess who could take a fall and come back swinging. Not 'Royal's Week Goes from Bad to Worse,' but 'Princess Shows True Grit.'

She chose the headline she wanted to read.

Thus, as she hit the deck and the collective photographers gasped, Victoria scrambled to her feet before they could even blink. Then she took her shot without giving it a moment's thought, and it arrowed past a startled Cam Holloway and into the net.

Victoria let out cry of satisfaction, and turned to see Ash stood behind her, applauding.

"I guess it's a draw," Victoria told her.

"I guess so," Ash grinned.

# Chapter Thirteen

Ash put the flat white in front of Victoria and settled on the wooden bench opposite. It was just the two of them, Cam and Sasha making their excuses. The good thing about Victoria's unplanned fall was that the press pack had mostly packed up and left, having got way more than they bargained for. Victoria had spent a good 15 minutes afterwards chatting to a few of them, making jokes at her own expense. Ash was still a public-eye novice in comparison to her.

"You handled that like a pro. I'm impressed."

Victoria exhaled. "I'm glad you think so. Although I'll have a mighty bruise for my troubles."

"But also a million new adoring fans who think you should play up front for the Lionesses."

"If you're trying to charm me, it's working." The skin around Victoria's eyes crinkled as she smiled. "Thanks for getting the coffee."

"You're still the heir to the throne. I have to show willing."

Victoria took a sip, and when she lowered her plastic cup, a perfect dollop of froth clung to the tip of her nose.

Without thinking, Ash reached across and wiped it away.

The moment her fingertips grazed Victoria's skin, she flinched.

Ash's hand froze mid-air, her heart stuttering as reality crashed back. "Shit, I'm sorry," she mumbled, her voice barely a whisper. "You had a bit of froth." Her eyes darted left, then right, scanning for the telltale glint of camera lenses, the whispered headlines already printing in her head.

Victoria gave her a tight smile, then touched her nose where Ash's fingers had been seconds before. "Has it gone?"

Ash nodded.

"Good. And don't worry, we're alone. No paparazzi. My security team made sure of that."

"Are they hiding?" Ash glanced around once more. "I half-expected that ex-SAS woman to be at the next table."

"Hoped?" Victoria raised an eyebrow.

Ash laughed. "I prefer my women a little less scary." She paused. "Anyway, it's good to see you." It was so much more than that.

Victoria cleared her throat. "You, too. Even with a muddy arse."

"Part of my everyday life." Ash shrugged. "You're fitting in already."

"That's my aim."

Ash stared at her, unsure of where this conversation could go. Victoria had to leave in 20 minutes. She had other places to be, as did Ash. What could they cover in that time? What should she broach?

"How are things panning out with the break-up?"

Victoria screwed up her face. "As well as can be expected. The public are heartbroken because they adore a straight love story, and Dexter was pretty. Of course he's pretty – he's gay!"

Ash snorted. "For what it's worth, you've looked sufficiently sad in any photos I've seen of you."

"Have you been looking?" But Victoria's smile was warm.

"Not in a stalkery way."

"Because I'm your stalker, not the other way around – we established that in Marbella."

Victoria flicked her hair and tucked it behind her ear.

"We did." Embarrassment tinged with warm familiarity flowed through Ash as she recalled her brash words. "I've been looking at your photos in a concerned-friend way. Wanting to make sure you're okay."

"No other way at all?"

Ash smirked. "I might have had an ulterior motive. But I don't want to assume. I know what princesses are like. I've watched the movies."

Victoria put her elbows on the table, then rested her face in her palms. "Do tell."

Ash took a sharp intake of breath.

*Those baby blues.*

"Demanding. Entitled. Extra." Ash stared at Victoria. "Everything you're not. For instance, I bet Elsa from *Frozen* would never sit on a wooden bench in a car park in muddy jeans."

"She'd definitely start singing. No discretion."

Ash shook her head, smiling. "The more I get to know you, the more I want to know."

Victoria dropped her gaze to Ash's lips.

Ash felt it everywhere.

"Have you thought about what I said? That if we're doing this, you have to be prepared for what comes next."

Ash gave a slow nod. She'd never be truly prepared, but she didn't want to stop now. "You've already shown me you're willing to step into my world. You just took a penalty in front of the country's press, fell over, and still made it a PR masterstroke. I'm prepared to walk into your world, too." She'd have to handle it, no matter what. "I've thought about little else since we were almost naked in a hot tub."

Victoria blushed and dropped her gaze. "When can I see you again?" Their stares connected. "Properly. Not with a crowd."

How Ash yearned to do it properly. But she couldn't.

"I'm in England camp for the next two weeks, and following that, the Ravens have a USA pre-season tour."

"Who knew a football calendar was as busy as mine?"

"I'm sure we can figure something out. The Lionesses have a friendly game in Sweden next week, then we're playing the USA at Wembley a few days after. Are you coming to that?"

"Let me check my calendar." Victoria exhaled. "But that's still not without a crowd."

With a courage that felt like freefall, Ash reached across the table, then trailed her little finger along Victoria's knuckles: a touch so light it could be denied, so deliberate it couldn't be mistaken.

Crucially, Victoria didn't pull away. Instead, her hand trembled slightly, like a corner flag in an unexpected summer breeze.

The surge of feeling that crashed through Ash at that whisper of contact – warm skin, trust, possibility – took her breath away. In that moment, she knew with bone-deep certainty this was worth everything. The press could circle, protocol could bind them, but this delicate, dangerous hope between them was worth every careful step.

From the look of pure astonishment on Victoria's face, Ash knew she felt it, too.

"Come to the game, and in the meantime, we'll work out when we can get together alone." Ash still stared at their hands, so close, but not touching. "Just you and me."

"I really want to kiss you." The look in Victoria's eyes was wild. Feral. "But I also don't want to rush it. When it happens, I want it to be real." She put her head in her hands, then peaked out through her fingers. "Do you feel like we're living in a 19th century romance?"

"Anne Lister would be proud."

\* \* \*

The July sun hung low over Stockholm as Ash and Cam walked the waterfront. Tourists crowded every corner of the capital, drawn by ABBA, the archipelagos, and the laid-back vibe. Grand hotels reflected golden light on their right, while the harbour stretched to their left, busy with ferries shuttling people between islands. The air was rich with salt water and laughter.

Ash's phone buzzed in her tracksuit pocket. Even before looking, she knew it was Victoria, their daily rhythm as predictable as her training sessions.

As Ash's England roommate, Cam had noticed the pattern of their messages. She'd asked, of course, and even though she knew Ash had gone to the barbecue, she hadn't said anything. Rather, Ash had cycled through a roster of fictional correspondents: her mum, her cousin, phantom school friends.

But the lies sat heavy. Ash told Cam everything. She'd trusted her with every secret since they'd met. This deception felt like a betrayal of their friendship. But more than that, Ash was bursting to talk to someone.

They dodged a couple on rollerblades, then Cam stopped and pointed at a jetty to their left. Comfy sofas covered its surface, cool jazz sailed out of the speakers, and a bar with an Aperol Spritz parasol stood nearby.

"Let's have a drink here, then you can tell me who's really sending you all these messages." Cam raised an eyebrow. "Just so you know, if you tell me it's your mum or your cousin again, I will grab the phone out of your hand and look for myself."

Ash swallowed hard, then stuck her hands in her pockets.

A staff member with a winning smile appeared as they sat on the sofas. She eyed them, then bit her lip before she spoke. "Can I just say, I absolutely love you both, and it's a true honour to be serving you here today."

Ash blinked. They'd walked around Stockholm all afternoon without being recognised.

"Thank you," she replied. "That's really kind."

"Once you knocked Sweden out of the Euros here last summer, I supported you after that."

Which was exactly what Princess Astrid told her at the party. The same one where she'd seen Victoria in a bikini. She pushed that image out of her brain.

They placed their drinks order – two Diet Cokes, they were still in camp – and the waitress returned, telling them the drinks were on the house. Then she gave Ash a receipt anyway. When Ash looked, it had the woman's name and number on it.

She glanced up and caught the woman's stare. Ash quickly looked away, then folded the receipt into her pocket. Even doing that felt like cheating.

Oblivious, Cam continued. "Here's what I don't understand. When you and Danielle were getting together, you couldn't shut up about it. 'Was it something you should do? Would it affect the team? Should you go for it'?" She paused. "Now you're getting messages all the time from someone, but I get nothing. Silence."

Ash jigged her leg up and down. "I haven't told you anything because there's nothing to tell. Yet. We're just talking, getting to know each other."

"Who are you getting to know?" She wasn't going to let this drop.

Ash didn't want her to. "If I tell you, can you promise you won't tell anyone else?" She paused, gauging Cam's reaction.

Cam frowned. "Of course."

Ash took a deep breath. Rip the plaster off. "It's Princess Victoria."

"I bloody knew it!" Cam sat back, eyes wide, shaking her head. "Princess Penalty."

Ash winced at Victoria's new tabloid name. "That's the one."

"I thought I clocked something when she came to the FA, but I shrugged it off." She paused to gather her thoughts. "I have questions. How, why, where, when? I know she invited you to the royal barbecue, but she was going out with Dexter Matthews and was apparently straight." She paused. "Hang the fuck on. Did she break up with him for you?!"

Clearly, Cam's thoughts were not easily gathered.

"Shit the bed, this is *huge*. You've started a thing with the one hot royal left, and she wasn't even available!" Cam's eyes were like saucers.

None of which helped Ash. "Please stop reacting so much, you're making me nervous."

"Since when is she queer?" Cam's speech was a strangled whisper. "I know a lot of people have wished. But she's had a boyfriend forever."

"She's had a beard forever."

It was a lot to take in.

Which was evidenced when Cam's mouth dropped open. "Really?" She licked her lips. "You didn't answer my question about the breakup. Did she do it for you?"

Ash shook her head. "It was a mutual decision. He's got a boyfriend and things were getting more serious there, too."

Cam flopped back on the sofa and let out a low whistle. "I cannot believe what I'm hearing. When I get over it, I'll tell you well done, because she is smoking hot. But also, how the hell do you date a princess when everyone thinks she's straight? How does that work?"

All of Ash's worries about what this might be and how it might go floated up to the surface. She wanted Cam to reassure her, tell her everything was going to be okay. But of course, Cam couldn't do that. Also, she was looking out for her friend. She wanted Ash to be happy and secure. Dating Princess Victoria was not the obvious way to achieve that goal.

"We haven't quite figured that out yet. She wants to come out, but her parents aren't so keen. We haven't even kissed yet. She told me she was interested at the barbecue. We've been messaging for the past six weeks, and it's been kinda romantic, getting to know her. But she was in Australia, then I'm away at camp, so we haven't been able to see each other properly."

"You were messaging when she came to open the centre the other week. When she took those penalties?"

Ash smiled as she thought of Victoria falling on her gorgeous arse. "We were."

"But is this what you want? Your every move raked over? No privacy? You hated it when Danielle splashed your life over her socials."

Desire mixed with a hint of unease knotted inside Ash. But the desire to see where this might go won the day. She knew Victoria came with conditions. She'd been very clear about that. But her honesty was refreshing. Plus, Victoria was not Danielle. Not by a long shot.

"All I know right now is that I like her like I haven't liked someone *ever*. I know I hated the exposure that came as part of being with Danielle, but I can't walk away from this without at least trying to see what happens. I don't know what it is, but there's a connection. A spark. She feels it, too."

A ferry arrived back at the dock, and tourists slowly disembarked.

"I'm dealing with it like I deal with football: one match at a time, one day at a time. If I flash forward, I don't know what will happen. But what I know is, I don't want to turn down something just because I'm scared of it. That's not who I am."

Cam sipped her drink, then shook her head. "You seriously haven't even kissed her?"

"Nope. She wanted me to be sure I wanted to."

"And you're sure now?"

Ash nodded. "As sure as I can be."

"You could be married to the future Queen."

"Shut up." But that made Ash smile. "I love how you go from no kissing, to us getting married."

"It happens. They'll take the Victoria And Dexter mugs and tea towels off sale, and start printing Victoria And Ash ones instead. I like it. It's got quite the ring to it." Cam paused. "Plus, there's precedent. Didn't one of the other royals marry a rugby player?"

"She did. But rugby is a posh, acceptable sport. Plus, he was a man. And Princess Arabella is tenth in line to the throne. I think this piece of news might make more headlines."

That brought another whistle from Cam. "You know I told you that it was time to get back out there? I didn't mean you had to shag a princess."

Ash grinned. "The heart wants what the heart wants."

"When are you seeing her again?"

"She's coming to the game on Saturday. She's the Women's FA Patron, remember?"

Cam shook her head. "Holy shit."

"Holy shit is right. I meant what I said at the start, too. You promise not to say anything? Keep it to yourself?"

"Of course." Cam balled her fist and tapped her chest. "I won't breathe a word. But you know once you start, you're going to be in deeper. Are you totally sure about this?"

"That train has left the station," Ash replied.

# Chapter Fourteen

Victoria had come to many sporting events at Wembley with her family, but now she was the Women's FA Patron, she was the one in the spotlight. Much as she was used to it, she didn't think she'd ever love it. She simply found ways to manage it, get through it.

Her therapist had told her to take a few moments to centre herself before she stepped out tonight. Victoria hadn't told her the added complication of Ash. She hadn't even told her brother, standing tall beside her. At least with him there too, he could share the limelight. Although as he always reminded her, "the only people interested in me are star-fuckers and middle-aged women. Everyone loves you. You are the country's great hope for the future."

When the country found out the truth about her, she was going to let everyone down.

She pushed that thought out of her head as she and Michael stood for the national anthem. The one praising their mother. The one that would one day praise her. The familiar notes struck up and Victoria and Michael sang with gusto, just as they'd been taught from a young age. Hearing a full stadium of 90,000 people singing it still gave her goosebumps. For her, it was a song of her past, her present, and her future.

The camera panned down the two teams, lingering on Ash. Victoria looked away when she saw her, knowing a blush was about to hit her cheeks. When the singing stopped, cheers filled the stadium, and then the game got underway.

Michael nudged her, his shirt unbuttoned one too many, showing a hint of his ginger chest hair.

"You scored two goals past the England keeper recently. I'm surprised you're not on the pitch."

Her penalty prowess had got a lot of media coverage, and she was now known as Princess Penalty. She had mixed feelings.

"Score predictions?" Michael asked as they settled into their seats.

"2-1 to England," Victoria replied. "Ash to score the winner."

He gave her a look. "You on first-name terms now you're a bigwig of the game?"

She shrugged. "We've met a few times and I like her. Plus, she's pretty good at football, which helps."

The first half flew by with no goals and not much goalmouth action, the two teams cancelling each other out. However, England came out for the second half all guns blazing, determined to make something happen and beat the USA, even if it was just a friendly.

Ash had messaged earlier in the week to say that training was going well, and that their set-piece specialist had come up with a new routine that, if it came off in-game, would be incredible. When England got a corner early in the second-half, Victoria rubbed her hands together and sat up.

"This is going to be good. I can feel it," she told Michael, slapping his thigh. "Get off your phone and watch." He did as he was told.

Sure enough, from the corner, Ash whipped in a curling ball that landed in the middle of the penalty area, causing mayhem. Sasha climbed highest for the knock-down, and young Lionesses' striker Nat Tyler spun and hit a shot that flashed into the net before anyone from Team USA could react. The stadium erupted as Victoria jumped to her feet and punched the air. She'd watched many Lionesses' games before, but somehow, now she knew the team, this one felt far more personal. Ash was in that melee of players, celebrating.

Ash, who'd chatted to her and kept her company when she was the other side of the world. Who'd made her laugh and shared bits of herself over the past few weeks.

Ash, who she was desperate to kiss.

Michael nudged her. "You were right." He raised an eyebrow. "Who's going to score the next goal then, Mystic Meg?"

"Sloane Patterson," Victoria replied without missing a beat. It was a fair guess, seeing as she was on the pitch and the US star striker. "But I'm still backing Ash to score the winner."

Fifteen minutes later, most of the stadium groaned as Sloane Patterson duly rounded Cam in a one-on-one and scored the equaliser. Victoria checked her watch. Twenty minutes to go. Plenty of time for the comeback. She made a fist in Michael's direction to show him she had faith, but he was on his phone again. She nudged him. It wasn't a good look especially when there were cameras everywhere.

He gave her a sheepish smile and put his phone away. "How long to go? Is it time for more champagne soon?"

"Twenty minutes plus stoppage time."

He looked less than impressed.

With each passing minute, Ash commanded more of the pitch. Every time she touched the ball, Victoria leaned forward, willing her on. Two perfect crosses had already sliced through the air, begging for a finish. What they needed was another Ash in the box. One to create, one to convert. Because those crosses deserved better than to die in empty space.

She checked her watch again. Five minutes to go. The crowd were giving it their all, trumpets blazing the familiar England song, and the singing as loud as Victoria had heard it. There would be one more chance, she just knew it.

Two minutes later, Sasha slalomed through the middle and threaded a peach of a ball to Ash. She still had a lot to do, but no time to dawdle, with three defenders on her. Victoria craned her neck even though she could see perfectly well, as Ash thumped a first-time shot towards goal, and the crowd held its breath. The ball was a low-slung arrow, and in the slick warmth of the evening it bent around the defenders, and nestled into the bottom left-hand corner of the goal before the US goalkeeper even knew it was past her.

Victoria shrieked and threw her arms around Michael. Pride and elation swelled inside. She knew the goal scorer. She was going to kiss the goal scorer. She'd never had a cool girlfriend before. Someone other people might look at more than her. She had no idea how that might feel, but she wanted to try.

\* \* \*

When the England manager showed Victoria into the dressing room, an arc of beer sailed through the air, liberally spritzing her. She'd had worse things thrown at her. However, the collective gasp as it happened, and then the stunned silence wasn't how she'd planned to make her entrance into England's post-match celebrations.

Cam was first to react, jumping up and offering Victoria a towel, but she shook her head. "I've been known to have a beer before, but I usually prefer drinking it to wearing it." She grinned, trying to be cool, and not like she wanted to jump in the shower and wash her hair immediately.

"So sorry, Your Highness." Cam patted Victoria down with the towel whether she liked it or not.

Meanwhile, the rest of the team stared at her with panicked faces.

Victoria turned up her grin to diffuse the tension. "Serves me right for coming in here post-game after such a great win."

Tentative smiles appeared on a few faces.

She crashed on, walked around the group and shook everyone's hands. "I just wanted to come in and tell you that being the patron of the Women's FA is one of the biggest honours of my life, and I plan to make sure the Lionesses are supported and paid properly every step of the way."

She gave Sasha a strong handshake and a "great assist", which she seemed thrilled with. When she arrived at Nat Tyler, the young star striker, she made sure to linger a little, even though Nat looked absolutely shocked to be speaking to her.

Right at the end of the handshakes was Ash. Looking sweaty and delicious with her socks rolled down, feet in sliders, shinpads and boots discarded. When they shook hands, the effect was quite different to everyone else who'd touched her before. Ash's handshake had weight. History. Promise.

"Well played." It wasn't what she wanted to say to her, but she figured this was the best in front of the group. Then she lowered her voice. "Good to see the corner routines paid off, despite you hating them over the past couple of weeks."

Ash treated her to a full smile. "They've been hit and miss in training, but it was nice one came off." She lowered her voice, although the rest of the team had recovered from dousing Victoria in lager and were chatting among themselves again. "I didn't know you were coming in," Ash whispered.

"Neither did I, but my PR arranged it. A photographer is turning up any minute."

Right at that moment there was a knock on the door, and a photographer walked in, camera strung around her neck. The team posed for a few photos, and then it was time for Victoria to leave. "Great game today. Persistence, tenacity, bundles of skill and talent. Thanks for a great evening, everyone."

She went to leave, then doubled back to Ash. "Are you around this weekend?" Her gaze dropped to Ash's lips before she could help it.

Ash winced, then shook her head. "Got some FA sponsorship stuff to do Saturday and Sunday, and I'm at the premiere of the new James Bond film on Saturday night."

A triumphant buzz fizzed through Victoria. "I'm there, too," she said. "We'll meet somehow Saturday night."

"I'll look forward to it," Ash replied, her voice low.

Victoria held her gaze, then slipped out of the dressing room, hoping nobody in there could read body language.

If they could, she was screwed.

# Chapter Fifteen

The August heat lingered in Leicester Square as dusk approached, the sun still high in the sky as Ash stepped from the black Range Rover onto the red carpet. The roar of the crowd hit her first. Hundreds of fans pressed against barriers, their phones raised high, their voices merging into one continuous wave of sound. Marianne had given her a quick once-over before she left, dabbing at a bead of sweat threatening to disturb Ash's perfectly applied makeup.

"Remember, straight down the middle, stop at the markers for photos," Marianne told her. "And smile naturally this time. Act like you've just nutmegged Sloane Patterson for the winning World Cup goal."

Ash rolled her eyes, but she could well imagine how wide her smile would be if that *actually* happened next summer in London. However, for now, she had a public to please.

She'd done this dance before. Perhaps not for a James Bond premiere, but she knew how to work a red carpet. The fact her heart was hammering against her ribs had nothing to do with the cameras or the crowd. It had everything to do with who would be walking this same carpet tonight. Their cars were due to arrive within five minutes of each other, so Victoria might be directly behind her.

The first camera flashes began as she moved forward, each step measured in her black heels, which she was surprisingly good at walking in, even if she hated them. The photographer pit erupted in a cascade of shutter clicks and calls of "Ash! Over here! This way!"

The turn was muscle memory now: hand sliding into pocket, lips curving into that camera-ready smile. They all wanted their piece of the captain, the golden girl, the face that had defined English football's summer of glory. But tonight, behind the smile that had launched her to Sports Personality of the Year, her thoughts were tangled in something far from this practised performance.

"Looking gorgeous, Ash!" someone called out. "Who are you wearing?"

"Alexander McQueen," she answered automatically, smoothing down the silk of her ivory summer tuxedo. She wasn't wearing a shirt underneath her jacket, just a low-cut waistcoat and a whole lot of boob tape. To the untrained eye, it looked like she was wearing nothing but silk and cleavage. Luke had taken about a week to persuade her this was the way to go. She just hoped she didn't have a wardrobe malfunction before she got into the cinema. Her look was going to send the sapphic football world into meltdown anyway, as it did any time she appeared out of her football kit.

She stopped in front of a BBC microphone and answered their questions about how good it was to beat the USA this week. "Was that a dress rehearsal? Are you winning the World Cup next year at Wembley?" the presenter enquired.

"If I have anything to do with it, we are," Ash replied, bold and sassy.

A few of the photographers behind her whooped at that answer.

Influencer Loella approached her. Ash had a lot of time for her, because her favourite things were football and fashion.

"You are looking fly tonight, girl." Loella fanned herself to show Ash how hot she was.

She smiled down Loella's camera lens: "I aim to please, and to represent."

"Tell me: do you think it's about time for another female James Bond, Ash? Any chance you might take up acting when you finish your football career?"

That made her properly chuckle. "I've still got a lot of football left in me," she said. "But yes, why shouldn't the next James Bond be a woman?" She could already see the headlines forming from this soundbite. "However, I don't think I should play the role. There are plenty of talented actors out there who'd fit the bill. I'll stick to football. And the occasional catwalk."

Loella laughed, then turned to look to the right of Ash.

A shimmer of excitement surged through the air. Ash didn't need to turn around to know what it meant. Victoria had arrived, and Ash's time in the spotlight was up. Victoria had messaged earlier, telling her she'd try not to steal her thunder too much.

Ash thanked Loella for her time, then forced herself to keep moving forward, to not break stride or give any indication that her pulse had just doubled its tempo. But she couldn't help stealing a glance over her shoulder, making it look like she was simply acknowledging fans on both sides of the carpet.

Victoria was a vision in flowing gold chiffon that caught the dipping evening sun with every movement. Her security crew kept a respectful distance, almost invisible unless you knew to look for them. Victoria's and Ash's eyes met for the briefest moment across the sea of cameras, and that familiar jolt of electricity zapped down Ash's spine.

Two months of flash meetings and never-ending messages. She'd always remember the Marbella balcony, and seeing Victoria with a beer in her hand like she was a normal person. Which, weirdly, she was turning out to be. Victoria blushing when Ash emerged from her bathroom in her bikini. Bumping thighs in Astrid's hot tub. Wiping froth from Victoria's nose in the FA car park. Each encounter charged, each goodbye heavy with things unsaid.

Tonight was different: they were determined to get some alone time, however that might happen. Victoria had messaged to say she had a plan.

Ash reached the next marker, turning to give the photographers their shots. Through the strobing lights, she could see Victoria doing the same two stages behind. The princess laughed at something, her head thrown back, throat exposed. Ash dragged her gaze away before anyone noticed.

"Final stretch." Victoria's aide, Tanya, appeared at Ash's elbow, steering her towards the cinema entrance. "You were originally seated in row Q. Victoria's in row F, with just me sat beside her," she added, her expression not changing one iota. "She's asked if you'd like to sit with her."

"In the cinema?" Dumbest question in the world.

Tanya frowned. "Yes."

Ash was about to sit next to Princess Victoria at a film premiere. The first time they'd done so in public, albeit in the dark. Her life was about to take a dizzying turn, wasn't it?

Her head filled with outcomes and permutations, but she shut it down.

"That would be great."

Tanya nodded and guided her to the VIP entrance. "Keep walking, wait on the right when you get in, and try not to look like you're about to rob a bank. I'll bring Victoria to you, then you've got 15 minutes in Victoria's private green room. I'll wait outside, and will bring you in separately."

Before Ash could respond, Tanya melted into the crowd, leaving her to navigate the final few metres of red carpet alone.

\* \* \*

The door clicked shut, and suddenly the world compressed to the size of this space. Just them, the low hum of the air conditioning, and the muffled sounds of the crowd. Victoria's perfume, something warm and musky, filled Ash's senses as the princess walked across the room and perched on the arm of a leather sofa. A bottle of champagne chilled in a silver bucket on the table, along with tubes of sour cream Pringles and a bag of Percy Pigs.

"Well," Victoria said, smoothing her gold dress over her knees, "here we are. One of these days, we won't have the world's media poised with cameras when we meet." Her voice carried that hint of humour that always made Ash's stomach flip, but there was something else there, too. A slight tremor that betrayed her own nervousness.

Ash remained by the door, her hand still on the handle, anchor-like. She needed something to ground her, to stop herself from crossing the room in two strides and doing what she'd been dreaming about for months. "Tanya knows?"

It was a statement more than a question.

"Tanya knows…" Victoria tucked a strand of hair behind her ear, a gesture Ash had come to recognise she did when she was trying to appear casual. "She knows that we've been talking. That I like you. I haven't specifically told her, but she's not stupid. She's caught me looking at my phone with a stupid grin on my face more times than I care to remember." Victoria gave her a small smile. "Don't worry, she's trustworthy. She's been with me for years, and there are some things I can't hide, no matter how hard I try. And I did try for years. But it gets exhausting. I don't want you to be exhausting."

"Neither do I."

"It was actually Tanya who suggested I needed a quiet moment before the film. Said something about how I wouldn't be able to focus otherwise if I didn't at least get to see you alone for a minute. She's right, too. I would have been craning my neck, looking everywhere."

"I'm glad you listened and took her up on her suggestion."

"Me, too." Victoria paused, her eyes dropping to Ash's chest. "Especially when you look like you're naked underneath that jacket."

Ash glanced down at her plunging cleavage, let go of the door handle, and took a single step forward. The air conditioning hummed against her skin, but heat still rose from her collar and crawled up her neck. Every tiny movement Victoria made – the shift of her dress, the flutter of her fingers against her knee, the slight parting of her lips – sent sparks dancing across Ash's skin. She fought to keep her breathing steady.

They stared at each other.

"Do you want some champagne?"

"Sure." Victoria stood up and smoothed down her dress.

Ash's mouth went dry. She moved forward, undid the foil and popped the cork. She poured two glasses, and handed one to Victoria. Her hands shook.

"Thank you. You're very skilled at that. I get scared popping bubbles after a cork nearly took my eye out."

"I've got many skills."

*Where had that come from?*

Victoria smiled over the rim of her glass. "I don't doubt it." She paused. "Skills I'm desperate to learn. But not in this *very* drab green room."

Victoria's lips curved into a smile that made Ash's pulse race. "Just know, when James Bond is running around chasing the villain with a gun as big as his head, I won't be concentrating on that." She took a step forward. In the bright light of the room, a slight flush crept up Victoria's neck, and her chest rose and fell with quickened breaths.

"What will you be focused on?" In what seemed like the most daring thing imaginable, Ash took a step forward, too.

"Oh, I don't know. Perhaps how this woman who's caught all of my attention of late is sat next to me, with the whole world behind us, and I can't touch her, which is driving me insane." Another step. "But it's also making me more determined than ever to make it happen. But this yearning is also kinda hot."

The way Victoria said 'hot?' Ash could listen to it all night. This green room might be drab, but there was something about it…

"Tanya described me as a cat on a hot tin roof. Which is probably pretty apt."

The princess's words reached inside Ash, pushing all her blood south.

She moved until she was close enough to see the silver flecks in Victoria's eyes. She could count her eyelashes if she wanted to. With them both in heels, Victoria was slightly shorter. The perfect height if Ash leaned down slightly...

"I want to kiss you, but not here. Somewhere more worthy. Will you come to the after-party with me?"

Ash coughed. "And kiss you there in front of everyone?" She couldn't quite imagine that.

Victoria shook her head. "No. We'd go, but then leave soon after. What do you think?"

Despite every bone in her body leaning in, Ash shook her head, an apology streaking across her face. "I have a super-early 4am call tomorrow with Pepsi Max for a shoot in Paris. Helicopter there and back in a day. I can't be out late tonight."

Victoria gave her a frustrated smile, and shook her head. "I get it."

Ash picked up Victoria's hand, drew it to her mouth, and kissed her knuckles one by one. A million magic crystals fell through her body as she did. Victoria was precious cargo. Every fibre of Ash's being told her so.

"How about I give you a lift home afterwards instead?" Victoria said.

"I live in St Albans. You'll miss your party."

She stared into Ash's eyes until Ash's knees almost buckled. "I don't care about the after-party."

A gentle knock at the door made them both jump apart. "Five-minute warning, Your Highness," came Tanya's voice, softer than necessary.

"Thanks, Tanya," Victoria called back, her voice tight. She looked back at Ash. Her pupils had dilated so wide, the blue of her eyes was just a thin ring, dark and dangerous. Ash's muscles betrayed her as the room tilted ever so slightly beneath her feet. She shifted her weight, trying to remember how her legs usually worked.

"You haven't answered me. Can I give you a lift afterwards?"

"I would love that."

"Great."

Ash still had hold of Victoria's hand.

Victoria dropped it, then gave a firm nod. "I'll go first. See you in there." She stepped towards the door, but paused with her hand on the handle. "Do you even like James Bond?"

"Can't stand him," Ash replied.

Victoria let out a throaty laugh that Ash was starting to know well. "Me either."

As Victoria opened the door, Ash caught Tanya's knowing smile, before the aide smoothly stepped in to guide her princess back to her public duties.

When the door shut, Ash closed her eyes.

This was about to be the longest few hours of her life so far.

* * *

The partition glass slid up silently, leaving Ash and Victoria alone in the back of the Rolls-Royce. The movie had been a long series of sighs and glances, but now they were alone, Ash wasn't any more relaxed. The leather seats seemed too pristine to touch, the air too refined to breathe. She sat with her hands clasped in her lap, hyper-aware of the crown insignia etched into every surface, catching the amber streetlights as they glided through London.

Ash's palms were clammy against the silk of her trousers. She snuck a glance at Victoria, cataloguing details she'd already memorised: the elegant curve of her neck, the way her lashes cast shadows on her cheeks, the slight smudge in her otherwise perfect lipstick from their quick sip of champagne on the way out.

Beside her, the leather creaked softly as Victoria got comfortable. Outside, London slipped by in a blur of summer twilight.

"So." Victoria's fingers traced patterns on the leather between them, then inched closer to where Ash's hand rested. "What did you think of the film?"

Ash swallowed hard, watching those delicate fingers move. "I have absolutely no idea what happened."

"You weren't paying attention?" Victoria's voice was low, teasing.

"Weirdly, no." Ash turned her head to find Victoria already looking at her. "I had a far better view than the film nearby. A front-row seat to a princess, no less." Ash leaned in. "Plus, you were doing that thing with your hair."

"What thing?" Victoria's tongue darted out to wet her bottom lip.

"That thing where you…" Ash's words faded as Victoria's pinky finger finally made contact with her own, the lightest brush of skin against skin. "Where you flick it, then tuck it behind your ear." Every time she did it, Ash was transfixed.

"I didn't know you were watching." But Victoria's smile

said otherwise as her hand covered Ash's. "I mean, I hoped you were." She paused. "To tell you the truth, I don't know what I'm doing when you're around. I wasn't doing that with my hair to flirt. I was doing it to occupy my hands. To redirect my energy. Anywhere that took my mind off the fact that my hands wanted to touch you."

The car slowed for a red light, and the shifting shadows from outside painted patterns across Victoria's cheekbones. Ash lifted her right hand, finally allowing herself to touch, to brush her thumb across that play of light and dark. Victoria's breath hitched, and her eyes closed briefly. The space between them crackled with possibility.

"I've been watching you for weeks." Ash's voice was barely more than a whisper. "Every time you walk into a room, every time I see you on TV, every time my phone lights up with a message."

She trailed a fingertip along Victoria's cheekbone.

Something fluttered in her chest.

A summer heat rolled through her.

Victoria turned her face into Ash's palm, pressing her lips to the sensitive skin of her wrist. The kiss was feather-light, but it shot straight to Ash's core. She shook her head. "Trying to get together with you is delicious torture, you know that?"

Ash exhaled. "I'm well aware." Her gaze dropped to Victoria's lips. They were inches away.

"You said you were going away on Monday? To the USA?"

It was a really, truly ill-timed pre-season tour. "For two weeks." But she didn't want to talk about that now. She wanted to stay in this moment. With Victoria so close. Her lips *right there.*

"I won't see you until the end of August."

Victoria shifted closer, and the fabric of her gold dress whispered against Ash's thigh. The effect was like a match strike in a dark room: sudden heat, the catch of breath, and the knowledge that everything was about to change.

"But we've got at least an hour if this traffic keeps up. I know it might not be the romantic setting we wanted, but honestly, I don't care. If I don't kiss you right now, I might actually expire." Ash leaned in and cupped Victoria's face. "And you don't want my death on your conscience, do you?"

Victoria shook her head, wordless, and leaned towards Ash. The car turned a corner, and Victoria used the momentum to close the final distance between them. Her lips found Ash's with devastating precision.

For one heartbeat, the kiss was gentle, tentative: a question being asked. Then Victoria's fingers slid into Ash's hair, nails grazing her scalp, and the question became an answer. Ash gasped against Victoria's mouth, and the princess took the opportunity to deepen the kiss, her tongue sliding against Ash's with an urgency that made Ash's head spin.

The world shrunk to points of contact: Victoria's hand tightening in her hair, their knees pressed together, the smooth warmth of Victoria's bare shoulder under Ash's palm. When Victoria pulled back slightly to take a shaking breath, Ash chased her lips, refusing to let even an inch of space come between them.

Victoria made a sound – half whimper, half sigh – and it rattled through Ash. She tasted like champagne and possibility, like every text message they'd exchanged at 3am, like every lingering touch they'd denied themselves in public.

When she dragged her thumb across Victoria's bottom lip, Victoria trembled beneath her touch. Ash's heart thundered against her ribs where Victoria's palm now pressed, burning through silk.

She kissed her again, slower, deeper, drowning in the reality of Victoria's mouth under hers, Victoria's fingers splayed possessive and wanting against her skin. Every fantasy paled against this: the actual taste of her, the small sounds she made, the way she touched Ash like she'd been aching for it, too.

The car hit a speed bump, jolting them apart just enough to remember where they were. Victoria's lipstick was thoroughly smudged now, her chest rising and falling rapidly, her pupils blown wide. Ash couldn't look any more composed.

She kissed Victoria's lips one more time, before drawing back. Every sense she possessed was ragged. She wanted to rip all her clothes off, and have sex on this leather seat. But that was not in the royal playbook, surely? Although, the way Victoria kissed her with such depth, such surety? Ash was beginning to rethink everything she knew about royalty.

"You sure I can't tempt you to turn this car around and come home with me." Her gaze burned hot. "I told you once we started, I'd only want more." But Victoria's words were laced with resignation.

Ash smiled. "After that kiss, there's nothing I'd love more." She checked her watch. It was already gone 11pm. "But I have to be up in a few hours and look pretty for the cameras."

Victoria leaned in and kissed her hard, pulping Ash's brain.

"There's no universe where you couldn't look stunning at any hour of the day," Victoria added minutes later, coming up for air.

Warmth bloomed in Ash's chest. "I could get used to your smooth talk."

"Do you turn into a pumpkin if you don't make it home by midnight?"

Ash nodded.

"I'll have to put that to the test one day." Victoria trailed a fingertip down Ash's cheek. "I've never dated anyone with a busier calendar than me. This is going to be interesting, isn't it?"

"You could say that."

"But when you're back, let me know, and you're coming round. I'll cook dinner. Banish Michael from the house. Deal?"

Ash gulped. "Deal."

# Chapter Sixteen

It'd been four days, and Victoria could not get that kiss out of her mind. The weight of it. The slight shake in Ash's hands as they touched her face. How it had started gentle, but soon turned hungry, desperate.

The problem was, she wanted to be able to focus on other things in her life, too. To not be constantly distracted. To chop an avocado without nearly slicing her finger off. To get out of the shower without nearly crashing to the floor. To put her bra on the right way, and not get waylaid thinking of the moment when Ash's fingertips grazed her nipple, and her mind had staggered left like it had just been shot.

Being able to function was the minimum requirement for Victoria. But multiple kisses in the back seat from England's captain, and she was a total wreck.

She wasn't sleeping well either, due to staying up late messaging Ash, who was five hours behind on the East Coast. The team were playing their first game tomorrow, so they were training every morning, and doing team activities in the afternoon. Yesterday, the Ravens had gone on a boat around the Hudson River. Today, somebody had booked them onto a Segway tour of the city, but their manager had quickly unbooked them, stating that was too dangerous for professional footballers.

Victoria had messaged earlier to say the same thing happened to her.

It was decided Segways were too dangerous for royalty. Did you know the man who invented them died on one a year after he sold the company?

We're both too valuable for a Segway.

Keep your legs safe for your job, and your hands and mouth safe for me, please.

Objectification!

It's getting to be a terrible habit.

She'd never understood the need to send tit pics to a partner, but now she did. She wanted to take her and Ash to the next level, and the temptation was overwhelming. But even though she trusted Ash, what if her phone fell into the hands of her more boisterous team-mates? Victoria could just imagine the briefing with her PR team for that one. It didn't bear thinking about.

Victoria's scattiness hadn't escaped Michael's notice, either.

"What's going on with you, Vix?" he'd asked this morning, after she hung up her wetsuit from her morning swim. He'd just made the world's strongest coffee which she loved him for, and presented her with a cup. "Every time I see you, you look lost in thought. And every time you wield a knife lately, I feel the need to duck." He zig-zagged sriracha onto his scrambled eggs as he spoke.

She waved away his worries. "I'm fine. I'm just a little preoccupied with work stuff. The homeless charity has nearly finished its first centre, so I'm going to visit them this week. Excitingly, we've managed to make half of the ten centres LGBT+, which I'm thrilled about. Plus, the Emir of Qatar and his wife are in town this week, and Dexter and I met them for dinner last time around. I'm going solo this week, but it feels a little odd."

What would it feel like to have Ash beside her as her partner?

Odd, too. She couldn't imagine it. She'd never gone into an event like that with a romantic partner by her side who she wanted to be with. She'd had Dexter, and she'd had Michael. That was it. But on the horizon, maybe that might change. Walking in with Ash would be a dream.

Michael took a bite of his egg-topped sourdough, then swallowed before speaking. "A homeless charity with a queer flavour, and the Emir of Qatar are two ends of the spectrum."

"I like to live my life with balance," Victoria told him. "Plus, if they meet me, they'll see queer people are just like them when I eventually come out."

His eyes widened. "Since when are you coming out?"

She waved a hand. "It's just a turn of phrase." Not strictly true.

He studied her. "You want me to come to dinner with you?"

She raised an eyebrow. "You're offering? Are you feeling okay?"

He narrowed his eyes. "You could do with some support,

that's all. This Dexter stuff is still rumbling on with the papers. Did you see they snapped him and Sid together at that polo game the other day?"

"I did. He messaged me and apologised. But they were just standing next to each other. Sid had a hand on his arm, but they were hardly humping in plain sight."

"Now that would be a photo to get the world talking." He paused. "Plus, now you've got a certain footballer in your sights, too. I heard you were playing footsy at the James Bond premiere the other night."

His words were like a bucket of ice over her head. "What?" All her blood drained south, and not for the right reasons. "Who told you that?"

He put down his cutlery and frowned. "You're going to have to practice your reaction to her name if this is going somewhere, because honestly, that was terrible."

"What have you heard?" If there were tongues wagging, she wanted to know.

"Nobody said anything. Tanya let it slip when we were chatting the other day that you'd sat next to each other. I put two and two together after I heard about you meeting in Marbella, and again when you went to the FA the other day. Once is nothing. Twice is a coincidence. Three times, and I know something's up."

He ate more of his food as Victoria squirmed.

"Am I warm?"

She pushed herself off the counter, then stood opposite him in the kitchen as Albert, their butler, walked in.

"Morning, Your Highnesses," he said, bowing. No matter how many times she and Michael had told Albert to call them by their first names, he refused. He was a classically trained butler and nothing would shake him from his old-school principles. "Just getting something from the pantry. Don't mind me, I'll be gone in a tick."

They waited for him to leave before they continued.

"Well?"

She nodded, not wanting to say anything out loud. The house had ears.

"You are. But please keep it to yourself. It's very early days and we haven't been able to get together because either I'm out of the country, or she is."

"Where is she?"

"America. Pre-season tour."

He nodded, then took a sip of his coffee. "And this is what to you? A dalliance? A walk on the wild side? I'm sure she's lovely, but she's not really your norm." He wound his finger in a circle in front of her face. "I'm not sensing casual here. Your face is scaring me. Last time I got anything like this was with Hermione…"

She folded her arms over her chest. She desperately wanted to talk to someone about Ash, but to do so before anything had truly happened didn't feel right.

However, her brother had just pointed out the elephant in the room. That Ash was not from their world. She didn't understand royal protocol. Had Victoria been getting too caught up in the moment to remember that?

No. If Ash didn't fit the royal protocol, perhaps royal protocol had to change.

Victoria shook her head. "I just know that it feels very different from Hermione. In a good way."

He raised an eyebrow. "Be careful, Vic. I'm on your side, but I also want to protect your heart. You know you can't go falling in love with just anyone. Dexter always told you that. Maybe without him in your life, you've forgotten."

"I can't help who I like, Michael!" Her head buzzed with conflict. "If you can't say anything nice, don't say anything at all."

He gave a sad sigh. "This *is* me being nice." He walked towards her. "Our family has a terrible habit of destroying anything that isn't deemed appropriate. You know that." His gaze held hers, daring her to contradict him.

She had to try. "We haven't had a chance to explore how we slot into each other's lives yet. We're both busy people. Once we do, I guess we'll know for sure."

Michael nodded, then put his mug on the side. "Take it slowly is my advice. This is a big deal. *You're* a big deal. Plus, the Dexter thing has just settled down. Public opinion is on your side. You need to lie low for a while. Play nice. Remember, you and Ash were seen together at the premiere by the people inside. Who all told their friends. Who all told theirs, too. That's strike one. Three strikes and you're out."

She wished he wasn't telling the truth, but she knew he was.

"I'm going to start laying the groundwork with mother. Because what I know is that I can't carry on this half-life I've been living. Can I count on your support?"

The look he gave her was filled with such tenderness, it almost broke her. "You can always count on me. From day one. It's us against the world, remember?"

\* \* \*

Victoria spent the following morning meeting with the new head of her homeless charity. David radiated positive energy, and the meeting had left her convinced he was the right person to lead her project to success. Ten centres around the country were due to open over the next six months, and she couldn't wait for the first one to come to fruition. The media had gone easy on her, not questioning the queer leaning of her charity too much. She was grateful for that, although she knew if she came out, that might change.

In the car afterwards, she'd fallen down a sapphic social media rabbit hole, where fans were currently speculating whether or not Ash and Cam were a couple. United were also in the US, along with the Ravens, and a shot had emerged where Ash's arm was casually slung over Cam's shoulder as they walked along a beach. Even though Victoria knew it wasn't true and that they were best friends, she was still irked by the rumours.

Ash was hers.

Almost.

Now it was lunchtime, and she was in the backseat where she and Ash had shared their first electric kiss. Michael's words from yesterday fizzed through her mind, as they had for the past 24 hours. However, being back on this white leather made all her doubts disappear. She knew what had happened with Ash. She knew how it made her feel. Maybe she needed to tell her parents that if she wanted things to change.

The car swung around Piccadilly Circus, on the way to Windsor, where she was meeting her mother for their monthly ride. They stopped at the traffic lights, the centre of town bursting with tourists all soaking up the summer vibes. To her right, a vendor sold hot dogs from a metal cart. Victoria had always hankered after one when she was little, but her mother had never let her. One day. The statue of Eros stood tall in the midday sun.

Victoria flicked her gaze to the huge curved electronic advertising hoardings, famous the world over. But what she saw took her breath away. It was Ash, In her ad for Tiffany's.

Victoria hit the button and lowered her window ever so slightly. She pulled down her sunglasses and inhaled. Damn, Ash was beautiful. She was also unapologetic, in your face.

Ash stared at her down the camera lens, as if daring Victoria to be bold, too. She was making change with her queer charity. Shouldn't that be echoed in her life?

Victoria put a hand to her chest as her heart thudded inside. Then she closed the window and leaned back.

It felt like a sign.

Maybe it was.

* * *

Victoria arrived at the Royal Mews earlier than necessary, as she always did when riding with her mother. She found comfort in the familiar routines: checking the girth on her saddle, running her hands along Artemis's flanks, the gentle huffs of horse breath in the warm afternoon air. Her mare nudged at her pockets, knowing there'd be treats hidden there.

"She already knows you have them." The Queen's voice carried from the entrance, more mother than monarch this afternoon. She was dressed in jodhpurs and a weathered Barbour jacket that was older than Victoria. "You spoil her."

Victoria gave Artemis a mint. "She deserves spoiling."

Her mother's mare, Venus, was already saddled: the staff would never leave the Queen to do it herself, even though she was perfectly capable. They led their horses out in comfortable silence, hooves clicking against the cobbles. The afternoon was pristine, hues of burnt butter and orange dappling the grass of Windsor Great Park, the castle rising behind them like a painting.

It wasn't until they were well away from the stables, mounted, that her mother spoke again. "How are you doing with the breakup and fallout?" She didn't wait for an answer. "I see Dexter's not wasting any time. He does know he can't be seen out with Sidney so soon?"

Victoria gripped her reins tight. "He does. He sent me his apologies. But they're on the same polo team. It wasn't a big deal."

"Small deals lead to bigger deals, Victoria. You know that. Don't leave a trail. What have I always told you? When I was growing up, we had more control over the media and what they reported. But these days, everyone's a reporter. It's the wild west."

She left a silence to put the matter to bed (for now), and the pair kept a steady walk, the August heat too oppressive for anything more ambitious. Even under the canopy of centuries-old trees, the air was thick and still, heavy with the scent of sun-baked grass and late-summer roses. Venus flicked her tail at flies, while Artemis tossed her head occasionally, sweat darkening her neck. A family of pheasants strutted unhurriedly across their path, too heat-drowsy to startle at the horses' approach.

Victoria gathered her bravery into a shield in front of her, then took a deep breath.

"Moving on from Dexter, though. Which I am doing, because I have to. We were never in love, never even in a relationship, as you know. I'm 33 now, Mother."

"Don't I know it. I've been reading all the columns on your age and the unfortunate nature of your relationship's demise."

*Great.* "I thought you told us not to read the tabloids? Or is that an instance of 'do as I say, not as I do'?"

The Queen didn't answer or turn her head.

It was the latter, then.

"I do want to find a meaningful relationship. One that will make me happy. Now Dexter is done, I need to think about what might happen if I meet someone." Ash's face on the Tiffany ad flashed into her mind. Strong. Gorgeous. Defiant. Everything she wanted in a woman.

"You know my feelings, Victoria. We talked about this."

"That was four years ago. Things change."

"The world doesn't."

"I have." Victoria gently pulled on the reins, and Artemis let out a puff of breath, then stopped. Her hands trembled, but she had to get this out. "It's not something you can just make a statement on, put it on a shelf and never revisit." Her voice cracked slightly on the last word. She straightened her spine, fighting against years of training that told her queens-to-be don't show emotion.

"This is my life. My future. My happiness. I could abdicate. Tell you I don't want to be a future Queen if I can't be myself. But I'm not going to do that, because that's not who I am.

However, I do want to be the best version of me. To do that, I have to live an authentic life."

Each sentence felt like removing armour she'd worn for too long, pieces of herself she'd locked away clattering to the ground between them.

Next to her, Venus's ears flicked back and forth. The horse sidestepped, forcing the Queen to soothe her with a practised hand.

"You always said that you wanted your children to be happy." The words tasted bitter now, childhood memories taking on new shapes in the harsh light of adulthood. "But it feels like that was something you said, rather than something you lived or truly believed. It was lip service."

Victoria met her mother's eyes directly, refusing to look away even as tears threatened to blur her vision. "But I need you to remember that when you and Father got together, it was groundbreaking. He wasn't the norm. He wasn't from your usual circle. I'm not going to fall in love with the norm, either. I need you on my side for this. I'm not going to hide away anymore. I *can't*."

Her mother's hands tightened almost imperceptibly on the reins. She stayed silent for a long moment, her eyes fixed on some point beyond Victoria's shoulder. When she finally spoke, her voice was low, careful.

"The monarchy survived the abdication, Victoria. It survived untimely deaths and a myriad of scandals. But this... This would be different. The tabloids would be relentless. The traditionalists in parliament would have a field day. Everything you do, everything you are, would be scrutinised through this one lens. Is that really what you want?"

"Of course it's not what I want." *Who would?* "But I don't have a choice. I get to be the person I am, or live a life that will break me. I'd rather die trying than never try at all."

Her mother looked at her. She'd always been on Victoria's side. Apart from this, the biggest hurdle of her life.

"What's making you bring this up now? Have you met someone?"

But Victoria wasn't ready for revelations. She didn't know what this thing with Ash was yet.

"There's nobody in particular. But there might be. Astrid and Sofia made me see that. As did Dexter."

The Queen raised an eyebrow. "Do his parents know?"

Victoria rolled her eyes. "They're more in denial than most people I know. This is your chance to show them the way. To really support your kids. It would also do wonders for all the queer kids in society. Think of how much this would help families worldwide if you come out and say, 'I support my queer daughter to be happy'."

Her mother drew in a long breath. "I worry about descendants. About the passing on of the throne."

"I can still have children, Mother."

There were times when Victoria was reminded her mother was from a different era.

When the Queen spoke again, her voice was quieter, stripped of its usual authority. "When you meet someone, come to me. We'll talk again then." Her internal battle danced across her face. "Until then, let me sit with this. Please." She looked up. "There's your grandmother to think about, too. I dread to think what she'll say."

Victoria had seen this before: her mother, usually so

composed, becoming that younger version of herself whenever Gran's disapproval loomed. Suddenly, Victoria understood the layers that were involved. This wasn't just about her own future anymore. This was about her mother caught between two generations: her gran's iron grip on tradition, and her daughter's plea for change.

Victoria had no idea how this would play out, but at least the ball was rolling. It was all she could do.

# Chapter Seventeen

The royal car that picked Ash up from her flat wound through Kensington's busy August streets. It was the final bank holiday of the summer, each turn bringing her closer to Victoria. She'd sent another message on the ride over.

> I'm attempting risotto. No guarantees it'll be edible.

As if Ash cared. A bottle of ridiculously expensive wine pressed against her thigh. Meanwhile, the memory of Victoria's hot lips against her neck pressed against her brain.

Eighteen days of nothing but texts and two carefully encrypted video calls. Eighteen nights of falling asleep with her phone in her hand, reading Victoria's messages until her eyes burned. The pre-season tour had dragged like no other. Ash normally relished seeing other countries, pitting herself against different rivals. Not this time. Sasha had shaken her head on numerous occasions when she'd told her to put her phone down and go to sleep. Unlike normal, the only goal Ash had been focused on was tonight.

The car sailed through the high iron gates, then drove up the short gravel drive before stopping outside the impressive tucked-away residence. Victoria had described it as a cottage, but Ash wasn't sure in what world a cottage stretched this wide and had six bedrooms. She jumped out, thanked the driver, then her stomach clenched. Behind this ordinary-looking black front door, Victoria was in the kitchen relentlessly stirring her risotto. Perhaps she was wearing a comedy apron Prince Michael got her for Christmas?

Ash stepped forward and pressed the doorbell. Somehow, she'd thought it might send a bell clanging, but that was because her parents had made her watch far too much *Downton Abbey*. Her mum had asked her to come for dinner tonight as it was her first weekend back. She'd lied, saying she was out with friends. She had no regrets.

She stood back, the weight of what was about to happen – dinner, yes, but after dinner, too – pressed against her chest, making it hard to breathe. They both knew what tonight meant. What it would change. The last text from Victoria, sent just minutes ago.

> I can't wait to see you. To have you here. To have you.

There was no ambiguity there. Ash wasn't sure what she'd expected from a princess, but it wasn't someone who was direct, devastating, dripping with promise. None of her previous girlfriends had made her feel this unravelled before she'd even stepped over their threshold. The thought of Victoria waiting for her, wanting her, made heat pool low in her stomach. Christ.

The door opened, and she was greeted by Prince Michael. All dressed up and on the way out, he smelt of expensive aftershave. He stepped back, bowed, then beckoned her in.

Ash stepped inside. "Shouldn't the bowing happen the other way around?" She'd liked him when they met at the England game. Nothing had changed, apart from the fact he'd clearly had his ginger hair cut recently.

He gave a nonchalant shrug. "I like to change things up. You look nice, by the way." He waved a hand up and down her body. "Very non-footbally."

"I'm not wearing my kit."

He snapped his fingers together. "That'll be it." He pointed down the grand hallway. "She's in the kitchen. Straight ahead, third door on your right. Follow your nose and your ears. Have fun, and don't do anything I wouldn't do." He winked, grabbed his car keys from a hook by the front door, and left, slamming it shut.

Unlike the outside, which was fairly traditional, the inside was far more modern. Dark wooden floors jutted against moody grey walls with sleek uplighting, creating a seductive entrance. Or perhaps that was just in Ash's mind? Expensive-looking art adorned the hallway walls, and a vase of sunflowers provided a pop of colour. In another room, someone sang along to Bon Jovi's 'Living On A Prayer'. Was it the princess? If so, she could hold a note. Ash recalled a message where Victoria had told her she liked karaoke. Ash, conversely, endured it, which was never a crowd-pleaser on tour.

Her chest tightened as she walked down the hall, wine in hand. When she reached the third door, she took a deep breath, knocked on the door frame, and stepped in.

The royal kitchen was larger than Ash's entire St Albans' flat, all gleaming copper pots and marble counters. However, that wasn't what caught her eye. That honour went to the princess herself, hair tied up in a messy bun, wearing a simple short-sleeved shirt and shorts. As Jon Bon Jovi hit the chorus, she punched the air and sang along. She had no idea Ash had arrived. Ash kept quiet, not wanting to spoil this party for one.

But then Victoria spun on the ball of her foot, wooden spoon in hand. When she clocked Ash, she promptly dropped the spoon, then screamed.

"Are you trying to give me a heart attack, sneaking up on me like that?" Victoria clutched her chest, her cheeks flushed. "Holy fucking hell!"

It was the first time she'd heard Victoria swear. The first time she'd seen her with a bun, too. She looked relaxed, which made sense. Ash had never seen her in private, with nobody else around.

This was the real Victoria.

She wanted to frame her.

Ash put the wine on the counter as the aroma of saffron and white wine filled the air, making her mouth water. "I'm sorry. I didn't want to disturb your singing. You never told me you could have been a pop star."

Victoria picked up the wooden spoon and rinsed it under the industrial metal tap in the sink. "I hardly think Taylor Swift is quaking in her boots," she said over her shoulder. "But if this princess gig doesn't work out, it helps to know I have options."

"Always good to have a plan B."

Their eyes locked, and the humour was instantly quelled. Now, Ash wasn't sure how the next part of the evening went.

They'd only kissed once, and that had been heated, furtive. Tonight was the polar opposite. Did you just walk in and kiss a princess? She didn't think so, even if Victoria looked at her with naked want. Ash picked up the wine and walked over to her. She felt naked, too.

"I brought a Chablis to go with the risotto." She held it up, ignoring the way her heart clattered against her ribs. "Shall I put it in the fridge?"

Victoria nodded. "Over there, left-hand door." She pointed. "Risotto is okay, right? I know you said it was, but you don't have to limit carbs or anything? I wasn't sure if I should do a protein-heavy meal, but Michael assured me athletes eat carbs."

"Every single day," Ash assured her, touched at her concern. "Can I do anything to help?"

Victoria shook her head. "It's nearly done. Shall we have a drink before I serve up? Wine or beer?"

"Whatever you're having."

Victoria poured her a glass of white and put it on the kitchen island. "Take a seat, please." She pointed at one of the three white stools in a row. "We're having a viognier. I'm told it pairs well with both risotto and nervous chefs."

Ash grinned as she took a seat. "I'm impressed you're actually cooking. You have many strings to your bow."

"Don't sound so shocked. I spent a term at Le Cordon Bleu. Part of the whole 'well-rounded royal education' thing."

"Did it work?"

"You can tell me later." She gave a nervous smile. "You're the first woman I've ever cooked for here."

Ash melted. "I'm honoured. If it helps, I'd be bricking it if it was the other way around."

"I doubt that. You're used to performing under pressure."

Ash shook her head. "That's just football. It's a whole lot easier than this." She gestured between them.

"What is this, exactly?" Victoria took a sip of wine and leaned on the other side of the island, her eyes never leaving Ash's. The kitchen was quiet except for the gentle bubbling of the risotto and the distant sounds of London beyond the cottage walls.

"A long-overdue official date?" Ash gambled.

A slow smile spread across Victoria's face. "I like that description a lot. I have a date with a footballer. Who knew I would get so cool?" She grinned deliciously at Ash.

"Who knew I had a thing for princesses?"

Victoria raised an eyebrow. "Plural? Should I be worried?"

Ash's laugh dissolved into a smile that was all heat and intention. "Singular. Very definitely singular." Her gaze lingered on Victoria's face, making it clear that no other woman compared. She sipped her wine. "This is good," she told Victoria. "What I know about wine can be written on the back of a postage stamp. But I like this."

"I'm glad." Victoria straightened up. "How was the tour? I know you told me bits on our messages. I watched your final match."

"You did?"

Victoria nodded. "Got Tanya to sign up to the Ravens subscription package. I paid £45 for the privilege. I hope you're impressed."

"I am." Warmth spread through Ash like the sweetest honey. It was like her manager, Jo, always said: you never knew who was watching.

"The tour was good. We're still rusty, but it did what pre-season tours should. Got us thinking a bit more, working on routines, and it got minutes in my legs, which is all I can ask after last season. I'm still bruised, but they're good bruises, you know? The sign you've been to work. That you're a footballer."

Victoria sipped her wine, listening intently. "I love hearing you talk about football. You're so passionate and dedicated. It's attractive." She paused. "A little like you."

The timer on Victoria's phone buzzed, and they both startled.

"Right." Victoria was back to business. "Let's see if I remember what I learnt in that one summer in Paris, shall we?"

\* \* \*

They ate dinner at the island, which relaxed Ash. She'd had visions of eating at a table set for 20, with grand candelabras down the middle, shouting to be heard. Conversely, the only two people she'd seen were Victoria and Michael, and Victoria was seated mere feet away.

"I think you paid attention in Paris." The creamy risotto coated Ash's taste buds. "This is delicious. Compliments to the chef."

Victoria blushed adorably. "Thank you."

"How do you get on living with your brother? I'm an only child, which means I like my own space."

Victoria shrugged. "We're hardly on top of each other, it's not too bad. He winds me up sometimes, and vice versa, but in the main, we get on. We have a chef come in three days a week. She cooks dinners and freezes them for us if we need them. We also have a full-time butler, Albert, who my parents keep on because he's been with the family for years. Michael and I don't use him like our grandparents used to, but he seems happy enough to be here.

"What about you?" Victoria took a sip of her wine. "No annoying family members to contend with?"

Ash shook her head. "Just me, demanding all of my parents' attention. I've got a couple of cousins I grew up with who I'm close to. But football demands most of my attention. I imagine it's a little like being a member of the royal family: football is all about routine, order, and consistency. Cam always says playing football is like the glorified army, with the battles on the pitch, rather than in real life. She might have a point."

"Were your parents always supportive of you playing? I know it was difficult for some players to find a girls' team, and sometimes still is. It was never an option for me, of course. Lacrosse or tennis, or nothing."

Ash put the last bite of risotto into her mouth. It really was spectacular. "They were, and they spent my entire childhood driving me to games, watching from the sidelines in the pouring rain, driving me to practice. I was always laser-focused. When I know what I want, I go after it."

She gave Victoria what she hoped was a sultry look, her heart racing at her own boldness. The wine had made her braver, but Victoria was intoxicating in her own right. "Although finding myself on a date with a princess who cooks a mean risotto wasn't in my plans this year. However, I'm glad it happened."

"I'm glad, too." Victoria's voice was soft, vulnerable, in a way that made Ash's chest tighten.

"What about you? Did your parents drive you to princess

classes when you were little? Were they always supportive of your career choice?"

Victoria gave her throaty laugh, the one that made Ash want to know more. "I've known since I was little that I'm being trained to be Queen. It's just my reality." She paused, uncertainty flickering across her features. "I hope that doesn't sound weird."

Ash shook her head, hating to see Victoria second guess herself. "It's the truth, there's no need to apologise."

Victoria's gaze settled on her, quiet and searching. "I seem to spend half my life apologising. To the world for my privilege. To my parents for wanting to live an authentic life. It's a hard habit to break." She dropped Ash's gaze, and sighed, the weight of her responsibilities visible in the slump of her shoulders.

"My exes – and I use that term very loosely as most women cut and run when the reality of my life becomes clear – never really got on board with who I am and what I have to do." She waved a hand, trying to dismiss the hurt that lingered in her voice. "But I'm not going to spend any more time on our first official date talking about my exes. There's only really been one of note."

Ash tapped her finger on the island, her stomach knotting with empathy. She recalled how her life had spun out of her control when she and Danielle broke up. "Was your ex out?"

Victoria's jaw clicked before she spoke. "She was. She was Danish, and we did everything there or at her place in London. One evening, she wanted to stay over at mine. To experience a slice of my life. That was four years ago, and I couldn't offer it fully. I was still too afraid of what being queer meant." She stared at Ash, hope and fear warring in her expression. "I'm older now. Definitely wiser. I know things have to change. For me, and for whoever I'm with."

Ash totally got it. "My ex, Danielle, is a pro, too. She understands football and all its challenges. But things started going awry with us when I was made England captain and she was dropped from the Ravens first team." The memory still stung, like pressing on a bruise that hadn't quite healed. "I started to get invited to events, and Danielle couldn't always come or didn't want to. Her career was going south, while mine was soaring. Our differences were magnified.

"What I'm trying to say is that I understand having a role in life that people can't understand. I had sponsors to please who didn't want me turning up with a girlfriend, and I let that happen. Plus, I had interviews and appearances to fulfil. Something had to give, and that was my relationship. Although Danielle cheating on me was still a surprise."

Victoria cringed, genuine compassion softening her features. "I'm sorry you had to deal with that."

"It was her way of getting out of the situation." It hurt like hell at the time, but in the long run, it had been the right thing to do. "It was a break. Not a clean one, but it needed to happen."

"How long ago did you split up?" Victoria's question was gentle, careful.

"Over a year."

"And you haven't met anybody since?"

Ash shook her head. "Plenty have wanted to audition, but it's not how I work. After three years with Danielle and thinking about a future together, I needed time just for me. I wasn't ready to go straight back into something."

Victoria cleared her throat, then reached over for Ash's plate. She carried both to the sink, then turned, hands still clutching the counter behind her. The buttons on the front of her shirt pulled deliciously around her breasts.

"And now?" Victoria asked.

It wasn't a question Ash wanted to answer with words. They hadn't even kissed again yet, and she'd been in Victoria's house for over an hour.

She pulled back her shoulders and got off her stool, then walked over to Victoria, heart racing. With no heels, they were around the same height. She hadn't noticed when they kissed before as they were sat down. But now, Ash noticed everything. The soft exhale that ghosted across Victoria's lips. The pink flush that stained Victoria's throat, the colour spreading down past her collar in a way that made Ash's mouth go dry.

She cleared her throat. "And now, I'm ready for something different. Something real. Do you know anyone who fits the bill?"

"Something real?" Victoria's eyes were glassy. "Reality can be scary, but I'm up for the challenge."

When Ash dropped her gaze, Victoria's knuckles whitened. She was nervous.

One of the most powerful women in Britain was nervous, *because of Ash*.

What could she do to put Victoria at ease? She stepped a little closer, then placed the gentlest kiss of her life on Victoria's neck. The warmth of her skin ignited something primal in Ash, a current that raced from her lips straight to her core.

Clare Lydon

Victoria jolted, too.

Ash brought her lips level with Victoria and stared into her eyes, daring her to look away. She was pretty sure neither was about to.

"I keep thinking about that kiss in the car," Victoria murmured, her voice lower than before, eyes glazed. "I've barely thought about anything else. I keep nearly tripping up, dropping things." She reached her hand to Ash's cheek and ran a solo fingertip down her skin.

Ash's whole body tensed with want, her breath catching as she pressed her face into Victoria's palm, needing more.

"Would kissing you again help you to stop dropping things?"

"It's got to be worth a try."

Ash's fingertips traced the line of Victoria's jaw, feeling the slight tremor there. "I'm here to serve," Ash said with a soft smile. "Plus, if it helps, I haven't been thinking about much else, either."

Victoria's breath stilled as Ash closed that final inch between them, pinning Victoria against the counter and pressing her lips to her.

Time seemed to stop: just the press of mouths, the thump of Ash's heart loud in her ears. This kiss was different from their first: slower, deeper, with an intent that rewrote everything Ash knew about kissing. Every nerve ending sparked alive, hypersensitive. Victoria's lips were impossibly soft, tasting faintly of wine.

Victoria's hands grasped Ash's hips as she drew their bodies flush together, and Ash's mind went blank. The heat of Victoria this close was dizzying. Her self-control, already hanging by a thread, dissolved entirely when Victoria's tongue slipped into her mouth.

A small sound escaped her throat: half surprise, half desperate need. French-kissed by a princess, and god, the reality of it was better than any fantasy. Victoria kissed like she had something to prove, like she wanted to consume Ash whole. Each stroke of her tongue sent lightning down Ash's spine.

When Victoria drew back, her eyes were alight with need, pupils dark. Ash struggled to catch her breath, her whole body humming with want. She'd been kissed before, but not to the point where it felt like she was burning from the inside out. Like her skin was too tight. Like she might die if she couldn't taste Victoria again.

"I can't fuck you in the kitchen. If Albert walks in, he'll never recover." Victoria fixed Ash with her gaze. "Bedroom?"

No protocol manual covered this: how to proceed with a princess who looked at you like she wanted to be ruined.

# Chapter Eighteen

Victoria's bedroom door clicked shut behind them, sealing out the rest of the world. Victoria caught Ash's gaze in the twilight and grinned. Yes, she was nervous, and she had no idea if that would come back and bite her. But she had to trust her gut on this. It was usually right.

In this moment, Ash felt every kind of right.

"You are nothing like what I expected, you know that?"

Victoria's chest burst with warmth. "In a good way?"

Ash closed the distance between them, then gathered Victoria in her arms. It was a gesture Victoria could relive all night. "You're the most unprincessy princess ever."

Victoria quirked her mouth. "I might be a pillow princess."

Ash's mouth curled in a delicious laugh that made all of Victoria's nerve endings wilt. "There's only one way to find out."

Then Ash's lips found Victoria's neck again, her teeth grazing the sensitive spot beneath her ear.

Victoria forgot to breathe.

"I've been dreaming about this for weeks," Ash said, nimble fingers popping the buttons of Victoria's shirt. "It also didn't help how you kept looking at me across the island. Like you wanted to eat me." Her fingers eased back the material, undid Victoria's bra, then her lips traced the line of Victoria's collarbone.

Victoria's response died in her throat as Ash's thigh pressed between her legs, and her thumb grazed the underside of her breast.

"Do you know," Ash whispered against her ear, "how many times I've imagined undressing you?" Her other hand gripped Victoria's hip, holding her steady as she rolled her hips forward. "Taking off all your clothes, piece by piece. Sinking into you."

Victoria's head fell back as Ash's mouth found her throat, sucking gently at her pulse point. She was already wet, desperately wanting more friction where Ash's thigh pressed between her legs, but also wanting this to last forever.

"Sinking into me sounds good." Victoria grabbed Ash's wrist, guiding her hand higher. "For now, just touch me."

Ash cut her off with a searing kiss, finally palming Victoria's breast as their tongues met. Victoria moaned into her mouth, fingers tangling in Ash's hair as she rocked against her thigh. The dual sensation – Ash's skilled fingers teasing her nipple, along with the solid press of muscle between her legs – made her drunk with want.

Moments later, Ash shed her top and bra, then got rid of Victoria's, too. They both stopped and stared. This was really happening.

"You are simply majestic." Ash's words were filled with sincerity, just like her face. She ran her palms over Victoria's perfect curves, drinking in the sight of her. "I thought you were stunning with clothes on, but without, you're spectacular."

Ash's voice went rough as she traced the constellation of

tiny freckles across Victoria's collarbone, as if memorising each detail. Then she backed Victoria onto the bed and pushed her down. Ash slid off Victoria's shorts, while Victoria shimmied her hips and pushed down her underwear, too. As she did, she kept her gaze on Ash's face, eyes wide, cheeks flushed. Then Ash took off her clothes, too, and it was Victoria's turn to gasp.

But she didn't speak. She couldn't. She didn't want to break the magic in the moment.

Ash slid up Victoria like a tide claiming the shore, and Victoria's heart clenched at her touch. The feel of Ash's skin against her own was pure overwhelm, not just desire, but the heady knowledge that this was real, that Ash wanted her just as desperately. When Ash drew level with Victoria, the kiss she laid on her was equal parts tenderness and hunger, and Victoria surrendered completely to the feeling of finally being exactly where she belonged.

Ash's hands travelled down Victoria's body, her fingertips dancing across Victoria's skin the way she'd seen her tease her way past defenders: deliberate, skilled, mesmerising. Each touch sent electric currents racing down Victoria's spine. The air was thick with anticipation, each movement deliberate. It was just a question of how long Ash was going to take without making her beg. When Ash cupped Victoria's arse, she pressed her head into the pillow and moaned.

Victoria was wet, ready. Her heart was beating out of time.

Ash's skilled fingers slid lower, skating up the inside of Victoria's thighs, tracing maddening circles.

Victoria grasped the back of Ash's neck and pulled her

close, kissing her with rough passion. When she pulled back, Ash's eyes were dark, curious.

They panted at each other, eyes locked.

Ash's fingers ghosted over Victoria's centre. A fleeting promise.

Victoria's heart thundered beneath her ribs.

"Please, Ash."

"Please, what?" she whispered, her hot breath slamming into Victoria with all the subtlety of a champagne cork at midnight.

"Touch me."

Ash placed her lips beside Victoria's ear. "What was that, Ma'am?"

*That word.*

Desire soaked her.

"Please, I'm begging you."

Ash licked her tongue up Victoria's neck, and then there were no more words, as Ash smothered Victoria's mouth with her own.

Victoria spread her legs, then locked her gaze with Ash: amber colliding with steel. No titles now, no careful manners. The kind of look that would've gotten them both exiled in another century.

Ash's fingertips brushed Victoria's clit. Then, with one fluid motion, she slipped inside.

Victoria's jaw went tight. She gasped, then reached out, pulling Ash towards her. All the pent-up tension of the past few weeks rippled through her at Ash's sure touch. Victoria never wanted this to end, but they had all night. There was no way she was letting Ash leave. Not after she'd felt the heat of Ash's skin against hers, the strength in her muscles as she curled more fingers into Victoria, slow and deliberate. The effect was dizzying, intense.

"This okay?" Ash whispered, her breath hot and explosive.

Victoria could only nod. This was more than okay. This was off-the-scale okay. It shredded the term, made it obsolete.

The world narrowed down to the point of their connection, Ash's movements rhythmic, with a foggy, dream-like quality. Her fingers slid in, out, and to just where Victoria needed them, driving her to the edge, then holding her there with an exquisite intention that was all-consuming. Victoria shifted her hips, then wrapped her legs around Ash's hips, pulling her in, wanting more, needing more. Ash's firmness sent thrills through her as the room filled with the sounds of their bodies finally merging.

When her orgasm hit, it hit hard. Victoria's back arched off the bed, one hand gripping Ash's shoulder, the other fisting the sheets. She bit her lip to muffle her cry, her body shuddering as waves of pleasure rolled through her.

Victoria squeezed her eyes shut, drinking in Ash's scent: all spice and dark promises. After months of wanting, the reality of this moment felt almost too much to grasp. When Ash moved inside her, each touch sent aftershocks rippling through her body. When she claimed her mouth in a bruising kiss and drove Victoria over the edge once more, Victoria could no longer deny how real this was.

The most real thing she'd ever felt.

She tried to bury that thought deep where it couldn't shatter the careful walls she'd built. But with Ash, those walls were already crumbling. The truth rose up, undeniable: she couldn't walk away from this feeling. More importantly, she couldn't walk away from this woman.

When Ash finally withdrew her fingers and rolled onto her side, she traced lazy patterns across Victoria's flushed skin.

Victoria turned to her with a dazed smile, her world slowly settling back into place.

"That was..." she began, unsure how to convey her feelings.

But Ash seemed to understand. At least, that's what her smile told Victoria, quickly followed by her words.

"I know." Her fingertips moved a lock of hair from Victoria's forehead. "That was delicious. Intense." She inhaled. "Perfect." Then something shifted in her face. "But I want you to know, if you want me to leave before morning, I will. It'll kill me a little, I won't lie. But I want this to be okay for you, and for both of us."

Damn, did she have to be so perfect? No woman had ever said this to her before.

For the first time in Victoria's life, someone saw her. Just her, the woman. Not her job, her life. Just a woman who wanted to be loved.

A lump formed in her throat, but she wasn't going to cry.

Instead, she shook her head. "You going is the last thing I want." She leaned in and kissed Ash's velvet lips, then pulled back. "I want to spend the next couple of hours wrapped in you. Also, in you." She gave what she hoped was a devilish smile.

In turn, Ash grinned. "That's a plan I can get down with."

Energised by the kiss, Victoria rolled on top of Ash, pressing their naked bodies together.

"You feel criminally good." Then she raised an eyebrow, and slowly moved down the full length of Ash's body, licking every part of her as she went. She settled between Ash's legs, nudging them apart with her shoulders.

Ash gasped.

Victoria kissed the top of Ash's firm thighs, then stared upwards. "Just so you know, I've admired your thighs from afar."

Ash's gaze locked with hers. "You have?"

Victoria nodded. "I've got a thing for footballers' thighs."

"Plural? Should I be worried?" She shot Victoria a languid smile.

In response, Victoria licked her way up Ash's left thigh, then her right, making her squirm deliciously beneath her.

"No, you're very safe. Singular. These are the only firm thighs my lips intend to touch." She stared upwards. "Just so we're clear, I meant what I said. I want you to stay." She dipped her head, then swept her tongue over Ash's hot centre.

They both groaned in unison.

"Does that work for you?"

Ash could only nod her agreement.

Victoria licked her lips and got to work.

# Chapter Nineteen

Sunlight danced across Victoria's sleeping form, casting her in the kind of ethereal glow reserved for those renaissance paintings Ash had seen at her investiture. She'd thought Victoria was dreamy that first day they met, but last night had shown Ash she was all that, and so much more.

But in the harsh light of morning, reality settled on Ash's chest like a lead crown.

Just over a year earlier, when the media and women's football crowd had picked over the carcass of her last relationship, she'd vowed not to get involved with another footballer. She couldn't take the constant speculation when they were together, and then when they weren't.

She'd kept to her word.

However, if she'd been trying to keep her next relationship quiet, she'd spectacularly failed by falling for literally the most photographed woman in the country.

When Ash had blinked awake in the darkness, reality crashed over her like a wave. These weren't her sheets. That wasn't her ceiling. And the soft, steady breathing beside her belonged to actual royalty. The knowledge fizzed through her blood, equal parts terror and wild joy.

She could have chosen someone who wasn't famous. That

barista at her local coffee shop who always slipped her free drinks. The lawyer who'd given her their card with too much lingering eye contact after finalising a lucrative boot deal.

But Ash had never been one to take the easy route. Her career told the story of that, coming as she had through the ranks of the Ravens, cleaning boots, going out on loan, taking every single step to get to where she was today. Perhaps that was what she needed to do with Victoria? Take it one day at a time.

Victoria stirred, her dark lashes fluttering against her cheeks, and Ash's heart performed its now-familiar stumble. Victoria's hand moved across Ash's body, her mouth kissing Ash's shoulder as she rolled into her with the kind of unconscious intimacy that already spoke of trust. The simple warmth of that touch scattered all Ash's careful logic like leaves in an autumn storm.

The most worthwhile things were rarely simple.

"Morning." Victoria's voice was coarse. "What time is it?"

"Eight o'clock."

She nudged Ash with her arm. "What are you doing awake? You need your beauty sleep so you can bang in the goals."

Ash felt Victoria's smile against her shoulder.

Victoria raised her head with an arched eyebrow. "Wouldn't the world be outraged if they knew you'd been up banging me instead?"

"They'd be surprised. I know that for sure."

Victoria reached up and kissed Ash. It was softer than last night's desperate heat, but no less devastating. "Also, you're thinking too loud," she murmured, propping herself up on one elbow.

The white sheet slipped down, and Ash forced her gaze back up to Victoria's face. Not an easy task when her breasts were that perfect.

"I can practically hear the wheels turning. 'What the fuck have I done; everyone is going to think I've corrupted the heir to the throne'."

"That's not—" Ash started, but Victoria pressed a finger to her lips.

"It is. And you look adorable when you worry, by the way. But here's the thing about being a princess in the 21st century: I'm not some delicate flower who needs protecting from her own choices. I knew exactly what I was doing when I asked you here." Her smile turned wicked. "I knew it the first time, the second time, and the third."

The blush that heated Ash's cheeks had nothing to do with embarrassment and everything to do with those memories. "Still. You have responsibilities, expectations—"

"You think I don't know that?" Victoria's expression softened. "Last night wasn't a rebellion or a mistake. It was me choosing something that made me happy. Someone who sees me as Victoria first, and Her Royal Highness second."

"But you know how it is. Social media makes it doubly treacherous. It's not just the regular media we have to worry about. When I was made England captain, I was told to dial down my sexuality. Be a little more mysterious. That's been easy while I wasn't seeing anyone." She glanced at Victoria. Had she said too much? "And I don't know what this is, and I'm not professing undying love for you…"

She'd said too much. Post-coital anxiety was not an appealing quality.

"Ash."

Ash moved her mouth, furious at herself for letting her thoughts spiral. "Yes?"

"It's normal to feel what you're feeling. This situation isn't normal. But then again, it really is. Just two people having dinner, being attracted to each other, doing what comes naturally."

Ash nodded. Victoria was being nice about it.

"I guess what I mean is, what happens next?"

She hated how vulnerable the question made her sound.

But Victoria simply kissed Ash's shoulder. "Next? It's a bank holiday weekend. I'm thinking breakfast. Then maybe a repeat performance of last night. And after that..." She shrugged, the gesture somehow both elegant and casual. "We figure it out. Bit by bit. Unless you're planning to run?"

The challenge in her voice made Ash smile despite herself. "Not a chance, Ma'am."

Victoria closed her eyes and groaned. "Why do I find it so hot when you call me that? When you did it on the pitch at the FA, I couldn't look at you." She bruised Ash's lips with a kiss. "We're never going to have breakfast at this rate. Because I'm not done with you yet. Not even close." She kissed Ash again. "Besides, how hard can it be to keep quiet that you're sleeping with the heir to the throne?"

"When you put it like that, I don't know what I'm worried about." Ash reached out and stroked Victoria's breast, then gathered her in her arms and pressed their bodies together.

Victoria groaned into her mouth. "I love the way you feel against me."

Ash ran her tongue along Victoria's bottom lip. "The feeling's mutual, Ma'am."

Her rough, throaty laugh followed. "Talk dirty to me."

A fire ignited within, and suddenly, Ash knew what kind of breakfast was now on the menu. She was just about to kiss her again when three curt knocks interrupted them.

"Madam? Are you up? I have your morning coffee and papers."

Victoria froze in Ash's arms, then pulled away. Alarm stained her features. "Shit. Shit, shit, shit! I thought I told her not to come in today. But maybe I didn't. I don't know." She jumped out of bed, and threw on a white silk dressing gown. "Shit, shit, shit." She glanced at Ash, then at the bedroom door.

"Hang on a minute, Tanya!"

She winced. "Do you mind going in the bathroom? Just for a minute? I know she knows about you, and I know what I just said, but I thought I'd have a little time to process what to do next after we took the next step." She shook her head. "I'm sorry."

But Ash was already out of bed, already collecting up any stray clothing from the night before, wiping away any trace of it.

"I understand. Knock when you're done." Unease circled in her mind.

Ash stood in Victoria's marble bathroom, bare feet cold against black tiles, hearing the muffled voices beyond the door. The irony of hiding like some dirty secret wasn't lost on her. Not when mere minutes ago, Victoria had been talking about choosing happiness and figuring things out together. Easy words in their intimate bubble. Harder to maintain when faced with the realities of royal life.

Even through the thick door, she could hear Tanya's crisp,

efficient tone reviewing the day's schedule. All duties that couldn't wait just because the princess had spent the night falling apart in her arms.

The worst part was how natural it seemed to Victoria. Like hiding her lover was just another part of the morning routine. Maybe it was?

Ash pressed her forehead against the cool mirror, her breath fogging the glass.

Last night she'd felt special, chosen, like maybe she could be more than just another secret lover. Now, standing naked in her bathroom, she wasn't so sure. She didn't want to be a secret, but also, she didn't want to be scrutinised. The real challenge of being involved with royalty started to dawn.

The door opening interrupted her thoughts, and Victoria stood there, her face torn in a way it hadn't been a few minutes earlier. She walked over and took Ash in her arms.

Ash let her. She was too winded to do anything else.

"I really am sorry." Victoria's hand settled on Ash's naked arse.

Ash should shake it off, but she didn't want to.

"I know I could have handled that better, but I didn't want to throw you right into it." Victoria shook her head again, then pulled back. "However, bundling you into a bathroom was hardly a skilled move." She licked her lips and stared into Ash's eyes. "Can you forgive me just this once?"

"I get it." And she did. However, that didn't mean it didn't hurt. "But I'm not interested in being your dirty little secret. If that's what this is going to be…" She trailed off as Victoria's gaze softened, becoming something raw and honest.

"You're not a secret," Victoria whispered, stepping closer.

"You're just new. And precious. And I want to protect this, *protect us*, until we figure out how to face everything else. But I handled it badly, and I'm sorry." Her hand came up to cup Ash's cheek. "Let me make it up to you soon? Are you free this week?"

Victoria's hand travelled up Ash's back, making it hard to focus on what her week entailed.

"Pre-season training. A few sponsorship things."

She pressed her thigh between Ash's legs, all the while never losing eye contact.

Ash's mind scrambled. "What about you?"

*When did her voice get so raspy?*

"Tanya just told me, but I've forgotten already. Because all I could think about was you, naked, in this bathroom. And what I wanted to do with you." With that, Victoria reached down between Ash's legs, and slipped two fingers inside.

Ash gasped, as glitter rattled through her. She pressed down on Victoria's fingers, grinding hard despite what she just said.

"After pushing you in here, I wanted to leave a different lasting impression on you." Victoria curled into her, then added a thumb onto Ash's clit. "One that will make you smile when you fall asleep later."

Ash pressed herself against the wall, her insides coiling tight. When Victoria swiped over her, she saw stars.

"You're not my dirty little secret, Ash," Victoria whispered in her ear. "You're someone I want in my life. I want to take you to Scotland, show you places I love. Say you'll come with me."

But Ash couldn't respond as Victoria started to fuck her hard in a way that was so all-consuming, she was surprised she was still standing. She clung to her for dear life, and as she came apart at the seams, she knew she was in this, whatever being with Victoria entailed. It wasn't going to be plain sailing, she'd known that from the start.

But the way Victoria had her in the palm of her hand?

It wasn't nothing.

*She* wasn't nothing.

Ash came all over Victoria's fingers with a guttural moan.

She knew then, this thing was bigger than both of them.

# Chapter Twenty

"Wait, what? You're taking her to Scotland!?"
Astrid nearly choked on her 2008 Dom Pérignon,
her blue eyes wide with disbelief across the intimate corner
table at the Devonshire Club, one of London's most prestigious
private members clubs. Its signature raspberry-coloured walls
and low lighting created the perfect cocoon of privacy, while
the gentle murmur of conversation from other members –
aristocrats and high-fliers, politicians, and carefully vetted
creatives – provided just enough cover for their conversation.
"Meeting your grandmother, too. You've never taken anybody
to Scotland before." The implications hung in the air.

"I took Dexter."

"Dexter, much as he's a darling, does not count. You've
never taken a woman."

Victoria's cheeks flushed hot at the memory of their night
together: Ash's hands, her mouth, the way she'd made Victoria
forget her own name. "It's more a chance to get away somewhere
far off the radar. I'm not going to tell Granny I'm with her, of
course. She's just a new friend."

Astrid furrowed her brow. "Your granny is not as stupid
as you think."

Victoria waved her comment away. "Granny was in love

with Dexter. She's probably still mad with me about breaking his heart. But taking Ash to Balmoral is part of my grand plan to wow her. I have some making up to do after I rather buggered things up the morning after our dazzling night before."

"What did you do?"

"There was a knock at the door and I panicked. Yes, I know Tanya *knows*, but she doesn't know about Ash yet. She knows I'm interested, but she doesn't know the full picture. And what if Albert saw something? I wouldn't be able to look him in the eye ever again." Victoria groaned, then covered her face. "I basically shoved Ash into the bathroom. God, Astrid, you should have seen her face. She looked so hurt."

She instinctively glanced around their alcove, although she knew the club's staff were legendary for their discretion. The silk lampshades cast a warm glow that made everything feel conspiratorial, intimate. Perfect for confessions.

"Oh, darling." Astrid's voice softened with understanding. She set down her glass. "What happened next?"

"I apologised. Properly. And then..." Warmth crept up Victoria's neck. "Let's just say I made it very clear how much she means to me. Against the bathroom wall."

"Victoria Elizabeth!" Astrid's delighted laugh bounced off the wood-panelled wall of their corner. "You absolute dark horse. I knew you had it in you." She leaned forward. "Tell me more about the night before. Some of us have been married too long and want to relive the first throes of lust."

Victoria shook her head. "Just because you're one of my oldest and dearest friends, you do not get all the details." But then, she couldn't help herself. She lowered her voice, aware of the people around them.

"I'll just say, she's known for being good with her feet, but she's no slouch with her hands or her tongue, either. And her body, my god. I have never dated a professional athlete before, and I don't know what I've been doing with my time. She's all lean muscle. When I ran my hands down her stomach..." She closed her eyes briefly at the memory. "Her abs are sent from heaven, and you should see her thighs. I notice footballers' legs, of course. But up close, they're something else."

Her friend raised a single eyebrow. "You're blushing, and I am loving every single second."

"She made me blush, believe me." Victoria's mouth quirked into a smile. Picturing Ash inside her made her feel like she was right back there all over again. She shifted in her seat then moved a little closer before she continued. Astrid did the same.

"The way she touched me, it was like I was precious, but not fragile. She kept asking if I was okay. Let's just say I'm fairly certain half of Kensington heard exactly how okay I was." She met Astrid's delighted gaze. "I've never lost control like that. Never wanted to."

"All hail Ash Woods."

"Shhhh!" Victoria put a finger to her lips and frowned at Astrid. Talking about Ash was one thing. Saying her name out loud was quite another.

"I went down a little social media rabbit hole looking into her after you messaged me all lusted up," Astrid told her. "There's a lot of photos of her with the Lionesses' keeper Cam Holloway, and women's football social media seems to wonder if they could be more. Nothing to worry about?"

Victoria shook her head. "They've been friends since they were eight. It would be like you and I sleeping together."

Astrid wrinkled her face like she'd just been served supermarket champagne. "Understood." She paused. "And now you're taking her to Balmoral?"

"I need her to know this is real." Victoria traced the rim of her glass, voice growing serious. "That she's not some secret I'm ashamed of. She's the first person I've wanted to share that place with, Astrid. The first woman I've ever..." She trailed off, unable to find the words.

"Are you close to saying the L word?"

Victoria's features crumpled at her friend's suggestion. "Don't be so ridiculous. We've hardly spent any time together."

"You've been flirting and messaging for months. It's like an old-fashioned courtship, and everyone knows that the slow build makes the best kind of relationships. You might have only slept together recently, but your feelings have been building far longer."

Victoria didn't deny it. She didn't want to. What Astrid was saying was 100 per cent true. Finally sleeping together had only confirmed what Victoria suspected.

"I want to give her something that's just ours. Somewhere we can just be. She's too high-profile to do that in London. We both are."

Victoria couldn't even bring Ash here. If she looked left, she recognised a cabinet minister, a pop star and a well-known actor. She was damn sure they knew just who she and Astrid were, too. However, seeing two princesses together wasn't really news. Seeing her and Ash Woods together totally would be.

"And you chose the one place you've never let anyone into." Astrid reached across the table and squeezed her hand. "I'm proud of you for opening yourself up."

"I know it's fast. We've only just started whatever this is, but when I'm with her…" Victoria paused, thinking of how safe she felt in Ash's arms, how right it felt to wake up beside her. "It feels so natural."

"Which is exactly how I felt when Sofia and I first got together."

Victoria's mind blared an alert. "Don't say that."

"Why not?" Astrid's face was a question. "I assure you, what Sofia and I have is the realest thing I've ever had in my life."

"I know. Of course I want that, but everything that goes with it? Coming out, placating my mother and the entire country when they find out the Princess Royal likes women? If I think about it too much, it makes my head hurt." She raised her gaze to Astrid. "I spoke to my mother the other day about changing royal protocols. About what might happen if I meet someone who matters."

"And what did the delightful Queen have to say for herself?" Before Victoria could answer, Astrid held up a hand. She cleared her throat, before changing her accent to mimic the Queen. "No, let me guess. 'The UK royal family is not the Swedish royal family. We have standards, and being a lesbian is not in those standards'. Am I close?"

Victoria gave a rueful smile. "At least I got her thinking about it."

A waiter appeared and refilled their glasses, disappearing into the shadows as stealthily as he'd arrived.

"The fact you had the conversation in the first place shows me this is different from anything else you've had before. That Ash might be someone worth upending your life for." She covered Victoria's hand with her own. Her soft touch made Victoria jump. "It had to happen sometime."

Victoria sighed. "You don't think it's too fast? That I'm rushing into it?"

"What do you think?"

"That I've waited all my life to feel like this. That I really like this girl. That I could easily fall in love with her." That was the plain, unvarnished truth.

"Then it's not fast. I think this is your time. You've put in the years of dutiful service, of pretending to be in love with someone you're not. But you can't do it forever. You deserve a chance to be happy. And if your mother doesn't see that, tell her to call mine. She can tell her the world will not collapse if you come out."

Victoria smiled. She needed to hear that from one of her oldest friends. She needed someone to tell her she wasn't wrong or going mad. That she could finally stop apologising for who she was and choose her own happiness.

"You really think so?"

"I know so."

# Chapter Twenty-One

The Range Rover crunched to a halt on the gravel, and Ash's first thought was that the photos didn't do Balmoral justice. The granite wasn't just grey: it sparkled in the weak Scottish sunshine, flecks of black and silver catching the light like stars trapped in stone. Three steps led up to a thick wooden door, propped open today with what looked like... was that a curling stone?

"Home sweet home." Victoria gave Ash's hand one final squeeze before climbing out of the car.

A red-coated footman nodded to them, and Victoria returned the gesture with the easy familiarity of someone who'd grown up in places like this. Inside, Ash's box-fresh Nikes squeaked against stone tiles as she turned slowly, taking it all in.

The fireplace was enormous, the dark wood mantel carved with thistles and stags and other things she couldn't quite make out. To one side, a small army of wellington boots stood to attention next to fishing rods and walking sticks, like some posh outdoor equipment shop.

"Wellies are essential." Victoria followed her gaze. "It can be absolutely Baltic up here, even in September. Last summer, I made the mistake of wearing trainers on a walk and ended up knee-deep in a bog." She glanced at Ash's feet with a grin. "When we walk, you might want to leave your Nikes here."

They moved down the corridor, every few feet another door opened into another room, each one looking like something out of a period drama.

"Now I really feel like I'm in Downton Abbey." Ash's mum didn't know Ash was here. If she did, Ash would probably hear the screams from St Albans. "It's so bizarre that you grew up here." Ash paused to examine an oil painting of Queen Mary.

"Summers and Christmases mostly, but I have nothing but fond memories. Father barbecuing on the lawn, Granny telling lewd stories and covering my ears, Mother actually relaxing. This is everybody's place to chill, away from it all."

Ash breathed in the smell of furniture polish, damp, and living history.

Victoria stopped in front of a statue, kissed her palm, then laid it on the stone woman's shoulder. "This is Queen Victoria, my namesake. I always give her a little extra love when I pass. Isn't it wild that centuries of my family have lived here?"

Her namesake. Because, of course, Victoria was going to be Queen Victoria eventually.

Ash pushed that thought to the back of her mind, and tipped her head to Victoria's ancestor. "Your Royal Highness."

Victoria grabbed Ash's hand and led her to the end of the corridor, through an enormous vestibule, and then into one of the most impressive ballrooms Ash had ever seen.

Scratch that: the *only* ballroom she'd ever seen. The space felt alive with centuries of memories, golden light spinning through crystal to dance across polished floors that had hosted many kings and queens.

"I wanted to show you this." Victoria's face lit up as she looked around. "I love it here. I learnt to dance in this ballroom, and we have parties here in the summer. Loads of people come, and my gran used to make the most amazing cocktails. They were very potent, so it's a good job she's mostly stopped now she's in her 70s. We need her fighting fit, especially with Granddad not here."

"Is she up here on her own?"

"With staff, plus she knows quite a few people round here who come and have dinner with her. She's a popular woman." Victoria paused, eyeing Ash. She pulled her close. "I'd love to dance here with you. I've only ever gone to formal balls with men. I'd love to go with you." She leaned in and placed the most delicate kiss on Ash's lips. "I bet you'd look extraordinarily hot in a tux."

Ash's mind melted, between the kiss and the image Victoria had just painted. Her in a tux, Victoria in a gown, spinning together under crystal chandeliers. She'd never considered herself particularly dashing before, but the way Victoria looked at her made her want to be.

"I've got the perfect one in my wardrobe. Gucci lent it to me last year and never asked for it back."

Victoria squeezed Ash's hand, her brow furrowing. "You know, there's a New Year ball every year at Buckingham Palace. Maybe we could go together. You in a tux. Me in a flowy chiffon number."

"The two of us in public?" Ash's heart thumped at what everyone would say. What the football world would say. Her parents' reaction.

Victoria held her gaze. "It's a stretch, and I haven't figured out the logistics, but just think about it. It's going to happen sometime. I would love to go to the ball on your arm. When's your winter break?"

"Mid-December to mid-January. But I should warn you, I'm a terrible dancer." Especially with the eyes of the world watching.

Victoria stared at her. "Having slept with you, I simply can't believe that." She kissed her one more time. "First, let me show you around. I can't wait for you to see everything properly. The castle looks incredible at sunset, and there's this little loch where we can go wild swimming."

"Wild swimming? In Scotland? In September? Are you trying to freeze me to death?"

"Says the woman who goes to work in shorts all winter long," Victoria countered. "Here was me thinking you'd be up for adventure."

Ash kissed Victoria's hand. "If it means getting nearly naked with you, count me in."

"I promise to warm you up afterwards."

\* \* \*

Ash had to keep reminding herself that when she'd woken that morning, she'd been in her two-bed flat in St Albans, and had started her day as she always did with a bowl of porridge, topped with chia seeds, berries, and a banana. In the 12 hours since then, she'd flown on a royal jet, been driven to a castle by a princess, and promised said princess she'd go to a ball with her.

Honestly, this was her life now.

Following an afternoon of clay pigeon shooting (at

which Ash had failed miserably and Victoria, after a lifetime of practice, was a sure shot), they were back at the castle. A real, live, honest-to-goodness castle. With turrets. She was glad she'd quelled her Instagram impulse, otherwise the impetus to share a story might have been too much. Instead, she was just enjoying being here, with a woman who was far from the two-dimensional princess the press made her out to be.

Princess Victoria was a fully formed human with a law degree from Oxford. She was also a devout Swiftie, loved women's football, swore by Orangina ("the best fizzy drink, often overlooked"), and had a penchant for bathroom sex, which she'd just demonstrated one more time to a very flushed Ash.

Victoria was currently stood beside her dressing table, wrapped in a luxurious fluffy white bathrobe, shaking her hair in the sexiest way possible.

The princess eyed Ash, then frowned. "What is it?" She brushed down her front. "Do I have something on me? Is my hair sticking up at an awkward angle? Am I sunburnt from that weird afternoon sunshine that appeared when I was shooting clay moulds from the sky?"

Ash was sure she was sunburnt, but not Victoria. "You look perfect, and I was just wondering how it was possible that you manage that so often."

Victoria did her laugh again. The one that made Ash's insides quake.

"You've got post-orgasm glow," Victoria said. "Anything I did would be incredible to you right now." She walked over to Ash and kissed her on the lips.

Ash breathed the princess in, all lime-scented shower gel

and shampoo. "You have a point, Ma'am, but so do I." She smiled at her clever word choice.

Victoria looked her in the eye, a faint blush bruising her cheeks. "I swear, if you call me that in front of my grandmother, you're dead. Save it for later." She grinned, then placed a firm kiss on Ash's lips. "Ready to go and meet the matriarch?"

"As I'll ever be, Ma'am," Ash winked.

Ten minutes later, Ash walked into the kitchen behind Victoria. She was about to meet another key royal. The Queen Mother, who'd been in Ash's life forever. A national treasure. She was also standing at the farmhouse sink in Balmoral's large-yet-cozy kitchen, wearing bright-yellow Marigolds and washing up what looked like the remains of afternoon tea. The Queen Mother was dressed in a tartan skirt and blue woollen cardigan, and her silver hair caught the overhead light from the window as she hummed to herself.

Even though Victoria had warned Ash that her family lived a far more normal life in Scotland, she still hadn't expected the Queen Mother up to her elbows in soap suds.

Victoria cleared her throat softly. "How's my favourite grandmother?"

The older woman turned, her face lighting up at the sight of her granddaughter, then breaking into an even broader smile as she spotted Ash.

"And here's my favourite granddaughter, although don't go telling Charlotte or Bridget that. Sorry I wasn't here to greet you, but I'm sure you've made yourself at home."

She stripped off her gloves and walked around the distressed farmhouse table big enough to seat eight, giving Victoria a hug before holding her at arm's length. "It's good to see you. And you're glowing, that's good to see." She pursed her lips. "I hoped you were okay after the whole Dexter debacle, but clearly, you are. Your mother told me it was your doing."

Victoria nodded. "It was, Gran. We're still good friends. He sends his regards." Then she turned. "This is my friend, Ashleigh Woods."

The Queen Mother's eyes, the same striking blue as Victoria's, sparkled with interest. "Captain of the Lionesses, I know who she is. Meeting you is something worth bragging about at my next bridge game. Far more interesting than those politicians who drone on about fiscal policy over the pheasant course." The older woman's handshake was firm, her smile warm. She was also far taller in real life than Ash had expected. Taller than both she and Victoria. "It's a pleasure to meet you, Ashleigh."

Ash wasn't quite sure whether or not to bow or curtsy, and ended up doing a mix of both and nearly tripping over one of the dining chairs. She grasped the back of one just in time to stop herself face-planting on the terracotta tiles underfoot.

"Are you okay, dear?" the Queen Mother asked.

Ash wanted the world to swallow her up as she steadied herself.

"She will be when she gets over meeting you, Gran. Remember, you're a living legend," Victoria said with a grin.

"Better than a dead one!" Her gran put an arm around Victoria's shoulder. "Let's go into the parlour and have a pre-dinner drink, shall we? I asked Chef to prepare your favourite this evening, and Edward brought a delicious bottle of red up from the cellar. A 1982 Château Latour. It's not every day my granddaughter pays me a visit with a new friend, is it?"

Was there the slightest of eyebrow raises from the Queen Mother to Victoria when she said that? Ash had probably imagined it.

The Queen Mother led the two of them out of the kitchen and down the breezy hallway to the parlour with its intricate cornices, corner bar and pair of cherry-red Chesterfields either side of a roaring fire.

"Please take a seat," the Queen Mother said, indicating the sofas before disappearing behind the bar. "I took the liberty of pre-mixing my new favourite cocktail. A Last Word. Have you had it before, Ashleigh?"

Ash shook her head. "I haven't. I'm afraid I'll have to pass on this round as I'm in pre-season training right now."

"A little sip won't hurt, will it? You should definitely save any alcohol tokens for the wine, but I'll just pour you a little one."

Ash glanced at Victoria, who gave her a tight smile.

She understood. "Just a small one, for a taste."

The Queen Mother grinned. "I knew my granddaughter would have good taste in… her friends."

Right at that moment, Victoria's phone blared in her pocket. She pulled it out, stared at the screen. "Shit," she muttered under her breath, before standing. "Sorry, Gran. I'll be five minutes. I just need to return this call. It's from a potential sponsor of my homeless charity, and I said I'd call her today. I've lost track of time." She glanced at Ash, knowing full well why she'd lost track of time.

"Don't you have staff for that?" Victoria's gran asked.

"Of course. But I wanted to provide a more personal touch for this project. I'll be as quick as I can."

"You do what you have to do." Her gran brought over two cloudy green cocktails of equal size in crystal martini glasses, and placed one on the wooden table in front of Ash. "It means that Ashleigh and I can get better acquainted, doesn't it?"

Victoria held up five fingers, mouthed the word "Sorry!" at Ash, and disappeared.

Then it was just Ash, the Queen Mother, and the crackle of the fire. Ash dredged her brain for all the media training she'd been put through. Some of it surely had to be useful here.

"A gorgeous home you have here. So full of character and history."

The Queen Mother nodded, her gaze intense. "It is. I'd love to claim it's all my doing, but we have interior designers come in every few years to cheer the place up." She glanced around the room with its dark green walls and antique rugs. "But this room is one of my favourites. Cosy, and perfect for reading, which is one of my favourite things to do." She paused. "Do you read?"

Ash shook her head. "I don't really have time. The last books I read were when I did my degree, but they certainly weren't for pleasure."

"What was your degree in?"

"Business."

"Smart girl. Just like Victoria. Getting a backup in a business like women's football is essential." She tilted her head. "Although somehow, with your skills and good looks, I think you're going to be okay. A little like Victoria, who has a job for life. But it never hurts to get educated and broaden the mind, does it?"

Ash shook her head. "It doesn't."

The Queen Mother shifted a little closer.

Ash's nerves and heartbeat rattled skywards.

"Shall we take a sip of our cocktail?"

Ash nodded. Anything to break the intensity of the moment. When the liquid hit the back of her throat, her eyes widened. This cocktail was potent. Definitely not on her list of things that would aid her football progress. But she couldn't say no to the Queen Mother.

"What do you think?" the Queen Mother asked, taking another sip. "Pokey, aren't they?"

"That's definitely a word for it." Ash's hand shook as she put her drink down.

"While Victoria's away, I wanted to let you know that I understand." The Queen Mother raised both eyebrows.

"You understand?" Was she getting at what Ash thought she was getting at?

The older woman nodded. "Yes." She paused. "I know. What this is." She looked very pleased with herself.

"What this is?" Ash was not going to fall into a trap.

"I mean, I think I do. Victoria likes to keep things to herself, and I understand that. We all have secrets. But I've been watching her all her life, and I know this secret is getting harder to keep. Dexter was a lovely boy, but quite clearly gay."

Ash choked out a cough. If she'd had any drink in her mouth, it would have landed on the opposite Chesterfield.

"Gay?" she spluttered, like it was the first time she'd heard the word.

She dimly recalled a module on this very topic. How

to deal with reporters who asked inappropriate questions on your sexuality. How to shut the conversation down. Those reporters weren't as hard to deal with as an insistent grandmother, though.

"Yes, gay. I'm sure you've heard of it. Likes a musical. Kisses boys. Or girls, if it's the other way around." She took another glug of her cocktail as if it wasn't blow-your-head-off strong. "Which I'm assuming you and Victoria are. Let's put it this way: I got Edward to make up the spare room for you because Victoria asked, but I know it won't be used. Whereas when Dexter was here it was expected he would share Victoria's room. However, the bed in the spare room was always ruffled and then badly remade in an attempt to cover up the fact they *weren't* sleeping together. That's not the case with you and Victoria, is it?"

Was there a right answer in this situation? If there was, Ash had no idea what it was. She cleared her throat, but no words came out. Instead, she gave the older woman the briefest shake of her head.

"Good." The Queen Mother put a hand on Ash's knee. "I want you to know, I approve. Of Victoria living her life, and of you."

"Thank you." Ash wanted to slap herself in the face for being so monosyllabic, but she simply couldn't muster up any other words.

"But I've read up on this. I understand I can't tell Victoria I know until she tells me. Hence, I'm waiting. This is our little secret, if you'll indulge me."

Ash nodded.

Still no words. But a cascade of relief washed through her

like a tidal wave. Maybe, with the Queen Mother on their side, this might not be such an uphill task.

Maybe.

"However, if you want to suggest I might be open to Victoria telling me, that would help. Just if it comes up, you understand. She's dancing around it. Her mother's dancing around it. And every time we meet, it's like the elephant in the room."

Ash had not expected any of this today. "How long have you known?"

The Queen Mother smiled. "Forever. She's dated a few men, all impeccably behaved. But none as lovely as Dexter. All as queer as a nine-bob note." She paused. "Not that I expect you to know what that is." The matriarch smiled. "I want Victoria to be a happy monarch, to love whoever she wants to. I wasn't allowed to do that. My marriage was arranged, and while we tolerated each other, it was never enough. We both looked outside for comfort. It was the way things worked in the olden days."

And now the Queen Mother was divulging extra-marital affairs? Ash glanced up at the door. Victoria was still not there.

She took another sip of her drink.

It burned all the way down.

She was suddenly glad of it.

"But with Victoria and Michael, I see a new dawn. They don't want to do things the old way. I allowed my daughter to marry outside her class because she begged me. Oliver has proved a good choice. Solid, reliable, and he knows his role is to support. Now I think she needs to do the same for her own daughter. The monarchy will only live on if the people in it are happy to be there. Happiness breeds happiness. For Princess Victoria to become Queen Victoria with a smile on her face, progress and change needs to happen. Just so you know, I'm on your side."

\* \* \*

Ash stood at the window, watching moonlight paint silver across the wilderness. Sleep eluded her, though today had been perfect: the company, the castle, even the wine she'd barely tasted.

When it was just them, hidden away with Victoria's irrepressible grandmother in this corner of Scotland, everything felt possible. Magical, even. But reality waited beyond these ancient walls, and that was their real challenge: not what they felt for each other, but what the world would make of it.

Having Victoria's grandmother in their corner gave Ash hope. It also reminded her of her own pending confession back home. She'd been avoiding her own mother lately, knowing those shrewd eyes would read her heart in seconds. But this weekend had crystallised everything. Victoria wasn't just another chapter in her story; she was the whole book. Soon they'd both need to face their truths, because Ash couldn't deny it anymore. She was falling completely, irrevocably in love.

Two hours later, Ash had proof of just how hard she was falling: only love could explain why she was up at 6:15am, wearing a borrowed swimsuit and heading to a loch for a dawn swim. She'd expected a chauffeur, but Victoria had gleefully taken the wheel herself. "No need on our private estate," she'd explained. Now, as the sun peeked over the horizon, Ash didn't regret allowing Victoria to coax her into this mad adventure.

The heather bloomed across the hills like spilled wine, deep purple against the grey Scottish sky. Ash pressed closer to the window, watching the ancient Scots pines rise dark and proud between patches of silver birch, their leaves just starting to edge into gold. A cluster of rowan trees blazed with red berries, bright as emergency lights against the forest's sombre green. The bracken was turning, too, painting the lower slopes in copper and rust, while the occasional juniper bush huddled dark and dense near the roadside. The whole landscape felt like it was holding its breath, caught between summer's last flash and autumn's slow advance.

Even though Ash was outside for her job every day, it never made her feel like *this*. Like she was a part of something far bigger. Like she could take in lungfuls of air and still never get full. Like she had the space and freedom to truly be who she wanted to be.

It seemed like the magic of Balmoral wasn't just for royalty.

"Play me your favourite Taylor song," Victoria told her, offering her phone. "I've got to warn you, I'll totally judge you."

Ash picked up the phone. "Challenge accepted." She cycled through the most-played, but then went for a lesser-heard album track that always spoke to her. When the intro filled the car, Victoria turned her head and raised an eyebrow, then nodded her approval.

"You pass the test, Ash Woods."

"So do you, Victoria Richmond."

Five minutes later, they were out of the car and stood on the edge of a large loch.

"My advice? Don't think about it. Take my hand, and we'll go in together. It's a shock at first, but you soon get used to it."

Victoria shrugged off her dry robe, and Ash was temporarily distracted by her tempting body that she'd spent another couple of hours exploring last night. Safe to say, the sleep specialists at the Royal Ravens would not be happy with the amount she'd clocked up this weekend. They would, however, be happy about this cold-water immersion.

"I might not wild swim, but I have to do hydrotherapy as part of my job. Which includes ice baths. I'm not a complete novice." Ash shrugged off her outer layer.

Victoria squeezed her hand. "Perfect!" she said, with the calm assurance of someone who rarely heard the word 'no'. "Ready?"

With that, she yanked Ash's hand and they broke the water. Ash gasped as the cold water climbed her thighs, but Victoria's steady presence anchored her. They counted down from three, then plunged shoulder-deep in unison. The shock punched the air from Ash's lungs, Scotland's ancient waters wrapping around her like a living thing. On the opposite side of the loch, a red deer paused at the water's edge, and for a moment, everything was wild and possible.

Suddenly, Ash got it. If Victoria could do this, she could do anything. Perhaps this was why she did it so often, to challenge herself. Taking the plunge was all about taking the first step. Being a professional footballer, she knew that more than most.

Victoria grinned at Ash, then leaned back, resting her head in the water, floating.

Ash did the same, reaching out for her hand. Her teeth chattered, but as she took deep lungfuls of air, her temperature levelled out.

They stayed like that for a few long moments, watching the day break through the scattered clouds.

"I sometimes wish I could stay here forever."

"I understand that now I'm here." Ash squeezed Victoria's fingers with her own. A few minutes later, they swam further into the loch, then stopped to admire the scenery.

"Drink this in. Nobody around. It won't be like this for a long while now." Victoria's jaw twitched as she spoke.

"Especially now I'm back in training. First proper league game in two weeks. And you're off to Wales to open factories, pat babies, and help to save the planet?"

"Something like that. One royal visit at a time," Victoria said. "That's why having this time was so important. You mean a lot to me, Ash." She licked her lips. "I can't wait to watch you play more often again. This time as your…" Victoria trailed off, then glanced at Ash. "Can I say girlfriend?"

The water around them rippled as Ash moved towards Victoria and took her in her arms, flushing their bodies together as one. "It would be my honour to be your girlfriend, Ma'am."

Victoria's eyes flickered with delight. She kissed Ash again, and the world swam around them.

When they pulled apart, Victoria stared at Ash like she hung the moon.

"There's no need to look at me like that," Ash said, heat rising to her cheeks. "My hair is plastered to my head, and it's still the middle of the night. I'm sure I look like a frozen sausage."

Victoria snorted. "That's exactly what I was thinking. Spot on." She rolled her eyes. "I have a question for my frozen sausage." She paused. "When you score a goal, do you have a celebration?"

Ash shook her head. "Not really." She had plenty of teammates who did, but Ash just went for the standard air punch.

Victoria licked her lips. "If you score at the weekend, will you do a special celebration to camera just for me?"

Her face was so full of joy, Ash couldn't refuse. "I'll do anything for you." She meant it, too. Even in these icy temperatures. "But I should warn you, I don't score that much. Although my creative coach and I identified it as something I should focus on this season."

Victoria's arms snaked around her neck and pulled her close. "I think you should listen to your coach, focus, and score. I have faith in you. Just remember how much you scored this weekend," she added. "I know you can do it again."

# Chapter Twenty-Two

The Palace breakfast room was bathed in September sunlight, streaming through the tall windows and catching the silver tea service that had been in the family for generations. Victoria had fond memories of eating here as a child, where it was always a treat to be with her grandparents. All the glamour, none of the responsibility. When she was small, the table was always laden with home-made cupcakes and scones with jam and cream, which she'd always loved. Now, the table often bowed with the weight of duty and things left unsaid.

However, this particular Saturday brunch, the Richmonds were in a pretty good mood. Her mother had already been for a swim, and her father had done his morning 5k around the Palace grounds. "A Park Run just for me," as he always joked.

In contrast, her brother's exercise this morning seemed to be chewing. Michael demolished his third pain au chocolat with the single-minded focus of someone who treated all meals as competitive sport. Also, someone who was mighty hungover. Victoria already knew she wasn't going to get much support from him today. Their "us against the world" support declaration only worked when Michael's brain was fully functioning. Crumbs scattered across his plate as he reached for a fourth pastry. At his feet, the family Corgis, Honey and Truffle, waited patiently for anything he dropped.

"Really, Michael?" their mother sighed, but there was fondness in her tone. "It's like you didn't just eat a whole Eggs Benedict." Not for him a comment on his weight, or if another pastry "was strictly necessary?". Because, as Michael always told her, what he did held no consequence.

Victoria picked at her avocado toast with boiled eggs, stomach too knotted with anticipation to eat much. She'd been awake since dawn, chatting with Ash, who was pissed off with her roommate Sasha, who'd spent all night coughing, hence her sleep had been broken. Ash was worried it might affect her performance in the season opener at Manchester City.

Victoria had sent her a reassuring message earlier.

> I'm sure you're going to be great. It'll be nice to see your toned thighs again, even if it's just on TV. Not close enough to lick.

Ash's response was in the forefront of her mind.

> My thighs are ready when you are, Ma'am. Make sure you're watching today. When I score, I've got a special celebration planned, just for you.

They'd managed to fit in a couple of nights together since Balmoral, where Ash's thighs had been thoroughly taken care of, along with every other part of her body. It had been a slice of heaven. Plus, Victoria had perfected her home-made ravioli with spinach, cream cheese, burnt butter and sage, and Ash had begged for more.

"So," her father said, buttering his toast with those precise, measured movements that characterised everything he did. "The foundation launch. The focus on youth homelessness is excellent. Very worthy issue that needs bringing to the fore."

Victoria straightened, grateful for the distraction. "Glad you think so. I want to specifically include queer youth programs because they make up a disproportionate percentage of homeless young people, and the current support systems aren't enough."

Her father nodded slowly, and Victoria caught something in his expression. Understanding, perhaps? Or resignation? "That seems very you," he replied.

Her mother shifted in her seat, the delicate china teacup clinking against its saucer. "Just ensure the messaging is balanced. We don't want to appear too political."

"Everyone should be allowed basic human rights, Mother. This has got nothing to do with politics." But Victoria wasn't getting into this now. She checked her watch for the umpteenth time since she sat down. Fifteen minutes to Ash's game. Her heart rate picked up. "Would anyone mind if we took our coffee through to the lounge? The women's season opener is on, and as the new Women's FA Patron, I should watch it."

"Of course, darling," her father said. She could rely on him. They'd always been close.

Michael paused mid-bite, eyes wide. "Are the Royal Ravens playing, by any chance?"

If she could reach, she'd have kicked him under the table. As it was, the best she could do was give him a small death stare.

"They are. Playing City away, so it's a big game. Last year's WSL winners versus last year's runner-up. New season. All to play for."

"Maybe you could apply for a job as a pundit if the FA Patron doesn't work out." Michael tilted his head. "Sounds like you've been doing your homework."

She honestly hated having a brother sometimes.

They finished up their food – Michael grabbing another croissant as he left – and the royal butler, Desmond, loaded their coffees onto a silver tray and followed them through to the lounge.

When people thought about how royals lived, this was probably the picture they had in their head: ancestral portraits, heavy velvet curtains, and carefully upholstered Victorian furniture, which was surprisingly comfortable. However, they probably didn't picture the 65-inch TV with surround sound her parents had installed. Or the bright pops of colour in the cushions her mother had ordered.

The Queen smiled to herself as she plumped one up before she sat.

Victoria positioned herself carefully, ensuring she had a clear view of the television while appearing casual about it.

"How was your official visit to Wales?" her mother asked, as Victoria's eyes tracked Ash coming out of the tunnel. Even in the wide shot, she could pick her out instantly. Something about the way she moved, that confident grace that had first caught Victoria's attention months ago. When the camera zoomed in, she felt the blood rush to her cheeks.

She had to remember her parents didn't know anything.

She definitely wasn't looking at Michael.

"Very forward-thinking." She leaned forward and made a fuss of Truffle. "The renewable energy project was super interesting. The locals were particularly engaged with the environmental impact assessments on the community. I think it's going to be a real coup for the area." She smiled at her mother, hoping she'd said enough to appease her. Her mother loved Wales, and was always keen to get progress reports from whoever visited.

On the TV, Ash tucked in her shirt and did a couple of warm-up jumps. She looked hungry, ready. Victoria knew that look very well.

The game kicked off, and the conversation drifted on. Victoria contributed enough to appear present, but her attention was increasingly drawn to the match. Ash was playing well, commanding the midfield. She smiled as she recalled Ash at Balmoral demonstrating her keepy-uppy prowess. Incredible that someone so coordinated with their feet was so terrible at shooting.

"Victoria? I asked about the hospital opening next week? Is it still going ahead as planned?"

But Victoria didn't hear her mother's question. Ash had broken free of her marker and ran clean down the middle.

Victoria sat up straight, body rigid.

Desmond took that moment to appear in front of her, holding the silver coffee pot. "Would you like some more, Ma'am?"

That word didn't have any effect when it came out of Desmond's mouth.

Victoria peered around him. "No thank you, Desmond." She tried and failed to keep the annoyance out of the tone.

When she caught sight of the screen again, Ash only had the keeper to beat. She swept it into the bottom corner with casual ease, and Victoria punched the air before she could stop herself.

"Yes!" she yelped, sloshing her coffee over the rim of her mug and onto the carpet. She didn't care.

At her feet, Honey and Truffle started to bark.

"Victoria!" her mother admonished.

Desmond scuttled off, muttering about getting a damp cloth.

But Victoria ignored them all, keeping her eyes glued to the screen. When Ash reeled away from goal, she ran right up to the camera, held up her palm, and blew a kiss right down the lens.

Victoria hadn't been expecting something so intimate. Perhaps she should have. "It's just for you," Ash had told her.

Her knees gave way and she sank back onto the sofa.

The celebration was perfect. After, Ash winked, then turned to celebrate with her team. Victoria's own heart pounded so hard, she could barely hear the commentators.

"You seem quite involved in this match," her mother observed, with that careful tone that always preceded difficult conversations. "More than usual."

Victoria pursed her lips, not sure how to answer. She went with duty. Her mother couldn't be annoyed at that. "Maybe I am. It's part of my role now, supporting women's sport. Plus, shouldn't the royal family support the Royal Ravens?"

"She's got a point, there, Cassandra," her father piped up, glancing up from his phone. They were strictly forbidden at the table, but once they hit the sofas, all bets were off.

Beside him, Michael stared at Victoria. Unease danced across his face.

The Queen frowned at her husband, then smoothed her skirt, before turning to Victoria. "I must say, I'm pleasantly surprised with the number of ponytails out there. I always thought football attracted a more…" She paused to choose her word carefully.

Victoria winced, waiting.

"Butch type. At least, it did in my day. But that seems to be changing. Which is good."

Victoria's hands clenched around her coffee cup, knuckles white. Her mother's casual prejudice made her stomach turn. But she had to pick her battles, she knew that. "I wish I could have played properly," she said, her voice tight.

"It's hardly appropriate for the future queen. It's a working-class sport."

"Don't be so ridiculous, Mother," Victoria snapped, years of frustration suddenly bubbling to the surface. "That's such an old-fashioned view. Like a lot of your views, actually."

The temperature in the room dropped. Michael sat up, his eyes darting between his sister and mother like he was watching a tennis match. Their father became very still, in that way he did when conflict was brewing.

"What's that supposed to mean?" her mother asked.

Victoria took a deep breath, her heart racing, all her hopes and fears rising up in her throat. She tried to swallow them down, but they appeared stuck, only one way out.

This wasn't how she'd planned this conversation, but watching Ash's celebration, then her mother's casual dismissal of women's football, something inside her snapped.

"It means that the royal family is stuck in the dark ages when it comes to a lot of things. Football might have been no-go when you were growing up, but the women's game is a different beast altogether. Very inclusive, safe, fan-focused. The players aren't spoilt brats, and a lot have degrees. It's more like the US model of sport." She paused, hands trembling slightly. "But it's not just football where this family needs to be brought forward. It also needs to take a giant leap when it comes to who we can and cannot be in a relationship with."

The Queen frowned, her face taking on that mask-like quality Victoria had seen so many times before. "We already had this discussion, Victoria. I told you then that when and if you meet someone who matters, come back to us and we can discuss it. But until that time—"

"I've met someone who matters."

The words hung in the air like crystal, delicate and sharp. On the television, they were showing replays of Ash's goal celebration. Victoria kept her eyes fixed on her mother's face, refusing to back down. Everything she'd been holding back – every careful deflection, every hidden text message, every furtive glance – all merged into this moment.

The portrait of Victoria's grandfather, King Henry, glowered down at them, a reminder of everything she was challenging.

Right at that moment, Desmond reappeared with a damp cloth.

The Queen stood, her face tight. "Not now, Desmond. That will be all."

He stopped, glancing down. "But the carpet, Your Majesty—"

"I said not now." The Queen's tone was a thunderclap.

He bowed, then left the room.

Her father leaned over and put the TV on mute.

The Queen's face was unreadable, but her hand shook as she set down her cup. "You've met someone since we spoke? Isn't that a little fast to be making declarations?"

Victoria shook her head. Her heart slammed against her chest. "It's not just since we spoke. We've been seeing each other for a little while. It's been going on for a few months. Which is why I can't hide it anymore."

She glanced up at the screen, where Ash was down on the grass, a grimace on her face. Victoria walked over, picked up the remote, and put the sound back on.

Behind her, the Queen cleared her throat. "Victoria. We're in the middle of what you told me was an important conversation. Yet here you are, dismissing it to watch the football?"

Victoria swivelled back to face them, and took a deep breath. It was now or never.

Besides, she'd never be ready for this.

"It's not unconnected." She pointed at the screen, where Ash was feeling her ankle, and being helped up. "It's her."

Her mother frowned. "What's her?"

"The one who matters."

From the opposite sofa, Michael gasped.

She didn't look at him.

"You're dating Ashleigh Woods?" her father asked, his voice soft.

"You know her?" Victoria was genuinely surprised.

"Of course I know her. Everybody knows her. We met when

the whole team came to the Palace after the Euros win. I've chatted to her on a couple of other occasions, too."

She'd forgotten that. Victoria pulled her shoulders back and stood up straight. Confident. Defiant.

Astrid would be proud.

"Yes, I'm dating Ashleigh Woods. I'm telling you now because she makes me happy, and this feels different. Like it could go somewhere. She sees me as Victoria first, and a princess second."

"Which would be lovely if that was how everyone else saw you, too." Her mother sat on the sofa, head high, face set.

"I don't care about what everyone else thinks, Mother. I care about Ash and me." She waved her arms. "I'm bored of waiting for my real life to begin. I want it to start now." She was also terrified of that happening, too. But she had to be positive to counteract her mother's negative. She wouldn't be cowed. She couldn't be any more. "You said we could talk when it happened."

"And we can. We are." Her mother couldn't hide her exasperated tone. "But royal protocol and crown duty doesn't change overnight. This is a huge step for the world to accept."

"But the world is ready, Mother," Michael said. "Loads of countries have queer leaders. You never thought marriage equality would happen in your lifetime, but here we are."

Victoria smiled at him. He might exasperate her, but there were also times she was happy he existed.

"Sit down, Victoria." It was an instruction from her father. "You're wearing a hole in the carpet."

She did as she was told, not yet brave enough to look her mother in the eye.

"What your mother is saying is, we understand, but we worry," her father continued. "The scrutiny is brutal. Remember when Uncle Tristan thought about coming out? He tested the water, but decided he couldn't."

"I'm not marrying a man and having women on the side." She'd done a version of that for years. All it had done was make her skin blotchy, her mental health fragile. Hell, even her hair had started to fall out. "I've seen how Bertie suffers." Tristan and Bertie had been together for nearly two decades, but to the outside world, Tristan was married to Sienna and had three children. "I want to be true to myself. I want to take Ash to the New Year Ball."

Now her mother did put her head in her hands.

"The scrutiny is not just from the press, but from within the family, the government, the Church," her father continued. "We're on your side, but are you ready for that level of attention? For that fight?"

Victoria looked up at the screen, and the camera focused on the goal scorer. Ash pumped her fist, oblivious to what was happening 200 miles south.

Watching her, a sudden realisation hit Victoria like a physical blow: she was falling for this woman. Scratch that. She *loved* this woman. She jolted with comprehension.

Was she prepared for the fight?

You damn well bet she was.

"I can't keep running," she told her father. "I have to stop at some point. Why not now? It's as good a time as any. Ash is the best reason I can think of."

"But is she really the sort of person you see yourself settling down with?" Her mother lifted her head, her skin pale.

"She doesn't understand our way of life. She's not from our world, Victoria."

The tired get-out clause was too easy to reach for. "You don't even know her. Why not give her a chance before judging her? She understands fame, and the pressure of public life, which is more than any of my other suitors did. We have that in common. Plus, she understands hard work and sacrifice. You don't get to where she is in life without all of that."

Her father sat forward. "There is that, Cassandra. Plus, I met Ashleigh last year in a more informal setting after an England game. She was great company. We chatted about football, about her business degree. She's got her head screwed on the right way." He paused, eyeing his wife. "And remember: your mother thought I was riff-raff. Probably still does a little, but we've mucked along all right, haven't we?"

Victoria risked a slight smile. She welcomed the spotlight being turned down a touch. She shot her father a grateful smile, and he shot one right back.

"Okay." Just one word from her mother, which was unusual.

"Okay?"

The Queen nodded. "Let's meet her. Bring her here for afternoon tea."

"To the Palace?" Victoria's face crumpled. Ash had been nervous about Balmoral. She could just imagine what she'd think of this plan.

"You said she understands your life. Who you are. If you see a future with her, Buckingham Palace is going to feature, isn't it?" Her mother's eyebrow raised on the final two words.

Victoria hated when her mother was right.

"Fine. I'll bring her to tea. Then I'll take her to the summerhouse and beat her at pool."

Michael snorted. "She's the England captain. Doesn't it follow she'll be brilliant at pool, too?"

But Victoria simply stuck out her tongue at her brother. Then she stood, with a smile.

For the first time in her life, she felt completely certain of who she was and what she wanted.

# Chapter Twenty-Three

Steam curled around them in the vast bathroom, Victoria's back pressed against Ash's chest in the claw-footed tub, water lapping at their skin. Despite their urgent reunion a few hours ago – all desperate hands and hungry mouths after a week apart – being in the bath felt somehow more intimate. Ash winced slightly as Victoria's shoulder found the spot where a Bayern defender had left her mark in this week's Champions League game. Ninety minutes of European football written in purple across her ribs. However, Victoria's lips had traced each forming bruise with such tenderness earlier, Ash had almost forgotten the pain.

"I told them about us," Victoria whispered.

Ash's finger froze mid-pattern on Victoria's shoulder.

There it was. The thing Victoria had been dancing around in her messages all week. She'd told Ash she had something to tell her, but wanted to wait until she saw her in person.

Ash flinched. "You did?"

Victoria's hand found hers under the water, gripping tight. "On Saturday. Just after you scored that goal against City. We were all watching it after brunch."

She'd told Ash that part, which Ash still couldn't get her head around. Of all the people she imagined watching her play football, the Queen and King had never figured in that equation.

"I couldn't keep lying to them, Ash. It wasn't fair to any of us."

Ash tried to remember how to breathe properly, which made her bruised ribs throb. *The Queen knew*. The actual Queen of Britain knew that Ashleigh Woods, daughter of a nurse and a civil servant, had slept with her daughter. Was in a relationship with her.

*Well, fuck.*

"What did they say?" Her voice was spaghetti-thin.

"They were surprised. But not angry. They want to meet you."

"Meet me?" Ash had known it would happen, of course, but this seemed a little soon.

Victoria stayed very still, just moving Ash's fingers to her lips to kiss them. It wasn't lost on Ash that she wasn't looking at her as they had this chat. Perhaps that made it easier.

"Properly. As my girlfriend."

Ash stared at the ornate brass tap and shower attachment at the other end of the bath. Her mind raced. She'd met the King before, of course: quick handshakes at official functions, polite small talk at post-match receptions. But this would be different. They'd be looking at her as the person their daughter had chosen. Measuring her worth. Finding her wanting.

"I'm not... I mean, I'm just..." The words stuck in her throat. Just a footballer. Just a working-class girl from St Albans.

At least she was sure which fork to use first.

Victoria twisted her body, and water sloshed over the

side of the tub. She knelt before Ash, breasts enticing as her hands cupped Ash's face, forcing Ash to meet her eyes. "You're everything. It's going to be okay." She kissed her lips, which calmed Ash momentarily.

She nodded, staring into Victoria's rich blue eyes. However, no matter how much she wanted to be worthy, she couldn't quite bring herself to believe it. "I know you think that. And when we're together, I do, too. But what if they don't think I'm good enough?" The fear that had been lurking since their first kiss finally voiced itself. "What if they're right?"

"Hey." Victoria's thumb brushed Ash's cheekbone. "You're one of the kindest, most genuine people I know. And if social media is to be believed, every queer woman in the country wants to sleep with you." She grinned. "And I'm the lucky one who actually gets to do it."

Ash gave a small smile. "You should definitely lead with that."

Victoria kissed her lips once more. The effect never failed. "They're going to love you." She went to say something else, then stopped.

"When?" Ash needed a timeline to her execution.

"Tuesday week. October 13th. You told me you had two days off after the Arsenal game?"

Ash nodded.

"They suggested afternoon tea at the Palace."

Ash let out a shaky laugh. "At Buckingham Palace?" Her mind shook, then collapsed. "Right. No pressure. Just a casual afternoon with the Queen and King at an actual palace."

Victoria licked her lips. "Pressure is a privilege. It means if things work out, you can effect change."

"And if things don't work out?"

"You try again."

Ash took a deep breath. "Okay. Let's try to effect change." She paused. "I'll come, on one condition."

Victoria tilted her head. "What's that?"

"If I'm meeting your parents, you'll have to meet mine, too. How do you fancy a Sunday roast in St Albans? I should warn you, they live on Victoria Street. Probably named after your ancestor. Mum'll make her famous Yorkshire puddings, Dad'll tell all his terrible jokes, and then they'll drag out every embarrassing photo from when I was younger. What do you say?"

Victoria's eyes widened slightly, and Ash saw a flicker of nerves cross her face. "Of course. Fair's fair. I'd love to get to know your family."

"They're not the Queen and King, but..." Ash trailed off, suddenly uncertain.

"They're just my parents," Victoria told her. "Just as your mum and dad are yours. They're important because you love them." She gave a jagged smile. "Do you think they'll like me?"

The role reversal wasn't lost on Ash, who couldn't help but laugh. "My mum already loves you. She's got every magazine article about you cut out and saved. Dad pretends he doesn't care about the royals, but he watches the Trooping of the Colour and the Queen's speech every year." She paused, her heart beating loud in her chest. The words she'd been holding back for weeks rose up, impossible to contain any longer. "But most of all, they'll love you because..." Ash took a deep breath.

"Because?" Victoria asked, holding her gaze.

Ash licked her lips. "Because I do," she said.

The moment the words left her mouth, the bathroom went absolutely still. Victoria's breath stilled, and Ash's own pulse roared in her ears. She'd thought it a thousand times, whispered it in her head as Victoria slept, but she'd never said it out loud before. Now it hung in the steam between them, real and raw and terrifying.

Victoria's eyes were huge, searching Ash's face. "You love me?"

Ash's throat went tight, a weird mix of fear and release flooding through her. No taking it back now. "Yeah. Yeah, I do." The words came out rough, honest in a way she couldn't control. "Have done ever since I heard your glorious laugh and held your gaze when you pinned a medal on me." Her hands shook, but she didn't try to hide it. Not anymore.

Victoria's reply was a kiss, fierce and tender all at once. When they broke apart, her eyes were glassy. "I love you, too. Which makes this doubly complicated, right?"

Relief flooded Ash. "You could say that." She took Victoria in her arms.

For a long moment they just held each other, the cooling water lapping around them, until Victoria laughed softly against Ash's neck. "You think we should tell our parents we're in love?"

"Mine have got to get over the fact I've seen the future queen naked, first."

Victoria kissed her again. When she pulled back, her smile didn't quite reach her eyes, and Ash caught that shadow in her glint again: that hint of something unspoken. For now though, she pulled her closer, careful of her own ribs, and let the water and Victoria's touch wash away her fears. They had two families to face, but at least they'd face them together. Plus, now she knew – *really knew* – that what they had was worth fighting for.

Victoria pressed herself back against Ash, kissing Ash's hands, before placing them on her own stomach. "Your mum's Yorkshire puddings," Victoria added. "Are they worth the trip alone?"

"Damn right they are," Ash replied.

The water cooled around them, but neither made a move to leave. Ash just hoped their love was enough to survive these first family meetings.

And then, everything that came after that.

\* \* \*

The familiar squeak of the side gate announced Ash's arrival before she appeared in the warm kitchen-diner at the back of the house. Nothing had changed since she was a kid: the same worn oak table dominated the space, its surface marked with 30 years of family meals and homework sessions. The Welsh dresser still displayed her mum's collection of chinoiserie porcelain, alongside a smattering of Ash's medals and trophies from her childhood.

October sunlight filtered through the home-made gingham curtains, casting long afternoon shadows across the slate-grey tiles. Outside, the cherry tree that had been there since before Ash was born was starting to flower, its pink blossoms cheering up the garden and everything around it.

"Look who's decided to grace us with her presence!"

Debra Woods wiped her hands on her apron as Ash walked in, still in her training gear, tracking bits of Hertfordshire mud onto the floor. The radio hummed softly from its perch by the sink, some Radio 2 afternoon show her mum always had on while she pottered. "I was starting to think you'd forgotten where we lived."

"I know, I'm sorry." Ash dropped her bag by the patio doors out to the garden, and accepted the crushing hug, breathing in the familiar scent of baking and lavender washing powder. "I've just been really busy, you know how it is once the season starts." She trailed off, her heart already racing at what she needed to say. "What are you baking?"

"Rhubarb and custard cake. First time. We'll see how it turns out." Her mum wiped down the counter before she continued, rinsing the cloth in the sink. "Saw your goal against City. Proper striker's finish, that. You must have been working hard in training." Debra pulled a couple of mugs from the cupboard above the AGA, the one that still stuck slightly in autumn dampness. "How's your fitness coming along? You looked sharp against City and against Bayern, although she still took you off after 60 minutes, didn't she?"

Ash nodded. "The knee's feeling virtually back to normal, now it's a matter of trust and confidence. But I'm getting stronger every day and starting every game, so hopefully, I'll be back to where I was soon. Everyone tells me I just need patience—"

"Not your strong suit." Her mum added milk to their teas.

"No," Ash smiled. "But I'm trying to trust the process."

Ash took her steaming mug of tea, warming her hands

around it as she leaned against the counter where she'd once needed a stool to reach the biscuit tin. Through the window, she could see their neighbour, Julie, hanging out her washing on her rotary line.

"Can we sit down for a minute?" Her mum definitely needed to be sat for this news.

Debra's eyes narrowed. "What have you done?"

"Nothing." But Ash wasn't sure that was strictly true. "I just want to talk to you."

"Which makes me nervous." But her mum took off her apron, pulled out a chair, and sat. "The cake's in the oven. I've got tea. I'm all ears."

Ash sat opposite and stared into her tea, then at her mum.

"You know how I haven't been around much lately?"

"I think we've already established that, yes. I put years into raising you, then you never come home. Noted."

"The reason is that I'm seeing someone."

Her mum sat up straight. "Finally!" She frowned. "That's good news, yes?" She waved her hand. "I'm not sure from your face." She paused. "Tell me you're not back together with Danielle, because I don't think I could go through that again."

Ash spluttered. "No, I'm not. But I am dating someone who you might not expect."

"Someone from Arsenal?"

"Not a footballer."

Her mum's shoulders relaxed a little. "That's good news. I kept telling you to fish in a different pond."

She'd certainly done that.

Ash took a deep breath, her fingers tracing the chip on her mug's handle. "The thing is, I'm seeing Victoria."

Her mum frowned. "Victoria who?"

"Victoria Richmond. Princess Victoria."

The silence that followed was deafening, broken only by the gentle tick of the kitchen clock above the door, and the distant toll of the cathedral bells marking four o'clock. Her mum's mouth opened and closed several times before she spoke. "The Princess Royal? Who's just broken up with Dexter Matthews? Don't be so silly. Plus, she's not gay." Confusion clouded her face. "Is she?"

"It would seem she might be a little bit."

"But she's only ever dated men…" Her mum shook her head. "You're not joking, are you?"

Ash shook her head, finally bringing her gaze to meet her mother's. "I'm not."

Debra blew out a long breath. "I can't quite wrap my head around what you're saying." She paused. "How long?"

She had no idea when they became official. "Maybe three months?"

"Three months!" Debra's voice rose an octave, making the cat sleeping in its basket by the radiator look up in alarm. "You've been dating the future Queen for three months and you're just telling me now?" If her mum had a top, it had just officially blown.

"We had to be careful. Nobody knows except her parents, and she only told them this week." She bit her lip. "Which is part of the reason I'm telling you. We really like each other. We think this might go somewhere. She wants me to meet her parents, and I'd like you to meet her, too." Ash paused, not missing the alarm that swept across her mum's face. "I've told her she'd be welcome for Sunday lunch this weekend.

Our game is tomorrow night, so it works out. Would that be okay?"

Debra gripped the edge of the table. "Is that enough time to repaint the house, buy a whole new crockery set and hire a Michelin-starred chef to cook for her?"

Ash smiled and reached across to cover her mum's hand. "She's really quite normal. I told her you cook a mean Yorkshire, and she's looking forward to that."

"She's royalty, Ash! I can't even begin to think about her being normal."

Right at that moment, her dad appeared at the patio doors, and walked in, his pink tie loosened over his grey suit. He worked for the local council, and, being an early riser, had negotiated his hours so he could start early and finish early, too. When he saw Ash, his face lit up. "Well, this is a lovely surprise!" He walked over and gave Ash a hug, then kissed his wife on the top of her head. When neither of them responded, he looked between them, noting the tension. "Who's died? What have I missed?"

"Sit down," Debra said faintly. "Ash has something to tell you."

Her dad sat at the head of the table between them, then turned to Ash, his face eager. "This sounds serious. I'm pretty sure you're not pregnant. Plus, you're already England captain, so I've no idea how you're going to top that."

This time, Ash ripped the plaster off in one go. "Dad, I'm in a relationship with Princess Victoria."

There was silence, quickly followed by her dad's big belly-laugh. He slapped his thigh. "Good one. What's really going on?"

"It's not a joke, Dad. We've been together a few months. She wants to meet you both."

The laugh died in his throat as he realised his daughter was serious. He looked at Debra, who nodded weakly.

"She's coming to meet us," Debra added, sounding slightly hysterical. "The Princess Royal is coming for Sunday lunch. In our house. On Victoria Street." She paused. "Oh god, will she think we're being funny, living on Victoria Street?"

"I think it makes it extra-special."

Her dad ran a hand over his goatee beard. "Bloody hell, Ash."

"I know it's a lot," Ash said quickly. "But she's just... she's just Victoria to me. She's funny and kind, and she makes me happy. Really happy."

Something in her voice made both her parents look at her sharply. Debra reached across the table and took her hand.

"Oh my god, you've fallen for her, haven't you?" It wasn't really a question.

Ash fought to keep her emotions in check, swallowing hard. "I don't know, Mum." But she did. "Maybe I have, but it's kinda scary. What happens when everyone else finds out?"

But Debra inhaled, patted Ash's hand, and stood up. "Then you deal with it like you do with everything. With honesty, grace and dignity."

"Your mum's right." Her dad jumped up. "Although it doesn't mean your mother won't be practising how to cook a roast in the run-up." He gave his wife a grin. "She's going to love your Yorkshires. She'll go home telling the Queen about them."

"Oh, shit." Her mum clutched the top of her chair. "The

good china. We'll need the good china down from the loft."
She clicked her fingers. "And the tablecloth your gran left us."
She stopped suddenly. "What if she wants to see the cathedral?
Does she want a tour of the city? How will she get here? She's
coming in the front door, not the back like normal. Will they
have to close the street, because if they do, we might have to
tell the neighbours…"

"Mum," Ash interrupted. "She just wants to meet you.
Both of you. As you are."

"As we are?" Her mum paled. "I'm not having the future
Queen eat off our normal plates. They're from Primark!"

That was when her dad put his arm around his wife, and
started to laugh. "Only our Ash could date anyone in the world,
and she picks a bloody princess."

"Language!" Debra swatted him. "You can't swear in front
of royalty!"

"She swears, Mum. She's going out with me."

Outside, the distant cathedral bells chimed quarter past.
Debra was already up, opening cupboards. "The silver needs
polishing. Or we need to buy some. Do we need to get those
little flags? What's it called?"

"No bunting!" Ash said. "It's just my girlfriend coming
for Sunday lunch." She was going to have to monitor what
they were doing, in case she turned up and the house was one
giant Union Jack.

"Do we have to bow?" her dad asked.

"One thing's for certain," her mum added. "We're going
shopping tomorrow. You need a new outfit, and I need…
*everything*. Everything needs to be perfect. The market will
still have some nice autumn flowers…"

"At least finish your tea first?" Ash dropped her head onto the table with a groan.

Her dad patted her shoulder. "Better get used to it, love. Your mum's going to be impossible all week."

"And you need a haircut before Sunday!" she told him.

Ash couldn't help smiling, despite everything. Through the window, the October dusk settled over the cathedral city, and the streetlights flickered on along Victoria Street. Her parents might be panicking, but they hadn't questioned it, hadn't judged.

They just wanted everything to be perfect for the woman she loved.

# Chapter Twenty-Four

Victoria adjusted her Chanel blazer one final time before stepping out of the Range Rover onto Victoria Street. Her bodyguards were in position, but on a street like this, they stuck out like sore thumbs.

Through net curtains, faces appeared and disappeared like nervous fish. Victoria had persuaded Tanya to take the day off, and she was going in with just Ash by her side. Nobody else. She wanted this to be as normal as possible. Even though she was scared witless.

If she and Ash were going to work, *this* had to work, too. She'd dated enough people to know that. The support of family was priceless.

"They're going to love you." Ash put a hand on her arm.

"Easy for you to say." Victoria adjusted her wide-brimmed hat, worn to stop too much recognition. Although now she was wondering how many guests turned up on a suburban street in a wide-brimmed hat.

"Just remember, they're very nervous, so ignore everything that comes out of their mouths." Ash had been warning her of this the whole way over.

"Got it. Let's get in before people cotton on and get their smartphones out."

The door opened before Ash even knocked. On the other

side stood a woman with a manic smile and the same eyes as Ash. She was wearing a new dress, too. Victoria could spot fresh-off-the-rail at 50 paces. She was also practically vibrating with nervous energy.

"Mrs Woods," Victoria began, offering a hand.

"Call me Debra, Your Highness," she replied, ushering her in while also doing a series of curtsies. Behind her, Victoria could almost hear Ash cringing.

"And please, call me Victoria."

The house smelled of roast beef and Sunday best. Victoria took in the family photos on the walls as she was ushered through to the kitchen-diner: Ash in football kits through the years, school photos, family holidays at British beaches. A normal family's normal memories, displayed without calculation or consideration of historical significance.

"We got the good china out." Debra gestured to the table. "My mother's Royal Albert. Seemed appropriate." She laughed. A high, anxious sound.

Victoria spotted Ash's wince, and hoped her mum relaxed soon. For Ash's sake, as well as everyone else.

This was exactly what Victoria had fretted about: the way her title walked into rooms before she did, reshaping everything and everyone around it.

"The table looks wonderful." Victoria removed her hat and Ash took it from her, along with her jacket. From behind the kitchen counter, Ash's dad strode around and offered his hand. He was wearing a suit, which Victoria was pretty sure wasn't his normal lunchtime attire.

"Great to meet you, Victoria." He frowned. "I shouldn't call you Princess?"

"Victoria is fine."

"Right you are. I'm Mark."

She shook his hand, grateful for a little honesty and normality. "Lovely to meet you, Mark."

"Drink?"

She nodded. "Whatever you're having would be great. Beer, wine, tea, water. I'm not fussy."

Mark's eyes widened. "Okay. But I still won't give you a Guinness. Seems wrong. Glass of chardonnay for you, sparkling water for my daughter."

Ash appeared back at her side, and relief flowed through Victoria. She needed an anchor in such unfamiliar circumstances.

Half an hour later, dinner was served, and Victoria was as relaxed as she was likely to get.

"You're a fan of women's football, Victoria?" Mark asked.

She nodded, cutting her beef. Still pink. She was impressed. "I am. A fairly new convert of the past few years, I must admit. But now especially, I have a vested interest." She glanced at Ash, who blushed delightfully.

"Do you get to many games?"

"When I can. I have a lot of commitments, but my aim is to get to see Ash play for the Ravens before Christmas."

"We're so proud of her," Debra added. "England captain by the age of 26. We didn't think she could top that, but then she told us she was dating you. We thought she was joking, didn't we, Mark?"

Ash's dad nodded, his smile tight.

"We just clicked from the start, didn't we?" Victoria told

223

them, squeezing Ash's hand under the table. Then she cut into her Yorkshire, and got what the fuss was about. They were melt-in-your-mouth good.

"Debra, I have to say, these Yorkshires are amazing. I can see why they're the talk of the town."

For the first time since Victoria walked in, Ash's mum was speechless.

The real questions started halfway through the main course. The ones Debra had clearly been dying to ask, after all the polite chit-chat.

"What are your plans for Christmas, Victoria? Your whole family usually spend it at Balmoral, is that right? Will you be doing that this year? We always watch the walk to church on TV." Her gaze bounced between Ash and their guest.

Victoria maintained her diplomatic smile, the one she'd perfected at age seven. "We used to go every year, but now Gran tends to come to London." She paused. "Balmoral at Christmas is so beautiful. I took Ash there last month. We had a lovely time, didn't we?"

As soon as the words left her mouth, she knew it was a mistake.

Debra's face paled, and she glowered at her daughter.

"You went to Balmoral?" Her hurt at not knowing was palpable.

"A last-minute weekend thing." Ash's smile was like glass about to crack. "You know I couldn't tell you anything. I have explained that. Similarly, you can't tell your friends about this lunch, either."

Her dad stepped in. "We know that, don't we?" He smiled at his wife. "This is our little secret. For now." He paused.

"Do you go skiing in the winter, too?" Mark continued. "I remember all those royal photos on the slopes from when you were younger. You and your brother, with your parents."

Victoria nodded. "Yes, in Klosters. I suspect we'll go again soon. It's family tradition, too."

"Mark and I went skiing once, didn't we?" Debra said. "Nowhere fancy, though. Just to France."

Ash's dad chewed his food, then nodded.

"Speaking of tradition," Debra continued, topping up Victoria's wine without asking, "what about children? I mean, not to be presumptuous, but I know Ash wants them, and with the succession and everything…"

Wow. She hadn't been expecting that question on first meeting.

Beside her, Ash coughed, then cleared her throat.

"Mum!" Her voice was sharp with embarrassment.

Victoria's composure cracked slightly. Children. The succession. The future of the monarchy itself. As if she didn't lay awake at night thinking about exactly this. Duty versus love, about what was possible and what was impossible. If the world wasn't ready for a queer princess, was it ready for one with children?

"I haven't really thought that far ahead." At least, not with Ash.

The rest of lunch passed in a blur of increasingly painful questions. What did she think about various politicians? Did she know certain celebrities? What do her parents do for Sunday lunch? Each question highlighted the gulf between their worlds more starkly than the last.

In the car afterwards, Victoria was numb.

"I'm so sorry," Ash said. "I had no idea your appearance would cause my mum to go on a diatribe to end them all. And the children comment: she doesn't even bug me about that often."

"It's fine," Victoria lied. "They were lovely. Really." She meant it, sort of. They were lovely. Painfully, awkwardly, desperately lovely.

"Come back to mine?" she heard herself ask, already knowing the answer.

"Not today. Early training tomorrow, and it's a big week. League cup and a league game. No late nights for me."

Relief flooded through her before she could stop it, then guilt at the relief. She saw Ash clock both emotions crossing her face.

They pulled up at Ash's flat pretty quickly, and she leaned over and kissed Victoria goodbye. It was short and swift.

"I'll message you."

But as the car pulled away from Ash's flat later, Victoria's mind churned. She loved Ash: her directness, her strength, the way she made Victoria feel. But today had shown her what they were really facing.

It wasn't just about them anymore. It was about worlds colliding.

Her phone lit up with a message from Ash. She must have written it as soon as she got in the door.

> Thanks for today. Sorry about
> Mum's 20 questions. xxx

Victoria's throat tightened as she typed back.

I've already forgotten about it. xxx

She loved Ash. She was sure about that. But as the car wound through London's darkening streets towards her Kensington home, her mother's words echoed in her head: "The monarchy isn't just about who we love. It's about who we *can* love. These are rules by which we live and die."

They were living in a bubble right now.

But bubbles had a horrible tendency to burst.

* * *

"You should have seen it, Dex. I mean, they were lovely, but it was a car crash." Victoria sipped her champagne (they were already well into their second bottle), then slumped forward, her head on her arm. "I so wanted to fit in. Merge into their ways. But me going there only seemed to magnify our differences."

Being home alone after lunch with Ash's family hadn't been ideal. Instead, she'd messaged Dexter to see if he could meet her at The Devonshire. He'd been more than willing.

"I'm experiencing the opposite. Sidney told his parents about me, but apparently they think I'm beneath him. They look at me like I'm a stain on society." He put his hand to his chest. "Me? Who used to fake-date you, which surely gives me some caché?"

Victoria raised her head and smiled. "What a sorry pair we are. Things were so much easier when it was just us, weren't they?"

"That's because none of it really mattered. Friendships

are usually far easier than relationships. Platonic love comes with less complications."

"Remember when I said I wanted it all? The woman, true love, to let the world know? Maybe I was getting ahead of myself."

"You don't mean that."

She exhaled. "No, I don't. Part of me is just really annoyed that my mother might be right. But it's not a deal-breaker. Ash's parents tried too hard. Asked weird questions. Hopefully that will only happen at first."

A tabloid gossip writer named Dan walked past, giving them both a perfect smile.

"Since when do they let him in here?" Dexter hissed. "We might need to get a new hangout."

Unease swept through Victoria.

They weren't doing anything wrong. Just two friends chatting. But if the journalist (she used that term very loosely) wrote about this, it would look bad to Ash and her parents. She wanted anything but that. She had others to consider now.

"What did they cook you?"

"Sunday roast. All the trimmings." She smiled. "I have to say, it was kind of nice not having servants buzzing around while we ate. Her mum made Yorkshire puddings the size of Mars."

"Did you eat it all?"

"If I'd eaten that whole Yorkshire, I wouldn't have been able to fit through the club door, believe me."

"Meeting the parents, though. It must be serious. And she's meeting yours when?"

"Next week."

"Good luck for that. It might make today seem like a cakewalk. Meeting Cassandra and Oliver is nerve-wracking. Take it from someone who knows."

Victoria pouted. "You're meant to be making me feel better, Dexter."

"Right." He stroked his stubble. "Things will get better." He didn't sound convinced. "I mean, they might get worse first, but they will get better eventually." He tilted his head. "And generally, apart from today, whenever I've seen you, you seem happy. Are you?" He kissed her hand. "I want that for you, darling."

Right at that moment, with Dexter clasping her hand and looking at her lovingly, someone cleared their throat beside them.

Victoria jumped, then registered who it was. Angela Fallon. The Prime Minister.

Of course it was.

"Sorry to interrupt," she said, face tangled as if she'd just interrupted a declaration of love.

They should be more careful.

"No problem, Prime Minister." Victoria stood, extended a hand, and Angela shook it.

"I just wanted to let you know that our meeting this week about your homeless project needs to be rescheduled. I'm wanted in Paris for a climate change meeting instead. But the week after should be fine. I'll have my secretary reach out." She dropped Victoria's hand, then glanced at Dexter. "Again, sorry to interrupt."

Victoria waited until she was out of the room before

sinking back to the sofa and closing her eyes. She had to hope the Prime Minister wasn't a gossip, but she'd heard otherwise. "If it's not out that we're back together by tomorrow, I'll be surprised."

"Great news. That'll really thrill Sidney." Dexter gave her a glum smile, gulped some champagne, then flagged down a passing waiter and ordered another bottle. It arrived mere minutes later, and their glasses were topped up. Victoria could already feel the alcohol loosening her up. Today, it was welcome.

"I was asking if you're happy? I saw Astrid briefly last month in Stockholm, and she told me you were glowing and in love." He narrowed his eyes. "I didn't know whether to believe her as you know that Astrid has a streak for the dramatic. But are you?"

"Happy or in love?"

"Either?"

"I'm in up to my neck, Dex." She held Dexter's gaze, her fingers tracing the condensation on her crystal flute. "Totally, hopelessly, in love. The kind that makes me want to tear up every rulebook I've ever followed." She shook her head. "I've spent my whole life being exactly who everyone needed me to be." She tucked her hair behind her ear, hope rising inside, pushing against the weight of reality. "Now all I want to be is hers. And I know it's going to be complicated and messy and probably cause an international incident, but I don't think I care anymore."

Wow. Maybe talking her doubts through with someone was what she needed. Yes, today hadn't been good, but what she and Ash had was. She needed to remember that.

"Does she love you?"

Victoria nodded. "Despite knowing what it entails, she does. I found her, Dex. The one."

"The one?"

Victoria nodded again as she pushed her fears aside. "I think so. I've never felt like this before. I took her to Balmoral, and Gran loved her. Today was the first bump back down to reality. Up until now, it's been bliss."

"There are going to be bumps in the road. There always are."

"I know, but I was hoping for none. Of being the exception to the rule. Princess privilege, you know?"

"If only that was how the world worked." He gave her a wry smile.

"What about you? Are you in love?"

"Hopelessly. But we're both struggling with parental approval now we're in the open." He held up a hand. "Don't worry, we're not open in full public. I know our agreement not to blow your cover."

Victoria felt bad about that, but it was necessary. "You're a good friend."

"What's this I spy? A reunion on the cards?" The voice was slurred, familiar.

Victoria looked up. Michael. Clearly worse for wear. She pulled him down to their sofa as he giggled.

"Not so loud!" she told him.

From feeling a little drunk, she was now suddenly *very* sober.

Michael put a finger to his lips and performed an exaggerated shushing noise. He had a smudge of something on his cheek. Was it lipstick?

"I've missed you, Dexter." He leaned over and patted Dexter's knee. "You should come over more often to see Vix. Bring Sidney. We can all get drunk together."

"You don't need any encouragement," Victoria told him.

He picked up their bottle, held it up to the light, then swigged some direct.

Victoria closed her eyes. Michael had these nights where he forgot who he was. Or perhaps, that was why he had them? In the past, she'd tried to coral him, like a cowgirl lassoing her herd. Now, she'd learnt to let him be. She couldn't control him, no matter how much she wanted to.

"Shall we order another bottle?" Michael asked. "This place is so dull sometimes. You know what it needs? A dance floor."

Victoria winced. Michael's arrival was about to hasten her departure. Plus, she'd had enough herself.

"Good luck finding that," she told him, downing the last of her drink. "Dex, I'm going home. Can I drop you off?"

"Yes please." He checked his pockets for essentials. "It's the thing I miss about dating you: a driver on tap."

"Then take advantage today." She paused, glancing at Michael. "What about you? Get in the car with me, call it a night?"

But she already knew the answer.

"You go. I was just chatting to a gorgeous woman next door. I was en route to the toilet when I saw you. I'll finish what I started."

She sighed. "Okay. But don't drink too much more. You'll thank me in the morning."

"Yes, Mother."

She hit his arm, and he let out an exaggerated squeal.

"I'll see you in the kitchen tomorrow morning." She got out her phone.

No new messages.

She missed Ash already.

"Ready, Dex?"

# Chapter Twenty-Five

"Your times are awful this morning. Plus, you were late this morning, and you're never late. What's going on? Were you out partying?" Jo Kendall stared at Ash.

She leaned on her haunches, getting her breath back. She knew that's exactly what it looked like, but it wasn't true. Rather, her shoddy performance today was down to her hardly having slept a wink, tossing and turning, still worrying about what Victoria had made of her parents. They hadn't been bad, but they hadn't been good, either. Oh god, her mum's comments about children. The tension in the car afterwards had left Ash reaching for oxygen. They'd left it on a strange note.

"No, I'm just having a day. Bad night's sleep."

Jo frowned, then nodded towards the byline. "Get over there and do some drills with the rest. Hopefully your touch is better than your sprinting today."

Lack of sleep wasn't the only reason she was feeling a little off today. When she got to training this morning, her phone lit up with notifications about Princess Victoria after she'd set up a Google alert for her. When she clicked them, she'd seen a slew of photos of Victoria and Dexter coming out of a private members' club in Mayfair, then getting into her car together.

Despite all logic, Ash's hackles were raised. The second

things got messy, Victoria had called Dexter and got drunk with him. No doubt poured her heart out to him. Did Victoria think it would be easier if they'd just stayed together?

For the next hour, Ash tried to put her worries out of her mind, and focus on today, this moment. She'd never had trouble doing that before. Whatever happened in her personal life, she'd always managed to keep it separate from her football. Once she stepped over the white line, she forgot everything else. At least, that's how it always *had* been. Before she got herself mixed up with Princess Victoria. She'd known being with a royal would make things different. She hadn't accounted for just *how* different.

In the dressing room afterwards, Sasha elbowed her gently.

"Everything okay, Ash?"

Her voice was so gentle, so unlike Sasha, it almost broke Ash.

She was on the edge, she saw that now. If anyone was too nice to her, she might fall apart.

"All good," she told Sasha, painting a smile on her face. "Getting ready for Saturday and the away trip to Salchester. Ready to show the northerners who really owns the WSL."

Sasha got up and started to strip off her training kit. "We do, of course," she said. "You know, if anything's bothering you, my door's always open." She paused. "I'm no good with this self-help stuff. Not half as good as Cam, I know. But apparently, it's good to talk. If you need to, I'm here."

"Thanks, I appreciate it."

Sasha saluted her, then headed for the showers.

She was a good friend, but this wasn't a secret Ash could share.

Half an hour later, Ash was showered and ready to go. Should she go and see her parents today? Her mum had messaged her last night to say she thought it had "gone well." To the untrained eye, Ash supposed that was true. They'd eaten dinner, chatted, and everybody had got on well enough.

But her parents' questions had only highlighted how different their lives were. She was due to meet Victoria's parents next week, and she was sure that was going to do the same. She wanted to fast-forward through the next nine days. Get the Salchester game out of the way, get the parental meetings done. Then she'd know the lay of the land.

Because after parental meeting number one, Victoria had gone silent on her, and then got drunk with Dexter. It wasn't a great start.

She got her phone from her bag and checked for any new messages from Victoria. She had none. Disappointment settled in her stomach.

Ash walked past the coach's office, and Jo beckoned her in. Her stomach rolled. It felt like she was back at school, being summoned to the head's office for something she'd done wrong.

"Sit down, Ash. Please."

She did as she was told.

"I just wanted to have a quick word. Everything all right with the knee?" Jo walked around her wooden desk, then perched on the edge as she studied Ash with a penetrating look Ash was sure had made many a player crack over the years. She wore a training kit, with the initials JK above the club badge.

"Yeah, fine. Just a bit tired today, didn't sleep well. Sure

I'll be better tomorrow." Ash focused on the half-eaten Bounty bar on the manager's desk. Those, and laughing at Sasha's bad jokes, were Jo's biggest weaknesses.

"You sure? It seemed like you were moving differently today."

Ash shook her head. "Honest. I'm feeling physically good."

Her manager folded her arms across her chest. "Big game Saturday. I need all my star players at their best."

"I will be. Promise."

"You said everything was okay physically. What about mentally? Something on your mind?"

For a split second, Ash almost told her. Spilled everything about Victoria, about their parents, about her fears that Victoria was going to cut and run. How she was falling so hard and fast, it scared her.

But she couldn't. Not yet. Not when they were being so careful. When even Victoria's security staff didn't know about half their meetings.

When she'd split up with Danielle, she'd told Jo about it, and asked for time off. Her manager had been very understanding. Ash was well aware the conversation would need to be had soon.

But not just yet. No matter how much it was eating her up.

"I just need a good night's sleep. I'll be better tomorrow."

Now, alone in the car park, she pulled out her phone, thumb hovering over Victoria's contact. In her phone as PV.

She opened their chat, started typing, deleted it, started again. Tried to think of something clever or funny. In the end, exhaustion won out.

> Miss you. Been thinking about you all day. Had a rubbish day at training.

She deleted the last sentence. That wasn't Victoria's fault. Her training was all on her.

The typing bubbles appeared and disappeared several times before Victoria's response came through.

> I miss you too. Today has been crazy. Sorry for lack of contact.

The apology lifted the weight on her shoulders a smidge. However, there was still a lot left unsaid.

None of which was going to be solved before the big meeting on Tuesday.

> I've got commitments this week on my day off. Then we're away at Salchester on Saturday. I hope you'll be watching?

> Wouldn't miss it. Even though Michael will moan I'm clogging up the TV watching football again.

> If I score, I'll do the heart celebration again.

There was a longer pause this time.

> You're impossible. In the best way. Don't spoil me, or I'll expect it every time.

Five seconds later, three heart emojis appeared, then three kisses. Ash took a deep breath, fingers moving across the screen.

> Speaking of impossible… I keep thinking about Tuesday. Meeting your parents.

'After the awkwardness of you meeting mine' was what she wanted to add, but she didn't.

> Just be yourself. That's who I fell for. Not some polished, perfect version trying to impress them. Just gorgeous you. They're going to love you.

Ash leaned her head against her car window. She really wanted to believe Victoria.

> You're good at this, you know. The whole making-me-feel-better thing.

> Years of diplomatic training finally paying off.

> I should go home. Rest up. Eat something healthy.

> Take care of yourself. Wish I was in your bed with you tonight.

> You're not the only one.

She didn't write 'Ma'am' at the end of that final message. She tried not to focus on that.

Ash slipped her phone into her pocket, the weight of the day lifting slightly. Tuesday was still terrifying, but at least she had Saturday's match to focus on first. One impossible thing at a time.

If the gaffer had noticed something off in her game today, she'd have to be sharper tomorrow. The last thing she needed was people asking questions, piecing things together before she and Victoria were ready. For now, their secret was still safe, still just theirs.

Even if sometimes Ash wanted to shout it from the rooftops of Buckingham Palace itself.

\* \* \*

The door to Salchester's away dressing room swung open just as Ash was adjusting the captain's armband. Sasha was sick today, so she was stepping up from her role of vice captain, to team captain. She glanced up, expecting the gaffer or somebody from the team. When she saw who it actually was, her blood froze.

Victoria stood in the doorway, flanked by two security guards, wearing a Royal Ravens scarf and looking entirely too beautiful for Ash to maintain her composure.

When everyone else saw who it was, the team fell silent. Royalty had that effect.

Ash didn't know where to look or how to act. Annoyance growled inside her, alongside delight at seeing Victoria. They'd messaged just a few hours ago, and Victoria had shared her plans for watching from her sofa with a Diet Coke and a bowl of sweet popcorn in her house in Kensington.

What had changed? What the fuck was she doing here?

Also, Victoria hated this sort of thing. She'd told Ash that dressing rooms intimidated her.

Ash knew the answer was her. But it wasn't like Ash could throw her arms around Victoria, or kiss her.

Why the hell had Victoria decided to surprise her before one of their most crucial games of the season?

But none of that could come across in Ash's face. She tried to maintain her composure, while inside, she was screaming.

"Ladies." Victoria gave her perfect royal smile.

Ash far preferred the languid sort she gave her just after she'd made her come.

*Stop thinking those thoughts.*

"I hope you don't mind me popping in to wish you luck."

Ash's hands trembled as Victoria made her way around the group, shaking hands and giving words of encouragement. Seeing her girlfriend – *her secret girlfriend* – chatting easily with her teammates filled Ash both with hope and despair. When Victoria reached her and their eyes met, Ash gave her a gritty smile.

"Surprise," Victoria whispered, gripping Ash's hand. "I hear you're captain today."

"You heard right, Your Highness." Ash's voice was steady, but the words were all wrong in her mouth, like chewing polystyrene. She locked eyes with Victoria. "Ma'am."

It had become one of their sex words. It drove Victoria wild when Ash used it.

Ash wasn't immune to its powers, either.

"I'm sure you're going to do great." Victoria licked her lips.

Ash followed every inch of the movement, her heart tripping over itself in her chest.

"I'll be watching and cheering."

She leaned in a little closer. Victoria's breath on Ash's skin made her body light up like a slot machine. She was too easy when it came to Victoria.

Even if she was annoyed.

"I'm especially excited for the celebration you might do if you score."

Ash flicked her gaze to one of Victoria's security at the door. She was ex-military, and no-nonsense. She was also watching Ash and Victoria's interaction with a knowing smile.

She knew. Of course she did. Because she'd seen Ash come and go at Victoria's house a number of times.

If she knew, who else knew? Alarm streaked through Ash, but she tamped it down. Could her teammates tell? Had Victoria spent an inordinate amount of time chatting to her than to everyone else?

The bell sounded, telling the teams to get into the tunnel.

At the sound, Victoria jerked, gave Ash a wink, then shouted: "Let's have a Royal win today, please!"

The visit lasted barely five minutes, but it threw Ash completely off-kilter. During warm-up, she kept catching glimpses of Victoria in the directors' box, and her usual pre-match focus scattered like leaves in the wind. Her touches in the warm-up were heavy, lacking their usual crispness. Her coaches said nothing, but she could see what they were thinking in their body language: was Ash going to get better or worse when the whistle blew? The answer soon became apparent.

From the off, everything felt wrong. The grass seemed too long, the ball too heavy, her boots too tight. Her first touch from Susie's pass bounced awkwardly off her shin.

Her second touch wasn't much better, skidding away from her and giving possession straight back to Salchester. The more Ash tried to over-correct, the worse she got. She wasn't playing on instinct. She was second-guessing every touch, and that was never good news.

Sloane Patterson – Salchester's star striker – seemed to sense Ash's uncertainty. She kept dropping deep, drawing Ash out of position, then spinning away with her trademark burst of acceleration.

Twenty minutes in, Patterson received the ball with her back to goal, 30 yards out. Ash stepped in to tackle, but Patterson had already whisked away, leaving her grabbing at air and falling on her arse. The striker drove forward, cut inside their keeper's desperate lunge, and curled the ball into the top corner.

Ash slammed her fist into the turf. That Victoria was watching made everything ten times worse.

Salchester's second goal came just before half-time. Another Patterson special, this time ghosting between two Ravens defenders to meet a cross with a diving header. In the dressing room at half-time, the gaffer tried to rally them, and her concerned glances at Ash said everything.

There was one half left for Ash to get it together, to make Victoria proud.

It didn't happen.

Patterson completed her hat-trick in the 65th minute, making Ash look foolish again with a nutmeg that drew groans from the crowd.

Something in Ash snapped.

The frustration of the day – of having to pretend, of

playing terribly, of being embarrassed by Sloane Fucking Patterson – crystallised into a red mist.

Five minutes later, when Patterson received the ball near the halfway line, Ash didn't think. All she knew was, she had to stop Sloane from making the whole team look like a bunch of muppets.

Or more specifically, her.

To do that, Ash launched herself into a tackle, studs up, far too late.

The crack of boot on ankle was audible, and Sloane went down screaming.

The referee's whistle pierced the air. Ash knew what was coming even before she saw the red card raised. She'd never been sent off in her career before, but there was no arguing this one. As she walked past the directors' box, she couldn't bring herself to look up, couldn't bear to see Victoria's reaction.

In the dressing room, she sat alone, still in her kit, head in her hands. Her phone buzzed several times – Victoria, probably – but she couldn't look. Not yet. Through the walls, she heard the crowd react to something, probably another Salchester chance.

She heard boots click-clacking on the concrete outside, but nobody came in. There was still at least another 20 minutes to go before she saw all her teammates again, and had to apologise. They hadn't lost because of her, but she certainly hadn't helped.

She still had her head in her hands, going through what she might say to her team, and also to Victoria, when there was a knock at the door. It was open by the time she looked up.

Victoria.

Ash jumped up, skittish in her girlfriend's presence.

Football, this dressing room, were Ash's world, not Victoria's. Ash wasn't sure how to meld Victoria into her realm on the pitch or off it. Was this why Victoria had gone radio silent after lunch at Ash's parents? Had she felt the same way?

"Hey." Victoria's face was a mask of compassion.

Ash hated it. She didn't deserve it.

"You okay?"

"Clearly I'm not."

Victoria walked over, and sat on the bench beside her.

If she moved to touch her, it might undo Ash. She might collapse into her arms. This was one of the lowest points in her entire career, and it had been televised *and* watched in the flesh by the woman she loved.

None of it made any sense.

"What happened out there?"

A flash bulb went off inside Ash's brain. She jumped up, and paced the dressing room, rubbing her hands together, shaking her head. "I don't know."

She glanced at Victoria. Her heart ached just looking at her.

"It was just..." Ash stopped. What could she say? That Victoria turning up was the reason she lost control? That everything about her life right now felt out of control, and it was messing with her head?

No, she couldn't say that.

"I honestly have no idea. Everything was off for me. It has been all week. It's normally fine once I cross the white line, but today, it wasn't." She shrugged like it meant nothing.

"Don't be so hard on yourself. It happens to the best of players."

Something jolted inside Ash, and her face set like cement. She stabbed her chest with her index finger. "It doesn't happen to me." The sharpness of her words surprised even her.

Victoria's face tightened. "I'm sorry if that sounded flippant. I didn't mean it to be. I know how important this is for you. I'm doubly sorry if me being here had anything to do with it."

Regret flooded every crevice of Ash's body. She shook her head. "You could have told me you were coming. I don't like surprises." Then she winced. "But it's not your fault."

It was simply the perfect storm. Ash's frustrations, this week, her need to impress. Her whole life had fallen on top of her in a precise 65 minutes. Unfortunately, it'd happened on the pitch.

That was new, and scary.

She needed to refocus, get her head back in the game.

Having Victoria in the dressing room was not helping.

"I wondered if I could give you a lift back to London? At least then we could spend a bit of time together before Tuesday?" Victoria's voice was not royal this time. It was whispered, worried.

Ash was shaking her head before she'd finished. "I can't. I have to go back with the team. It's not a good look if I don't travel back with everyone. Especially after I let them all down today."

"Of course." Victoria's face fell slightly, but she recovered quickly. She stood up, but didn't take a step towards Ash. She bit her lip, then looked up at her. "Will you call me later? I want to check you're okay."

"Of course," Ash said, though she wasn't sure she would. She needed time to process this, to deal with the shame of losing control like that. "I'm sorry about today. That it didn't go our way. That I didn't score for you."

Victoria stepped towards her now. "You never have to be sorry for that. You go out there and do your best. It's all anyone can ask." She reached out a hand.

Ash shook her head. "Don't. Not here." She couldn't.

Outside the crowd roared. Ash's stomach rolled. Had they scored again?

"You better go. Before the team gets back. I don't want people knowing you're here."

"Hillary is outside. She'll let me know if anyone is coming." Her chief of security.

"Even so." Ash tried a smile, but it wasn't successful.

Victoria's eyes got glassy, but she took a deep breath. "I'll message you later."

Ash nodded, not trusting herself to speak. She held her breath until Victoria left, then crumpled to the bench, desperately trying to stop her tears. She couldn't be in here crying when everyone else arrived. That wasn't who Ash was at all.

She was Ashleigh Woods. Midfield dynamo and Lionesses captain. For the next few weeks, perhaps she'd have to focus on that to get her game back together. Her career had to come first, as it always had. She'd taken her eye off the ball.

Her game had never let her down yet.

She wasn't about to let it start now.

# Chapter Twenty-Six

Victoria slumped against the leather seat of the royal car as it purred away from the stadium, replaying the image of Ash's devastated face as she'd trudged off the pitch. And then how awful it was in the dressing room afterwards. She'd thought turning up would be a gorgeous surprise. That Ash would be thrilled. But instead, Ash had got a red card. In 12 years of professional football, it was Ash's first one. Fair to say, the surprise had fallen a little flat.

Her phone buzzed. It was Faye, her press secretary. Victoria's heart stuttered. Faye never called on weekends unless something was wrong.

"Your Highness." Faye's voice had that careful tone Victoria had learnt to dread. "We have a situation."

The streets of Salchester flew past. "Go on."

"Someone's been following you. There are photographs. You and Ashleigh Woods at a small cafe in Scotland a few weeks ago. Also, outside your London residence. Multiple occasions of her car leaving your gates."

The world tilted on its axis. Victoria's fingers dug into the armrest. Beside her, Tanya turned her head, concerned.

Victoria imagined her own face had drained of blood.

Could this day get any worse?

That morning at the small cafe flashed through her mind. Driving from Balmoral to Aberdeen airport, and they'd both needed the toilet. As the place was practically empty, they'd decided to get a coffee before they got back on the road. Victoria recalled Ash's sleepy smile across the Formica table, the way her baseball cap had been deliciously wonky. Victoria had wanted so badly to reach across the table and touch her hand. Maybe she had, she couldn't recall.

She sunk down in the back seat.

"How many photos?" Her voice sounded distant to her own ears.

"Enough. Also, one very blurry shot of the two of you embracing on your doorstep. It's taken with a very long lens, of course, and it's hard to make out exactly who it is. That on its own wouldn't be anything to worry about. But someone's been talking to the Mail, claiming they talked to a source close to you both. They're saying you and Ashleigh are involved. That the relationship with Dexter was orchestrated from the start."

Victoria's stomach lurched. She thought of the handful of mornings Ash had left her place. It'd mostly been early. On a couple of her days off, she'd donned a beanie and gone for a run, before returning for breakfast.

"Can we get an injunction?"

"Too late. The gossip sites are already having a field day. Especially after you showed up at the Ravens game today. I think that's what sparked the tabloids deciding to run with the piece and the shots. People are putting two and two together."

Victoria closed her eyes. She hadn't thought it all through, had she? Michael's words about three strikes and you're out came back to her.

"I have to ask, Ma'am. Is there truth to these rumours? Just so we know how to deal with them? Because the photos could be taken that you're friends, but the optics don't look good."

Victoria almost snarled. How was she meant to answer that? And how dare her press secretary ask it so quickly. Yes, she needed to know, but *not right now*.

"I'll call you back," Victoria managed, ending the call.

Tanya let out a breath she'd clearly been holding. "Bad news?"

Victoria filled her in.

She turned to Tanya, her cheeks ashen. "You haven't said anything to anyone?" As soon as the words were out, she wanted to take them back.

"Goodness, no. I would never." Tanya's eyes were wide, honest. "Victoria, you know you can trust me."

Victoria nodded. She did. Tanya had covered for her countless times, had turned a blind eye to late-night visits, had rearranged schedules to create those precious moments alone with Ash.

Her phone buzzed again: Faye.

"Sorry for the endless stream of bad news, Ma'am. Just to confirm, they're running it," her press secretary said without preamble. "The photos are already online. The story breaks properly tomorrow in the papers, but it's spreading on social media. We need to get ahead of this."

Victoria's heart plunged through her body. She held the top of her nose between her thumb and index finger. She thought about Ash and the effect this would have on her. None of it was any good.

"What do we do?"

"Standard response. We deny any improper relationship. Say these are normal social interactions between friends. Ashleigh was at your residence for a charity planning meeting. It's well known you're supporting queer homelessness, and it's a cause close to Ashleigh's heart, too."

Fuck. They were going to use that against Ash, weren't they?

"She was also there to discuss FA stuff: very normal between the Lionesses captain and its patron. You get on. You're friends. Which is why you had coffee when you accidentally met at the service station." She paused. "Not that any of those details will come out unless we're completely cornered. Less said, the better. You know the drill."

Each lie felt like acid in Victoria's throat, but she heard herself agreeing. What choice did she have? She thought of Ash again, how everything she touched seemed to turn to gold until Victoria came along. Including today's match: Ash completely off her game, losing control, getting sent off. Was this what loving a royal did to people?

With trembling fingers, she opened her messages to Ash. Then she dropped her phone and put her head in her hands. What was she going to say? She had to tell the truth. That if Ash thought getting sent off was the worst thing that could happen this weekend, she better buckle up. But not in so many words.

> I don't know if you've seen the news,
> but someone has leaked us to the press.
> I don't know who.

Maybe Victoria's phone had been hacked? It wouldn't be the first time. Maybe that tabloid reporter at the club last week had something to do with it. Or perhaps her brother...

No. She couldn't go there.

> Photos are already online. My press secretary, Faye, says we have to deny everything. I'm so sorry for dragging you into this mess.

She stared at the words she hadn't sent. Somehow, after the week they'd endured, this felt make or break. Even thinking that cracked her heart a little.

> I love you.

She pressed send.

It didn't seem enough.

Ash would be travelling back on her bus right now, feeling terrible about letting her team down. She hoped someone on that bus put an arm around her when the news broke.

The notifications started flooding in before Ash could reply. Victoria's thumb moved against her better judgement, opening the *Daily Mail*'s website. The photos hit her like physical blows: moments she'd treasured turned tawdry by grainy long-lens cameras.

Ash leaving her house at 6am, hair mussed, her smile wide. Victoria remembered that morning: how they'd overslept, how Ash had kissed her goodbye with promises of seeing her the following week. Her heart had been so full of hope. The photographer's lens made it look sordid, shameful.

Their 'secret' meeting at the Scottish cafe. Ash's hand briefly touching Victoria's back as they walked inside. Victoria had been so happy that morning: in love, getting a brief taste of normality.

She'd kidded herself, of course.

Her life could never be normal.

There was always a whirlwind ready to suck her in.

*The Sun*'s headline turned her stomach: *BEND IT LIKE WOODS: Princess Royal In Secret Lesbian Tryst!*

*The Daily Star*'s wasn't much better: *PALACE'S LESBIAN BOMBSHELL: Victoria's Secret Lesbian Love Match!*

She knew what her mother would say. "Do not click on these sites. It only ends in heartache."

But today, Victoria simply couldn't help it.

Her fingers scrolled through the comments, each one worse than the last.

*No way the Princess is a lesbian. This Woods woman must have corrupted her.*

*Disgusting. What would her grandmother say?*

*Always knew that Woods was a dyke. Should never have let women's football get so big.*

*The Dexter thing was obviously fake. He's clearly a tooty fruity!*

*Abolish the monarchy. I always said they're depraved. This proves it once and for all.*

Victoria blinked back tears. No matter how much she thought she might be ready, she wasn't. Plus, this wasn't just about her, Ash and the monarchy. This was about Dexter and Sidney, too. She quickly messaged him.

> It's breaking. Just to let you know, your name is being dragged, too. Sorry. x

His reply was almost instant.

> Saw it. Don't worry about me. I'll survive the revelation that I'm not actually dating a princess, and am in fact, gay.

> She's meeting my parents on Tuesday. Perfect timing, right?

> They say the thing you've been dreading is never as bad as you imagine.

> I guess I'm about to find out. Thanks for being a sweetheart.

> Of course. Anything for you.

Hours later, when the Palace gates closed behind her car, centuries of tradition pressed down like a physical force. Beyond these walls, the world spun forward; but here, time stood frozen, bound by rules etched in stone. An emergency meeting with her parents loomed ahead tomorrow, and she knew the conversation would be unlike any they'd had before.

Her phone lit up with a message from Ash.

> Just saw everything. Coach took my phone after the red card to stop me doom-scrolling. I'm so sorry about today. About all of it. But I'm sorry you're having to go through this, too. Not sure how this works now?

Victoria's heart was like a tyre slowly losing air. What did that last sentence mean? This was exactly what she'd feared: Ash backing off.

> Still want me to come Tuesday?

Victoria stared at the message. How Victoria had promised that her parents would love Ash once they got to know her. Things had just taken a different turn, but she could handle it.

> Come. Didn't we say we'd face it together? None of this changes how I feel about you. It just means that more people have an inkling. My thoughts haven't altered: I'm tired of pretending.

The car stopped at the back entrance, because photographers had gathered at the main gates, their cameras dark in the night gloom. Her phone buzzed: her father's private secretary requesting her presence in the King's study first thing tomorrow morning.

A notification popped up. Another article, another set of photos. Victoria closed her eyes, remembering what it felt like today, watching Ash play, before everything fell apart.

How proud she'd been, even when it was clear Ash wasn't herself. Victoria still loved that Ash got on the field and gave it her all.

This afternoon, Victoria had visions of the pair of them walking out of a ground hand in hand within a few months.

Now, everything had been thrown in the air.

She clicked on to the *Daily Mail* again. Mistake. She was on the front page. So was Ash.

This wasn't just about her anymore. This was about Ash's career, about the monarchy, about two worlds that were never supposed to collide.

To get to the other side, she had to go through it. They both did.

Even if it meant walking the whole way on a tightrope.

# Chapter Twenty-Seven

Ash stared at her reflection in the studio mirror, adjusting the sponsored training gear with practiced ease. The photographer called out directions, and she moved automatically: twist, smile, look determined, show the gear in action. After years of doing this, she could perform on autopilot, which was exactly what she needed today.

"Perfect!" The photographer lowered his camera. If he was thinking anything about the revelations of yesterday, he'd kept his thoughts to himself. Ash was grateful. "That's a wrap."

She'd managed to lose herself in the shoot for two blissful hours, pushing away thoughts of the press camped outside her flat and her parents' house, along with tomorrow's royal showdown. But reality came flooding back as soon as she checked her phone: missed calls from Victoria, texts from teammates, and an endless stream of notifications from news sites. The one good thing to come from this shitshow? Nobody was focusing on her red card and how her game had gone down the pan.

"There's my star." Marianne appeared at her shoulder, iPad clutched like a shield against her charcoal trouser-suit. Her pristine bob didn't move as she glanced around the studio, sharp features set in their usual sceptical expression. "Even when I was your age, I never looked as good as you do in everything you wear."

"Thanks." Even Marianne's big-upping couldn't comfort Ash today. She started gathering her things. "We need to head out the back way. There were photographers round the front when I arrived."

Marianne pushed her reading glasses onto her head. "My car's waiting. We'll take the long way round. It'll give us time to chat on the way to your parents' place."

Ash guessed this was the first of many interrogations, so she better get used to it.

They made it to the car without incident, and Marianne waited until they were moving before turning to face her client of eight years. Her Apple watch buzzed continuously, but for once, she ignored it.

"So," she said, traces of Manchester bleeding into her polished accent. "Were you planning on telling me about you and Victoria?"

Ash's stomach clenched. She didn't respond right away. She didn't have to.

"Is that why you got sent off yesterday? Why she was there?"

"I don't know what I can say right now." The edges of Enfield blurred past the window. "Everything's complicated."

"Complicated is my job, Ash." Marianne's voice softened, the laugh lines around her eyes crinkling with concern. "That's literally what you pay me for. To handle complicated."

"I know." Ash rubbed her temples. The headache that had started yesterday hadn't let up. "I need to meet with Victoria first. Work out what we're doing."

"There's a 'we'. That answers my question." She shook

her head. "The press are having a field day. Your sponsors are calling. The FA wants a statement. I need something to tell them."

"I know." Ash's voice cracked slightly. "I know, okay? But I can't have anyone else questioning this right now. My parents are freaking out, the team's probably pissed off about yesterday, and tomorrow I have to go to Buckingham Palace and meet the actual King and Queen while their daughter's sexuality is splashed across every front page in the country. And when they see me, they're going to think it's all my fault."

When she said it out loud, it really was A LOT.

Marianne set her iPad aside, something she rarely did during business hours. "How long?"

Ash shrugged, then closed her eyes. If only the world had a mute button.

Marianne laid her fingers on Ash's arm, causing her to jump. "Ash, I'm asking as your friend. How long?"

Ash exhaled. "We met in Marbella in June, but nothing happened until August."

Marianne counted on her fingers. "June, July, August, September, October." Her eyes widened. "Five months, and you've said nothing?"

"I told you, we were waiting until the right moment." It sounded nuts now, she knew.

"The Dexter thing? Is that true?"

Ash nodded. "They're good friends. It was never more than that."

Marianne let out a low whistle. "And what is this for you? I assume it's serious, because you don't get involved with a princess and risk all of this blowing up for a quick fuck?"

A weak smile danced across Ash's face. "Serious as I've ever been."

"Okay. At least I know what I'm dealing with now. In that case, we'll figure it out." Marianne reached over and squeezed her hand. "But you have to let me help. No more secrets."

"I need to meet with her first. See what the Palace wants to do," Ash replied. "But yeah, after that... I'll need you."

"And you've got me."

"I know." Ash's phone buzzed: another message from Victoria about tomorrow's security arrangements. Doubts circled as she put her phone away.

"Okay?"

Ash shook her head. "I just worry. I've never had a red card before. What if this is too much, and I can't cope?" *What if we can't cope.* "I can't let anything affect my game in a World Cup year. Plus, the homophobic shit online is disgusting."

"Hey." Marianne's voice carried a steel that had faced down countless boardrooms. "One bad game doesn't define you. And if anyone gives you shit about being gay in women's football, they clearly haven't been paying attention."

"It's more the royal thing. The scrutiny. Having to hide, then getting caught anyway. She's going to be Queen someday, and I'm just me."

"You're the England captain. One of the most respected players in the game. Stop selling yourself short."

The car turned onto Ash's parents' street. Even from here, they could see the photographers camped out front.

"Shit, there are quite a few, aren't there?" Marianne peered out the front windscreen.

Ash nodded. Her parents had experience of it when their

daughter led the country to European Cup glory. Then, it had been good-natured and a novelty. This time around, the vibe wasn't quite so positive.

"Can you drop me round the back?" Ash told the driver.

"What time is it all kicking off tomorrow?" Marianne's glasses slid back down to their proper place as she reached for her iPad.

"It was going to be afternoon tea, but that's been abandoned in favour of a full-on morning crisis meeting." Ash attempted a laugh that came out more like a sob. "FML."

"None of that FML shit." Marianne slapped Ash's thigh as her car pulled up behind Ash's parents' house. "You've never backed down from a challenge before. Don't start now. Yes, the public are confused, but they'll calm down. They love both you and Victoria. Once they get used to the idea of you together, it'll make sense. Plus, just so you know, the women's football community are standing with you. Loads of your teammates and Lionesses have posted messages of support. The women's football community is on your side, and that's a start."

For the first time today, Ash smiled.

It wasn't nothing.

She had to cling to that.

\* \* \*

The White Drawing Room lived up to its name, all cream silk, stuffiness and gold-framed mirrors, with massive chandeliers casting judgement from above. Ash perched on the edge of a Regency sofa, its ivory upholstery exquisite. Beside her, Victoria sat straight-backed, while across the low table, the King and Queen mirrored their posture with royal precision.

Ash wore her lucky suit – the one from the European Cup final – but today she felt less like a football captain, and more like an actress who'd stumbled onto the wrong stage.

Maybe that's exactly what she was.

Victoria sat beside her, close but not touching, and Ash ached for the easy intimacy they'd previously shared. Now, every movement was calculated, watched, judged by the King and Queen sitting opposite them like judges at a trial. It had all started civilly enough, but quickly descended into an interrogation.

"Who knew about this relationship?" The Queen's tone was solid granite. "We need to know how this information got out." She addressed the question to Ash.

Ash's throat went dry. "I only told my parents and one teammate." She hated how small her voice sounded. Her mind flashed to Cam's fierce loyalty, her mum's protective anger. "People I trust completely."

"And you're certain they wouldn't—"

"Mother," Victoria interrupted. "We've been through this. Someone's been following us. Professional photographers. This isn't about who told who."

"People will do all sorts of things for money, Victoria."

"And I told you both Ash and I have been very careful."

"Is Michael not coming?" The Queen couldn't hide her irritation.

"He's on his own schedule," Victoria replied, her voice carefully neutral.

The Queen huffed her disappointment. "The press

hounds you mercilessly, while he gallivants London without consequence."

Ash's gaze flickered between mother and daughter, catching the layers beneath their exchange. She was pretty sure there was support buried in the Queen's criticism?

Ash glanced at Victoria, seeing the fresh hurt Michael's absence had carved. Another betrayal on a day already heavy with them. Her hand twitched, instinctively wanting to reach for Victoria's, but even that small comfort felt impossible here.

"And you're sure your family didn't say anything even if they didn't mean to?" the King asked Ash.

Something inside Ash snapped. She sat up. "I'm 100 per cent certain, Sir," she told him, holding his gaze. She wasn't going to be cowed on this. "I need you to understand what this is doing to my family. People are posting hate mail through their door. Journalists won't leave them alone. They didn't ask for any of this. They would never bring it on themselves."

Victoria's hand twitched towards hers, then stopped.

"I'm so sorry, Ash," she said. "We were supposed to have time to plan this properly. After New Year."

"I know." Ash swallowed hard. The weight of it all pressed on her chest: her parents' fear, the headlines screaming about her sexuality like it was public property. Staring into the faces of Victoria's parents, she saw now they were just two more parents wanting the best for their child. They didn't know how to handle this any better than she did.

She'd known it would be complicated. But this ambush, this violation of their privacy, had left them exposed, vulnerable, scrambling to protect not just themselves, but everyone they loved.

"Perhaps," the Queen said, standing abruptly. "I might have a word with my daughter. Alone."

Victoria shot Ash an apologetic look as the King rose, gesturing to Ash.

"Come with me."

Was this where she was excommunicated?

The King led her through corridors with centuries of history, finally arriving at a study that felt lived-in, personal. Books lined the walls, family photos sat on the desk. He went straight to a cabinet, poured two measures of scotch, and handed one to Ash. She thought about refusing, but then thought better of it. If nothing else, the glass was something to cling to.

"Sit. Please." He indicated a leather chair. "I think we need to talk."

Ash took a careful sip, grateful for the burn.

The King settled behind his desk, studying her. His fingers formed a steeple beneath his chin.

"I want my daughter to be happy," he said finally. "And if you make her happy, then so be it. But you need to understand what being with Victoria means."

Ash let him talk. The carefully measured tone told her he'd rehearsed this speech, probably while she and Victoria had been creating headlines neither of them had meant to make.

"This scrutiny you're experiencing now? It's just the beginning. When I married the Queen, I knew what I was getting into. I was prepared for it. But I was also a man marrying a woman. The path was clearer."

Ash stared into her glass as the amber liquid caught the light. "We knew it would be complicated."

"Complicated doesn't begin to cover it. Your family will always be under scrutiny. Your past relationships, your friendships, your career decisions: everything will be seen through the filter of your relationship with Victoria. Money can help with security, with legal protection, but it can't stop the rumours. Or social media. It definitely can't stop people forming opinions about you. The pressure may well be too much."

"Someone wise once told me that pressure is a privilege."

He gave her a steely stare.

"I understand the magnitude of this, Sir." The words felt hollow in her mouth, inadequate against the magnitude of what she really wanted to say: that Victoria was worth it.

He smiled, but it didn't reach his eyes. "Do you?" His voice was gentle but firm. "Because right now, you have a choice. Victoria doesn't. But you? You can still walk away."

Her fingers tightened around the crystal tumbler. "Are you asking me to?"

"No. I meant what I said about my daughter's happiness, and she's made it clear that she wants you. What I'm asking you to do is to think very carefully about what you're willing to sacrifice. Think long and hard."

He leaned forward. "For now, we're going to deny everything. You and Victoria will need to keep your distance until this dies down. Then, if your feelings are real, we'll put together a staged plan of action, one where we control what's known. That's not a request. Once you leave here today, you can't be seen together again."

"For how long?" Her voice cracked on the question.

"As long as it takes." He stood, moving around the desk

to put a hand on her shoulder. "You seem like a nice person, Ashleigh. But we don't live in a nice world. Maybe this time apart will give you a chance to really think about what you want."

Tears pricked the back of her eyes, and she blinked them back furiously. "And what about what Victoria wants?"

"Victoria has a sense of duty and responsibility that goes beyond personal desire. She always has."

He squeezed her shoulder once before stepping back, the gesture almost paternal, which somehow made it worse. Almost as if, in another world, he might have welcomed her.

# Chapter Twenty-Eight

"I'm so sorry about today. I didn't know they were going to do that. But I had a hunch it might not be the afternoon tea we'd planned." Victoria rolled the black ball down the middle of the pool table and it rebounded softly. She and Ash both stared at its course until it stopped.

Ash glanced around the summerhouse, taking in the surroundings. "I remember you telling me about your pool den when we were in Marbella. You undersold it. Any other day, I'd be thrilled to be here." Her face clouded over. "But not today."

"No," Victoria shook her head. "Not today." She caught Ash's gaze. "What did Father say?"

Ash put both palms on the side of the table, dropped her head, then took a deep breath. When she raised her gaze to Victoria, her blonde hair framed her face.

"That we need to deny everything and not see each other again for a while. That I should 'take some time to think about what I want'. Like I haven't done that already." She shook her head. "I won't lie, it felt like I was on an episode of some mob show. With your dad in the lead role as the mob boss."

"Not far off the truth, except my mother is always the boss."

Ash gave a heavy shrug. "Maybe they switched roles for a day? Whatever, I got the impression this was our last hurrah. That if I wasn't off the premises within an hour, they might set the dogs on me."

"Licked to death by Honey and Truffle?"

"Something like that." Ash's gaze was intense. "Did your mother give you the same speech?"

Victoria nodded. "Mother has always laid down the law. Then my father usually softens it. But this time, they put on a united front. One with zero flexibility."

Victoria walked around the table until she was next to Ash.

"They want us to deny it. Keep apart." She could smell Ash's shampoo, that mix of citrus and something uniquely her. Victoria's fingers found Ash's, and a familiar rush of desire fizzed through her.

The last thing she wanted to do was lose this closeness. *This feeling.* Losing Ash was like losing oxygen. It was unthinkable. "Just so you know, I don't want to."

Ash took a sharp inhale of breath, then withdrew her hand.

When Victoria peered closer, she could see Ash looked exhausted, with shadows under her eyes that hadn't been there a week ago. She hated being responsible for that.

"I don't think we have a choice," Ash said. "Your parents seemed pretty set on the idea, and I don't fancy going against them." Ash's green eyes met Victoria's, full of worry. "If we tell them no, what happens?"

Victoria walked over to the window. There had to be a way out of this she hadn't considered. The sunshine wasn't helping. She drew the blinds, then started pacing. "I haven't thought that far ahead. I just know I don't want to be without you."

"I don't want to be without you either," Ash said. "But I don't know how we can push back against this. If we deny the Palace, we alienate your family. I hate to be the one to break it to you, but in a fight of this scale, you're going to need them."

Victoria ran both hands through her hair and closed her eyes. Ash was facing the truth far better than she was. Conversely, Victoria was searching for a solution that simply wasn't there.

When she opened her eyes and stared at Ash, Victoria could already feel her slipping through her fingers. Just like everyone else.

She wasn't going to let it happen.

She *couldn't* let it happen.

"We can figure this out. I'm sure of it. We can get through it together. Just not right away."

Ash didn't move towards her. When she raised her hand, Victoria could see it was shaking.

"Victoria, I'm 29, and that plays into this. I might not have another World Cup in me. This is a huge season for me, one where I need my full focus to ensure I make the England squad. The only way that happens is by playing well for the Ravens. I haven't been doing that lately."

"It was one game, Ash." The words came out more sharply than intended. She hated hearing Ash doubt herself.

But Ash shook her head. "It's been going on for weeks, and in the game you were at, I couldn't control my emotions. I have to put my career first. This season is my big shot." Her face spelled anguish. "Plus, I can't keep living like this. Half in, half out. I owe it to myself, to every young queer person watching. I told my agent I wasn't going back in the closet when I became England captain, but I did tone it down. I regret that. Now you're asking me to deny what I'm feeling."

Ash's voice caught, and Victoria's heart with it.

"It's not just me, either. There's my family. I can't put them through hell for no reason."

"No reason?" Victoria couldn't believe what she was hearing. "How about the fact I love you?" The words burst out, raw and desperate. "Don't do this, Ash. I'll come out, I promise. I'll do it all, whatever my mother thinks. I just need time. A couple of months, maybe more—"

"Isn't that what your father suggested?"

Was it? Victoria's heart threatened to down tools and leave.

"I'll talk to my aides, and my parents." Panic flooded her. "Try to work something out. Maybe you can come back for the New Year Ball, and we can be a couple? Or at least by Valentine's Day."

But even as she said it, she knew she was making the same promises her parents always made.

Later.

Soon.

Just wait.

"The Ball is just over two months away. Don't make promises you can't keep." Ash sighed. "I never wanted to be your dirty little secret, you knew that. I was beginning to come around to the fact of the inevitable spotlight. But what I can't do is go out with someone who denies her feelings daily." Ash dropped her gaze. "Maybe we're just not meant to be."

Now, Victoria's heart did crack. She heard it, loud and clear.

"Don't do this." She walked over to Ash and stood before her. "We knew this was always going to be hard."

"You knew more than me."

That was true. Nobody prepared you for the royal commitment. "I know it's a lot to ask. You're not just dating me." She reached down to squeeze Ash's fingers. "You're dating the country's future."

Ash gave her the saddest smile imaginable, then kissed her knuckles, her eyes misty.

Victoria's ribs seemed to cave in around the space where her heart used to be.

"I want this so much," Ash whispered. "I really do love you. But it's affecting everything. My training. My game. My mental health. Your dad told me what he suggested wasn't a recommendation, it was an order. I don't want to piss off the King and Queen, even if I am in love with their daughter. Maybe we should take their advice, and cool it for a while."

Victoria ducked her head, trying to hide her tears.

She wanted to scream, but she had to respect Ash's wishes.

"If that's what you really want."

The biggest issue? Victoria understood. That was the hardest pill of all.

"Are we breaking up?" Her voice was heartbreakingly small.

"For now, maybe," Ash whispered.

They stared at each other.

Victoria memorised every detail of Ash's face: her smooth skin, her dark eyebrows, the flecks of gold in her sea-green eyes.

"You know, I once told Astrid I'd invited you over to have my way with you on this pool table. It was a joke, before I even knew you."

Something shifted in Ash's expression.

"Really?" Ash stepped close enough for Victoria to breathe her in. "Do you remember what happened?"

Before Victoria could answer, Ash crushed her mouth to Victoria, who wrapped her arms around Ash's neck as the kiss deepened, desperate and hungry.

They kissed like there was no tomorrow, which was the actual truth.

Victoria banished that thought from her mind, as Ash pushed her back against the pool table. Her fingers fumbled with Ash's buttons. She was usually better at this, but her hands wouldn't stop shaking.

"Here?" Ash breathed against her neck.

"Here," Victoria confirmed. "I need to feel you."

They shed clothing without words. Ash pushed Victoria against the pool table, the edges cold against her bum as Ash pressed into her. She trailed kisses down Victoria's throat, across her collarbone, lower.

Then Ash sank to her knees, looking up at Victoria with such a look of love, it crushed her. With no fanfare, she sank into Victoria with her tongue, licking her top to bottom, circling her like she could never get enough. Like she wanted to make this time count, imprint it on both of their brains.

Ash's hands clasped the back of Victoria's bum, pulling her closer, her tongue causing tidal waves of pleasure to rise up within. It didn't take long for the edges of Victoria's world to flicker, then blur. She hummed with anticipation as her insides caught alight, then buckled under the delicious sweep of Ash's tongue.

"Oh my god, Ash," Victoria whispered, fingers tangled in Ash's hair. Then her whole body jerked and she dissolved into the moment, riding Ash's gorgeous mouth. All they had was now, and she was going to live it, however much it simultaneously thrilled and devastated her.

Moments later, Ash rocked back on her heels, kissing her way up Victoria's flushed body. When her mouth landed on Victoria's, hot and soft, Victoria tasted herself, the effect intoxicating.

She tried not to focus on what came next. She wanted to freeze time. Stay in this moment. She was the future Queen. Why didn't she have that superpower at the very least?

But when she looked into Ash's eyes, she gasped. They were glassy, and she knew then that Ash was barely holding it together, too.

"We're not done," Ash said.

They both stared, knowing those words held a double meaning.

Ash lifted Victoria onto the pool table, the felt rough on her bum. She wrapped her legs around Ash's waist, pulling her closer.

Their gazes connected, just as Ash eased two fingers into her. When she hit Victoria's wetness, she let out a warm moan.

Victoria shifted, ground down, then put both arms around

Ash's neck. She put her mouth next to Ash's ear as her girlfriend thrust deep into her.

"I love you," she gasped.

Ash moaned again, then fucked her harder, just the way Victoria liked it.

As Ash moved inside and around her, Victoria cried out, not caring who heard. She wanted to shout to the world that this was a love she deserved. The one that was being cruelly taken away from her. Everybody had an opinion about them, but nobody knew who they were and what they felt.

If they truly knew, they'd never say this was anything but perfect.

"Look at me." Ash's breath was hot on her ear.

Victoria forced her eyes open.

The intensity in Ash's gaze made her chest tight. She was looking at her with hungry eyes. It was what Victoria had always wanted.

"I love you, too," Ash said. "Don't ever doubt it."

Everything sped up, then blurred. Ash's hands and mouth were everywhere, the pressure building inside. Victoria saw stars as she came in a rush, her face buried in Ash's neck, muffling her cry against her skin. Her tears mixed with sweat. She couldn't tell if they were from pleasure or pain anymore.

Moments later, Victoria flipped their positions, slipped a hand between Ash's legs, and fucked her until she clamped down on Victoria's fingers, coming hard on her pool table just like she'd always dreamed of.

Only today was no dream. This part, maybe. But overall, it was a living nightmare.

Ash's chest was red as she fought to calm her breath.

They stared at each other for a few long moments, not knowing what to say.

After, Victoria rested her head on Ash's chest, listening to her heartbeat slow, pretending they could stay here forever. But reality crept back in.

"I should probably go." Ash's voice was rough. "Before Truffle arrives."

"I know." There was so much more to say, but then again, there wasn't. Victoria pressed one last kiss to Ash's collarbone before sitting up. They dressed in silence, stealing glances, each trying to memorise the other.

At the door, Ash pulled her in for a final kiss. Victoria cupped her face, brushing away tears with her thumbs, tasting goodbye on Ash's lips.

"I love you," she whispered, because what else was there to say? "Just so you know, you'll always be my queen."

Ash nodded. "I'll never be sorry."

Victoria stood frozen as Ash walked away, taking Victoria's heart with her. She wanted to call out, to run after her, to promise anything, but she couldn't. Some things were bigger than love.

She lifted the blinds and the afternoon sun streamed through the windows, highlighting the empty space where Ash had been.

Victoria touched her lips, still feeling that last kiss, and let the tears fall.

# Chapter Twenty-Nine

The following week, Ash threw herself into training, and tried to ignore the press who were following her every move. Sasha had really pulled through for her, insisting she pick her up from the car park at the back of Ash's flats, so that Ash could avoid driving through them every day.

"I don't know what's happened, and if you can't tell me, you don't need to. But what I do know is that you need a friend, and I am that friend."

Ash had thanked her, and not said a word. She'd received firm instructions from the Palace not to talk to anyone. She wasn't going to do anything that might inflame the situation for Victoria. Even thinking about Victoria, and her stricken face when Ash left on Tuesday, made Ash's soul crumble to dust.

She'd lain in bed at night, tossing and turning, but had decided to press the situation down gently, put it in a box, and put it away. She couldn't speak about it to anyone, so what was the point? If she thought about it too much, she'd come undone. From now until the New Year, Ash was going to focus on football: the league and the Champions League.

Just as she had her whole life.

Her aim was to get through. When the calendar ticked

over, she'd refocus again, this time with eyes on the World Cup. With that in mind, her decision made sense.

On Friday especially, her boots hit the turf with extra force, every tackle fiercer than necessary, every sprint faster than usual. She channelled it all – the hurt, the anger, the heartbreak – into pure physical intensity. Then she stayed late, running drills until her legs burned. After, she hit the gym until her arms shook. Anything to exhaust herself enough that she wouldn't think about Victoria.

When the boss pulled her aside as she left, she expected praise for her dedication.

Instead, she told Ash to take a few days off. "You're suspended after your red anyway, so you're not playing. I don't know what's happening in your private life, but I've learned over the years there's normally no smoke without fire. I think it's best if you take an extended break. You're not coming with us for the game on Sunday, or the next week." Jo's expression softened. "Whatever's going on with you, sort it out. Talk to someone. You're needed around here, but only when you're 100 per cent."

Her flat felt empty when she finally got home. She'd barely closed the door when her phone pinged: another news alert. Before she looked at that, she checked her messages. There was nothing from Victoria. The Palace press secretary who'd called her earlier had told her there was to be no communication at all. No messages, no phone calls. "Just in case they're hacking your phone." It made sense, but it didn't make it any easier. Especially not when their pool table goodbye was on repeat in her head.

Ash clicked on the news alert: *Ashleigh Woods will NOT*

*play against West Ham on Saturday amid royal relationship rumours.* She let out a groan and threw her phone on her sofa, before slumping beside it.

She wasn't playing because of the red card she'd received while trying (and royally failing, the irony) to impress her girlfriend. Ash wanted to email and tell them to get their facts right, but she was pretty sure the Palace wouldn't approve. She couldn't quite believe that her life now needed royal approval for everything.

Her intercom buzzed. She frowned. Then remembered that Marianne had told her to look out for a care parcel after she heard the news of her enforced leave. Ash wasn't sure some bath salts and hot chocolate were going to cure her ills this time.

She pressed the call button. "Yes?"

"Queer Princess fucker!"

At least it was accurate.

Ash pressed her forehead against the wall, too tired to even feel angry anymore. It had been like this all week: shouted slurs, press camping outside, her parents getting hate mail. But there'd been good moments too. Her parents' entire street had formed a human barrier, chasing away photographers with garden hoses, brooms and choice words. Her mum had called, voice thick with pride, describing how Julie from next door had threatened to release her German Shepherds if they didn't clear off. Never mess with Julie.

Telling her mum about the breakup had been harder than expected. "Oh, love," she'd said. "Please tell me this isn't because of us, because of the harassment. It's already dying down, and we can take it. I know how much you liked her."

"It's not," Ash had assured her. "And you're right, I did

like her. A whole lot. But it seems like we're just wrong time, wrong place."

She grabbed her phone and called up her favourite food delivery app. She scrolled through the options. Italian reminded her of Victoria, who loved to cook it. Burgers reminded her of the incredible ones they'd shared in Scotland. Indian? Chinese? She wasn't hungry.

The whisky bottle caught her eye: a birthday gift from her uncle, still unopened. She remembered the King pouring her one in his study, before he ripped her world apart.

Ash had a week off, with nowhere to go. Now seemed as good a time as any.

The intercom buzzed again just as she poured her first glass. She ignored it, but it was insistent.

"Fuck off!" she shouted into it, patience long since gone.

"Charming way to greet your best mate." Cam's voice crackled through the speaker. "Let me up. I've brought curry."

Ash nearly dropped her glass, but did as she was told. When she opened her front door, Cam held up the takeaway, along with a bottle of merlot. "I come bearing gifts."

"But you live three hours away." Ash was still stunned.

"And you've been ignoring my messages, and are clearly in need of a friend." She kissed Ash's cheek, then walked through to her kitchen. She'd been here many times, she knew where she was going. "I can see I'm just in time." She nodded at the whisky on the counter.

"I'm allowed."

"You are. It's just not like you, drinking in season."

Ash knew that was true. She had strict rules.

*Had* being the operative word.

"This is not a normal season."

Minutes later, they sat on Ash's couch, takeout containers spread across her mid-century coffee table. Cam handed her a plate, then started spooning food onto her own. "I'm starving, and traffic was the usual crazy Friday night crush." She glanced at Ash with worried eyes. "I got chicken tikka bhuna, prawn biryani, sag aloo, tarka dhal, rice and a garlic naan. How did I do?"

"Perfect."

"Great." Cam took a mouthful, and nodded. "Not as good as up north, of course, but decent for the south." She grinned. "Eat some food please, then tell me what's going on, red-card girl."

Ash put down her plate, and took a swig of whisky. It burned on the way down, just like her cheeks at the red-card mention.

"I don't know, Cam." Telling her coach was one thing. Telling her best friend was quite another. "Everything just got on top of me and I lost control that weekend."

"I've never seen you play like that. You were reckless. You could have really injured yourself or Sloane. You're lucky you're both okay."

She nodded. "I know." The memory still scared her. "That's why the boss has put me on leave, to get my head together."

"Jo is very wise." She'd been Cam's manager when she played for Sunderland, and Cam had nothing but praise for her.

"But enough about the football. What about the story that's on the front page of every newspaper and website? I never expected to see my best mate's love life all over the news. They were even talking about it on the *Radio Five Live* phone-in today."

Ash closed her eyes. She usually turned off phone-ins, because they always attracted the over-zealous type. "What was the verdict?"

"The usual. Half of them couldn't care less; the rest said you're going to hell, along with everyone involved in the devil's sport that is women's football."

"Good to know."

"But I know you, and I know the truth. At least, some of it. You want to fill me in?"

There was a pressure building in Ash's chest, had been all day, and Cam's gentle concern was making it worse. The whisky wasn't helping like she'd hoped it would, either. Instead, it was loosening everything she'd tried so hard to push down. The words bubbled up, dangerous and honest. All week she'd kept a straight face, pushed through, stayed strong. But here, on her rust-coloured sofa with her oldest friend, she was just plain old Ash.

And Ash was breaking.

"You know what happened. I fell in love with the wrong woman at the wrong time. And vice versa." She drew a deep breath. "We've been ordered by the Palace to cool things off." She put her head in her hands.

"Ordered by the Palace? What are you, in *The Crown*?"

Ash peeked through her fingers. "Not far off. I went with it, because what else could I do? Plus, I've got my career to think about. This season of all seasons, I can't let it all go sideways."

To her horror, tears started falling. In 20 years of friendship, she'd never let Cam see her cry.

"But I just…" Ash took another drink. It tasted all wrong, but she emptied her glass. She sniffed, then took the tissue that Cam wafted under her nose.

"I've never felt like this before. But how fucking stupid am I? Falling for the future Queen? I mean, how was that ever going to go down? Badly, that's how." She blew her nose, then wiped her eyes. "You know what's really pathetic? There was going to be a Ball. An actual fucking ball, like in a fairy tale. I was going as Victoria's date, in a tuxedo. Only real life isn't a fairy tale, it turns out."

She reached for her phone, then put it down. "My head is a mess. I keep hoping for a message from her, but there never is one. It's only been three days. On all the news outlets, sports sites, entertainment pages – in fact, *everywhere* – there are tons of people weighing in with their opinion of us, even though there is no 'us'."

Cam reached over, took Ash's phone, and stuffed it under a cushion. "Lay off your phone. You can't message Victoria, and reading comments on the internet gets you nowhere. You know that."

"I haven't even checked what the women's football community are saying." They always had a lot to say on players' personal lives.

Cam chewed her mouthful before she answered. "You should. That is the one corner of the internet that's super-supportive. They all think it's really cool that Victoria is sleeping with a Royal Raven, obviously."

Ash frowned, then flopped back on the sofa. "I just miss her, Cam. I miss us."

"It'll take time to get over it."

"That's the thing. I don't want to get over it. But there's also no way I can be in it."

"Which means you have to find a way to go around it," Cam told her. "Have you split up?"

Ash shrugged. "Not officially, but kinda. I told Victoria I had to focus on my career and this was a distraction." She winced now at her words.

So did Cam. "How did she take that?"

"We had sex on a pool table." Ash smiled at that memory at least.

"That's one way to try to work things out."

Ash exhaled. "It's just so confusing. I love her, but everyone hates the idea of us. Plus, I have a job to do, and I don't think I can do that and date a princess, too." That was what her rational brain told her. "But then, my heart wants her. Desperately. I can't believe I left and didn't fight more. That's what's been eating me up."

Cam stroked her back. "The Palace told you to back off. What were you meant to do?"

"But what if she's the one, Cam, and I just made a huge mistake? What if time passes, we're both still unhappy, but we can't do anything to change it?"

"Then maybe that's your cue to fight for change."

Ash had backed off at the first sign of trouble. She doubted she'd be able to cope with it ongoing. "People think I 'corrupted' the princess. That's some homophobic shit. Like that's what we do, sit and wait, then pounce on any unsuspecting royal." She paused. "Another one I heard is that I'm part of a socialist plot to destroy the monarchy from within."

"Fuck them," Cam replied. "You're one of the best people

I know, Ash. The way I see it, this is like an injury. It floors you at first, but then you make small changes every day, working towards a larger goal, and eventually, you come back. You're different, forever changed, but sometimes, better than you were in the first place."

Ash knew what Cam said was true. She couldn't control this no matter how much she wanted to. The chips had to land where they fell, whether she liked it or not.

"I know you're right. I just need to focus on my fitness and my football. Try to forget how it feels when she smiles at me. Pretend I'm not in love with someone I can never really have. But I'm still annoyed I can't play or even train for the next week."

"Maybe that's for the best," Cam said. "You've been playing angry."

"I know." Ash closed her eyes. "I miss her so much. Is that mad? It's been less than a week."

Cam pulled her into a hug, and Ash let her. "It's not mad. It's love. The real kind, the kind that hurts because it matters."

Ash buried her face in her friend's shoulder, finally letting herself properly cry. For everything they could have been, for everything they'd never get to be.

# Chapter Thirty

Victoria's heels clicked against the polished floors of the queer homeless centre, the sound echoing off walls covered in rainbow murals and affirmation posters. Her security team hung back at her request, giving her space while maintaining their watchful presence. Inside, the walls hummed with life: music playing softly, a hoot of far-off laughter, the hiss of a pan from the kitchen.

"The kids are all so excited you're here today." That was David, the centre manager, who wore his hair dyed like a rainbow. What would the *Daily Mail* comments section say if she did the same? At least it might stop people commenting that there was no way she could be queer because she had long hair and painted nails.

You could have long hair and painted nails, and also fuck women.

Victoria was living proof.

For the past two months, she'd dragged herself to all her appearances: the mind-numbing dairy-farm tours, the hospital ribbon cuttings, the excruciating FA meetings where everyone pretended not to know about Ash. In contrast, this felt real. Important.

A group of teens huddled near a door, trying to look casual

and failing spectacularly. One girl with close-cropped ginger hair and too-big clothes caught Victoria's eye, then quickly looked away.

Victoria recognised that look: the mixture of hope and wariness that came from too many betrayals. This was why she'd fought so hard for this project. The first of what she hoped would be many centres: safe spaces for kids thrown out for being who they were. Beds, counselling, education, and most importantly, acceptance.

"We're at capacity already," David said softly. "Forty beds, and a waiting list that keeps growing."

Victoria nodded, her throat tight. "Then we'll build more." It wasn't a royal platitude. It was a promise.

A timer buzzed from the kitchen, followed by the smell of something baking. Home smells. The kind of ordinary comfort these kids had been denied.

"Would you like to meet everyone?" David gestured towards the group. "They're nervous, but hopefully they'll open up and tell you their stories."

The main lounge housed a tall Christmas tree in the corner, with a stack of presents already underneath it. Her team had arranged for those to be delivered this week, to ensure that all the young people had a present to open on Christmas Day. She couldn't imagine what it must feel like waking up on December 25th without your family at such a young age.

The teenagers bunched at the door, ready to shake her hand.

"This is Maya, Your Highness." David waved a hand to the young girl who'd caught her eye. Victoria was drawn to redheads, because her brother told her they were usually overlooked. "She's 15, and arrived at the centre yesterday."

Clare Lydon

"Call me Victoria," she told them both.

David blushed. "Victoria."

Maya bowed her head, her ginger hair catching the fluorescent lights. When Victoria shook her hand and sat, Maya's eyes widened with recognition, then narrowed with curiosity.

"You're a real person. I always thought you might be made up," she whispered. "Especially now you've come out as queer?"

Wow, straight in, no messing.

But actually, Victoria found her statement refreshing.

Maya had none of the outrage Victoria had heard whispered around The Devonshire and her wider circle.

"So pleased to see you here, after those vile rumours that did the rounds," Victoria's old school friend Alicia had told her at the club last week, when she turned up with Dexter. "Honestly, people have nothing better to do than sling tawdry allegations that you're sleeping with a *footballer*." She said the final word like it was a disease. "As if that would ever happen."

Another acquaintance told her: "Just so you know, I don't believe a word. Dexter, *maybe*. But you sleeping with a woman? Penalty Princess to Lesbian Princess? I don't think so."

Homophobia and elitism were alive and well in the 21st century.

The rumours had certainly marked out who was actually Victoria's friend, and who was not. Invitations she'd normally receive to festive events had not arrived. It didn't matter she was the heir to the throne. In some of her circles, it mattered who she loved. She was glad she'd found out. Maybe it was time to form some new circles. Maybe Maya could be in one.

That idea made Victoria smile inside. She and Maya had more in common than she thought.

Maybe in another life.

"I didn't know you were queer," Maya continued, her voice barely above a whisper. "It was nice when I heard. It made me feel like you understood."

The familiar denial rose in Victoria's throat. practised, protective, perfect. But looking at Maya, seeing the fresh hurt in her eyes from her parents' rejection, Victoria couldn't bring herself to hide.

Not here.

Not now.

Maya deserved better.

Scrap that, Victoria deserved better.

"I don't tell everyone everything about myself, because as I think you know, not everyone wants to hear it." Victoria picked at her jeans, even though there was nothing on them. She was glad she'd worn them. Tanya had suggested it, to be more relatable. However, perhaps the most relatable fact of all was that she was one of them.

That revelation ripped through her.

*She was one of them.* She was someone having issues living her life because of family expectations. Because she was gay.

"At least you don't have to worry about being homeless."

Victoria's chest tightened.

She was one of them to a point.

"No," she agreed, "but it comes with its own price. And it shouldn't. None of this should happen: not to you, not to anyone." The words felt inadequate against the weight of Maya's experience, against all the hurt in this room.

But as Victoria looked around the other teenagers, it hit her. She *could* do something about it. And if she did, the ripples it created might encourage change. Victoria usually didn't back down from a challenge. Why had she done so with this one?

Outside in the back courtyard, the winter sun cast long shadows across the fresh concrete. Someone had set up makeshift goals using jackets, and a game was forming: chaotic, joyful, free.

"I can't tell you what a difference the centre has made." David put his hands in the pockets of his yellow trousers – David was a colour evangelist – and squinted against the winter sun. It was the shortest day of the year, but the sun was still making the most of it. She'd first spoken to Ash properly on the longest day, back in June. Six months that had changed her life. She wasn't going to brush them all under the carpet.

"Some of these kids were sleeping rough, with nobody to turn to. Now, we're supporting them physically and mentally. You should be really proud of pushing this project into fruition. Without you, the money doesn't appear," he spread his hands, "and these kids don't have anywhere to live. Plus, they're sharing their experiences. They're no longer alone. That's incredible."

Victoria knew that alone feeling well. It had almost suffocated her as she shuffled around her house over the past two months, trying not to visualise Ash drinking a coffee and laughing in her kitchen, or spread naked on her sheets with come-to-bed eyes. Her parents were too caught up, as was Michael, his mission seemingly to party as hard as he could.

"I'm so glad I could do something positive." A stray ball rolled towards her, and without thinking, Victoria trapped it with her foot, the movement smooth and natural.

"You've clearly had extra practice with your girlfriend!" shouted one of the kids, with a grin.

The memory hit Victoria like a punch: Ash at the FA, patient and focused, showing her how to position her body to score a penalty. The warmth of her hands adjusting Victoria's stance, the electricity that had crackled between them.

She took a deep breath and swallowed down threatening tears. This morning had been joyful. She didn't want her personal life to leak all over it, literally.

"Can I use your bathroom before we leave?"

David nodded. "I'll take you to the staff room."

Once inside, knowing this was the only alone-time she'd get today as she had the family carol concert at Westminster Abbey to attend later, she exhaled and tried to compose herself. This visit had been too close to the bone. Too personal. But she was so glad she'd come.

She looked at herself in the mirror, a rainbow sticker in the top-left corner. Maybe that was what her bathroom needed to cheer her up.

A flash of fucking Ash against the bathroom wall flickered in her brain. Quickly followed by them in the bath, promising each other the world. Victoria closed her eyes and inhaled deeply.

Her phone buzzed in her bag.

When she pulled it out, her grandmother's name lit up the screen.

> Darling, how are you? Your mother tells
> me that you and Ash are taking a break.
> I wanted you to know, I liked her very
> much. You were good together.

Her grandmother knew?

> Did you know all along?

The response came quickly, her grandmother's words carrying decades of wisdom.

> Of course, dear. I wasn't born yesterday,
> and you're not the first gay person I've
> ever met. Or is it queer these days?
> I can't keep up. Besides, I know love
> when I see it. It was written all over both
> your faces when you visited.

A single tear rolled down Victoria's cheek as those words struck home.

If her grandmother could accept it, surely her parents and the wider world could, too?

Later, in the royal car with Tanya by her side, Victoria's carefully built walls finally crumbled. Without a word, Tanya steered the driver to a McDonald's drive-through, shouting out Victoria's emergency order: double cheeseburger, fries, chocolate shake. They parked in a far corner of the out-of-town shopping car park, away from curious eyes, the car's tinted windows offering rare privacy.

"I don't know what I'm doing, Tan," Victoria whispered,

stuffing some fries in her mouth with shaking hands. The admission hung in the air, simple and devastating. "Did you get ketchup?"

"Of course." Tanya pulled back the foil top of the tiny ketchup portion and held it for Victoria. Just that small act of kindness made Victoria start crying all over again. "I can't keep living like this. Watching her on TV. Not speaking to her. Carrying on as normal. Pretending I don't love her when I do."

She'd tried to suppress it, but it was no use.

"Then why did you walk away?" Tanya's voice was gentle, free of judgement.

"I didn't." Victoria's voice wavered. "Ash did. After some cajoling by my family. But when do I get to start living? I just wanted to go to the New Year Ball with her on my arm. Like princesses do in the fairy tales. I want my own fairy tale."

An hour later, Victoria was home. Alone.

She heard the front door slam, then footsteps on the wooden floor. When she looked up, Michael stood in the doorway.

"The wanderer returns." She hadn't seen him for over a week. All his "we're in this together" talk had fallen by the wayside when the shit really hit the fan. It wasn't something she was going to forget.

But tonight, there was something different about his appearance. He looked haunted. His tie hung loose, his hair dishevelled. He looked like he hadn't slept in days. He walked over and sat. Then he took her hands, and looked into her eyes. He smelled like he'd taken a bath in IPA.

"I can't do this anymore, Vix. It was me." He ducked his head.

She knew immediately what he meant. She'd probably known since it happened, but she'd been pushing that niggle down, along with so much else. All of it had to stop. It wasn't good for anyone.

However, she was still going to get him to say it.

"What was you?"

"I told the reporter about you and Dex, about you and Ash. I let it slip months ago. I thought they'd forgotten it, but it turned out, they'd been building the story behind the scenes. I'm so sorry. I was drunk, and probably a little jealous, as Astrid made me see. You found Ash, and she was lovely. Even your fake relationship with Dexter was better than anything I've managed. It irked me."

Victoria sat up. "Astrid?"

He ran a hand through his hair. "I've been in Sweden this week. Avoiding you. She collared me and wouldn't stop until I spilled. She convinced me I had to tell you." He held up a hand. "But I would have anyway."

"Would you? Or would you just have kept travelling and getting drunk for the whole of next year?"

"No! I've felt so bad. He asked me directly about it that night I saw you and Dex in the Club. The next morning, I didn't even remember it until I saw the headlines. Then I hated myself. The Palace went into full-on denial mode, you and Ash split up, and I couldn't look you in the eye. I never set out to wreck it for you."

His confession spilled out in a rush. He promised to do better, to be the brother she deserved, his words echoing countless similar promises over the years.

"Words are cheap, Michael. Actions speak far louder.

You said we were in this together, but it turns out, we're not."

However, her anger ebbed away as quick as it hit. She was more disappointed than angry.

"You're an embarrassment to the family. Look at you." She motioned to his trousers, stains on the front. "Sort yourself out before it's too late. Maybe then, somebody will love you. But nobody's going to do that until you love yourself." She raised her chin, defiant. "But you know what? Maybe you did me a favour, gave me time to see what it is I really want. I want Ash. Maybe it's time to fight for her."

When she stood, her brother looked up at her, small. She wasn't in the mood to placate him, tell him everything was okay, that she forgave him.

Because she didn't. She would in time. But not just yet.

In her room, the echoes of Ash were suffocating. Victoria kicked off her slippers, sank into her favourite armchair, and pulled out her phone. She typed out a message to Ash.

> Michael confessed. He leaked it. I hope the press have backed off you and your family. I'm so sorry for everything. I still miss you.

Her thumb hovered over the green button, but then she deleted it, character by character.

Ash had been the one to end it. If they were going to try again, it had to come from her, because she had the most to lose.

Victoria couldn't be the one to make the move.

Even if she desperately wanted to.

# Chapter Thirty-One

The plane cut through grey December skies, leaving London and its ghosts behind. Ash pressed her forehead against the cool window, watching the city shrink until it disappeared beneath the clouds. Beside her, Marianne flipped through a magazine, periodically shooting concerned glances her way. Her agent had suggested this trip to get Ash out of her funk. Ash doubted a few mugs of glühwein were going to cure anything.

Three hours later in Munich, the Christmas market sprawled before them in a sea of twinkling lights and wooden stalls. The air was crisp, carrying the scent of mulled wine and roasted chestnuts. It should have felt magical. Instead, Ash felt hollow, going through the motions. Last week, she'd been given courtside seats at a special USA vs Rest of the World basketball game in London. Not even seeing such peak athleticism up close had raised her spirits.

Her performances on the pitch for the past two months had passed muster, but no more. Some had described her as "mechanical" (that had stung), stripped of the joy that'd always defined her game. Her assists and goals hadn't suffered too much, but her usual football zeal had, and substitutions were commonplace for her now. Speculation ran rampant in the women's football community. Some blamed fatigue, others pointed to the mysterious fallout with Princess Victoria. Ash had perfected her response: "We were friends, working together for the common good of the game." She'd repeated it so often she could say it in her sleep. However, the lie never got easier.

She and Marianne found a quiet corner in a cosy beer hall, away from the tourist crowds. Steaming plates of schnitzel arrived, along with tall glasses of wheat beer. Marianne waited until Ash had taken a few bites before launching her interrogation.

"What's next on your horizon, Ash? You've got through the first half of the season with everything that's happened. Through the latest England camp. But next year, it's the World Cup, and I want a happy, smiling client. As does the country. Something has to give."

Ash pushed potato salad around her plate. "What's there to say? I'm scoring and providing assists, and Gill has assured me that barring injury, I'm going to the World Cup."

"What about how you're feeling?"

The shrug came automatically, a defence mechanism honed over weeks of deflection. But this was Marianne, who'd been there through all of Ash's recent triumphs and low points.

"How I'm feeling doesn't matter. Football comes first. There's no room for anything else. Not this season."

"It's been two months, Ash. You've been miserable. You need to ask yourself: is Victoria something you want to pursue?"

Ash took a long drink of beer, letting the question settle. When she spoke, her voice was barely audible over the cheerful Christmas music. "It doesn't matter." She stabbed at her schnitzel. "I made the decision. I have to stay on track. Being with her was putting me off my game."

"Not being with her is putting you off your game."

Marianne's words hit home.

"I want you to be happy. You're not playing with any love. To get that back on the pitch, you need to sort your heart out off it."

Outside, snow began to fall, dusting the market stalls in white. They finished their meal, then wandered through the crowds, stopping occasionally to admire handcrafted ornaments or sample local treats. Ash bought some gifts for her family even though she wasn't really in the Christmas spirit. The festive atmosphere felt surreal against the weight of their conversation.

"What if it's impossible?" Ash finally asked, voicing the fear that had haunted her since walking away.

Marianne smiled, catching a snowflake on her gloved hand. "I like to say that nothing's impossible if you imagine it. The only thing stopping it working is you."

Later, in her hotel room, Ash scrolled through her phone. The team's WhatsApp group was full of holiday plans: some heading home, others to warm beaches. Nobody mentioned the New Year Ball at the Palace, because nobody else knew about it. Ash had marked it on her calendar the moment Victoria had told her. Maybe she should do what Marianne said: visualise walking in with Victoria, dancing with her on the ballroom floor, cheek to cheek.

It would be a bigger victory than the Champions League games they'd won, putting them top of their group going into the New Year. Even the Ravens' recent league wins brought no joy: they'd succeeded despite her, not because of her.

The winter break stretched ahead, two weeks of freedom from the pitch, from the press, from everything. Christmas with family, then maybe New Year with Cam in Manchester. Anything to avoid thinking about where she really wanted to be.

She opened her camera roll, scrolling back through photos until she found one from earlier. She was stood before a towering Christmas tree in the market, fairy lights reflecting off her hair, a genuine smile on her face for the first time in weeks. Her fingers moved automatically, opening a new message to Victoria.

'All I want for Christmas is you,' she typed, attaching the photo.

Her thumb hovered over the green send arrow, heart pounding. Through the window, Munich glittered beneath a blanket of snow, a Christmas card come to life. Somewhere in London, Victoria was probably preparing for another royal engagement, surrounded by family obligations and expectations.

Ash stared at the unsent message until her screen dimmed. It would be so easy to press send, to take that first step. But what then? Their lives would become a circus.

Was Marianne right? Nothing was impossible if you could imagine it. And Ash could imagine it now: standing proud beside Victoria, no more hiding, no more pretending. Playing football with joy again, her heart full both on and off the pitch.

But she didn't press send. Instead, she locked her phone, set it aside, and lay back, listening to the distant sound of laughter floating up from the bar below.

# Chapter Thirty-Two

The kitchen door swung open as Victoria poured batter into the hot pan. It was Christmas morning, and she'd woken up with a determination to start the day with something that would cheer her up. She'd already told her parents she wasn't going to the service at Westminster Abbey, which they'd accepted without too much fuss. Even they were choosing their battles these days.

Victoria had landed on a cold-water swim to clear her head. It had done half its job. The next step on her plan to cheer herself up was pancakes. They had no connection to Ash, and their chef had brought her back a jar of maple syrup from a recent trip to Canada that was begging to be used. Today was going to be a challenge from start to finish. The least she could do was start it with something she wanted.

Michael stumbled in, wearing jogging bottoms and a Ramones T-shirt that was well loved. At least he'd made it home last night, which was an improvement on recent events. However, his eyes were still bloodshot, a telltale sign he'd been out late last night.

"Good morning and Merry Christmas." Victoria filled the coffee machine with water. She grabbed the jar of coffee and spooned some into the machine, then set it to brew. When she looked up, Michael was sat on one of the island stools. "Is this the new leaf you were talking about?" She waved a hand. "Because from where I'm standing, it looks surprisingly like the old one." She turned back to her pancakes. She was not going to let him ruin her mood.

"Can we call a Christmas Day truce?" Michael said. "Last night was a final hurrah. I am turning over a new leaf. I will be sober at the New Year Ball, and I'm not drinking today, either."

"Do you want a fucking medal?" The words came sharp and quick, cutting through the sizzle of pancake batter. She turned to him. "I'll believe it when I see it."

Her phone lay face-down on the marble counter, and she wasn't going to touch that, either. The only person she wanted to hear from did not want to hear from her.

She'd seen Ash play in the Champions League this week, unable to tear herself away despite knowing how much it would hurt. Her heart had ached watching Ash move across the pitch, her movements so graceful. Victoria had caught herself reaching for the TV screen, wanting to touch Ash through it somehow. To tell her how much she missed her. But she couldn't. The distance between them felt greater than ever.

She flipped the pancake, the first one breaking as it always did. She'd learned this recipe from YouTube videos late at night in her university flat, back when she could pretend to be normal. The muscle memory remained: the right consistency of batter, the heat of the pan, the exact moment to flip. Small victories in a world where so little felt within her control.

"I really am sorry," Michael tried again. "I bought you a Christmas present."

She spun on the ball of her toe, glowering at him. Did he really think he could solve everything with a gift?

"I will be civil to you today, because it's Christmas, and because Gran's here." She poured some more batter into the pan. "I will even give you a pancake as I have enough batter, and I have a stupid need to look after you. I blame my genetics."

He smiled at that.

"But I will not forgive you unless you *do* something to show me that you care. That you've changed. You and I share a life and two parents that nobody else can possibly understand. I needed your support with the biggest challenge of my life, and you made it worse. You can't just say sorry and expect everything to be fine." That had worked in their childhood. But Victoria was sick of always being the one who had to forgive and be the better person. It was the same with her parents, too.

When the machine beeped, Michael poured them both a coffee. She drizzled maple syrup onto their pancakes, watching it pool on the plate. She added a dollop of Greek yoghurt and a handful of berries. It was important to make this breakfast pretty, even though she had nobody to impress but her brother.

They ate at the kitchen island. The pancakes tasted delicious.

"Remember when we were kids, and Mum and Dad laid out all our presents for us in the lounge at Balmoral?"

They'd always spent Christmas up there when she was little. After her grandfather died, her mother had decided they'd spend it in London now and get Gran to come down. She missed the picture-postcard snow of the Highlands.

"I do. Those days seem so long ago. So innocent."

Those were idyllic Christmases, before her mother became Queen, when they had time for family. Maybe she wouldn't go to the New Year Ball this year. What was the point when she'd have to go as arm candy to another man?

Victoria was done pretending. Which was going to make today all sorts of difficult.

\* \* \*

The Palace dining room stretched out beneath glittering chandeliers, the long mahogany table set with the best Meissen china and heavy silver cutlery that had graced royal Christmas dinners for generations. Steam rose from a line of dishes – roast turkey, glazed ham, mountains of roast potatoes, and all the traditional trimmings – but the food remained largely untouched despite the staff's meticulous presentation.

Victoria pushed brussel sprouts around her plate, avoiding her grandmother's shrewd gaze from the head of the table. The Queen Mother sat ramrod straight in her high-backed chair, her perfectly coiffed silver hair framing her face, her triple strand of pearls cool and luminous around her neck.

"I must say," Gran broke the suffocating silence, her Scottish lilt sharper than usual. "If I wanted frost, I would have stayed at Balmoral." She paused, eyeing Michael's untouched wine glass. "And since when do you turn down a prime Bordeaux, dear boy? It's not like you. Last time you came to see me, you put a severe dent in my cellar."

Michael managed a weak smile. "Just not feeling it today, Gran."

Victoria's mother shot Michael a warning look across the

table, while their father became suddenly very interested in cutting his turkey into precisely even pieces.

"No festive cheer at all," Gran continued, picking up her own wine glass. "Victoria skipped church, Michael's not drinking, and everyone's acting like we're at a funeral rather than Christmas dinner." She took a deliberate sip. "One might think something's happened that nobody's telling me about."

The silence that followed was broken only by the soft clink of silverware against china. Victoria could feel the weight of unspoken words pressing down on them all: Michael's guilt, her parents' concern, her own heartache. She caught Michael's eye across the table, saw him open his mouth as if to say something, then think better of it.

"Nothing's happened, Gran," Victoria finally said, her voice steady despite the lie.

"Actually, that's a lie, Gran."

Victoria's eyes widened and she put down her cutlery.

Michael looked around the table, making sure he had everyone's attention before he continued. "I wanted to let you all know that from today, I've decided to live a sober life. Drinking wasn't doing me any good, as you've all told me over and over. From now on," he turned to his father, then his mother. "I'm going to be the son you want and deserve." He eyed Gran. "The grandson, too." Then finally, Victoria. "And the brother, which is long overdue."

Victoria couldn't quite believe he'd declared it in front of everyone.

"I was quite fond of the man you were, dear," Gran told him. "But if not drinking is what you need to do, then good for you. That's one grandchild making a positive change."

She turned to Victoria. "Now, what are we going to do about you?"

"What do you mean, Gran?"

"Yes, Mother. Victoria is fine. Everything has worked out after a sticky situation." The wobble in the Queen's voice betrayed her.

"Really?" Gran put down her cutlery. "I'll need this microwaved if we're having this discussion now. It's delicious, and you know I hate cold dinners."

The Queen tried not to roll her eyes, and Victoria tried not to laugh. She loved her gran for breaking the tension.

"The thing is, I think this is far more than a 'sticky situation'. We have newspapers in Scotland, Cassandra. I have staff and friends that I chat to who look at social media. I understand what's going on more than you think." She turned to Victoria. "The elephant in the room is Ashleigh Woods. I can see you're still upset you're not together. That she's not here."

Butterflies took off in Victoria's chest at the mere mention of Ash's name. She decided to honour them. "Mum and Dad scared her off, then Michael finished the job. I'm doomed to be a spinster forever, it seems. Or take a husband for show. Neither of which are appealing, but apparently that's my royal duty."

"Don't be so dramatic, Victoria," the Queen said. "We've told you that eventually you can be with who you want. But it has to be on a royal timeline, not yours."

"And in the meantime, both Victoria and Ashleigh are heartbroken and miserable?" Her gran wiped her mouth with her napkin. "Also, do you think Ashleigh is going to wait around for your daughter? She might, because she does care for her, but what you're offering is hardly a glittering pot of gold, now is it? Honestly, Cassandra. I thought I brought you up to be a little more caring to your children than that. You begged me to be able to marry Oliver, and I let you. Your daughter is doing exactly the same, and you're shutting her down."

The Queen opened her mouth, then closed it.

There was silence for a few seconds, while everyone weighed up what had been said. Victoria's gaze darted around the table, then settled on her gran. Right at this second, she couldn't have loved her more.

"Gran's right," she said finally, drawing inner strength from somewhere. The pancakes hadn't made her truly happy, so she needed something else to do the work.

Or perhaps *someone*.

"I don't know if Ash will wait for me. I wouldn't blame her if she didn't. But that breaks my heart. You always tell me that things can change later. Well, later is too late for me, Mother."

Victoria stared at the untouched roast potatoes, then pushed her plate aside. What was Ash doing right now? Probably in her parents' kitchen with the lovely oak table, paper crown askew, telling terrible jokes from crackers, laughing with her family.

Was Ash happy? Even if she was missing Victoria, at least she was experiencing a real Christmas. Not here in this suffocating room, navigating Mother's intakes of breath, and Michael's cagey stares.

"Listen to your daughter, Cassandra." Her gran turned to Victoria's dad. "You, too, Oliver. I know I was hard on you when you wanted to get married, but I had to be. I had to know you understood what you were getting into. You can shake up the monarchy if you want to. Times change, and while people will initially be startled, they'll get used to it. Look at Victoria's friend, Astrid. Sweden doesn't bat an eyelid."

"With all due respect, we don't live in Sweden, Mother."

"Then it's your job to shift the country that way. To support your daughter, because eventually your job will be on Victoria's shoulders. Isn't the job hard enough *with* someone by your side, loving you? Don't make it harder for her. Let her bring Ash to the New Year Ball and show their faces to the world."

Victoria took an audible intake of breath. "How do you know about me wanting to go to the Ball with Ash?"

Her gran smiled. "I heard whispered conversations in the halls when you two were at Balmoral. But also, I saw the way you looked at her. Like she was made of gold, like you never wanted to let her go."

How had her grandmother managed to glean all of this from one weekend? Victoria vowed never to sell her short again. But then reality hit.

"I want to come out. That's a given. But Ash does understand what being with me means, and I'm not sure she wants such a poisoned chalice."

Her gran frowned. "Dear girl, you are not a poisoned chalice. You are my incredibly strong and vibrant granddaughter. If Ash intimated that at all, it's because she's scared. Who wouldn't be? But she's a strong woman with bags of charisma, empathy and charm. Also, remember: she'll only play football for another few years. Then she's free to do whatever she wants, which might include being a supportive wife for Victoria, as well as a force for good in the country. She's your match, Victoria. I can feel it. It's time this whole family woke up and saw that, before she slips through our fingers."

# Chapter Thirty-Three

Ash curled up in the corner of her parent's cream sofa, not really watching *The Holiday*. Kate Winslet was falling for Jack Black, but she couldn't focus on the story. The Heroes tub had made several circuits, and Ash had claimed all the Eclairs, their wrappers scattered around her like crime-scene evidence. Her nutritionist would not approve, but she'd given herself three days off over Christmas. She deserved some joy in her life.

The knock at the door was sharp and uninvited. Whoever it was didn't know them, because everybody knew the Woods didn't use their front door.

Her mum frowned, pausing the film.

"Mark!" she shouted, but Ash's dad didn't answer. He was in the den, watching the first Ashes test.

"I'll get it, Mum." Ash jumped up, nerves jangling. She didn't know why, but she had a notion this knock was for her. If the sweary door-knockers were back, she was going to give them a piece of her mind turning up on Boxing Day.

However, when she opened the door, she wasn't prepared for who was on the other side.

Prince Michael, in jeans and a blue jumper. And next to him, the Queen Mother, who looked all sorts of out of place in their parents' street.

"Beatrice!" Ash clamped a hand over her mouth. "I mean, hello again." She sort of bowed, then cringed. She hated the bowing business. It really wasn't her.

"Lovely to see you, too, Ashleigh," the Queen Mother said. "Might we come in?"

Ash stood back. "Of course."

The Queen Mother stood in their living room doorway like it was the most natural thing in the world, black handbag hanging from her arm. Michael hovered behind her shoulder. The older woman was dressed like she was about to go walking in the Highlands, tartan skirt and thick woollen jumper. Her makeup was immaculate, and her grey hair didn't move as she turned her head.

"Oh my goodness, you are not who I expected." Ash's mum scrambled to her feet, picking up the chocolate wrappers from the sofa and scrunching them in her fist. "You must forgive the mess."

"Nonsense." The Queen Mother sat where Ash indicated, in the armchair nearest the door. "It's Boxing Day. Homes should look lived in." She glanced at the TV. "And may I congratulate you on your film choice. One of my favourites of the season, too. Jude Law is just divine, isn't he?"

The paused frame of *The Holiday* showed Jude standing in the cottage kitchen, trying not to cry.

Michael caught Ash's eye as he sat beside his grandmother, giving her a small smile that did nothing to settle the riot in her stomach.

"Would you like a cup of tea, Your Royal Highnesses?" Ash's mum bowed, then took an audible breath and wrung her hands.

But Michael shook his head. "That's very kind, but we

can't stay long. Victoria doesn't know we're here and she'd probably kill us if she did."

"But we felt like we had to do something, and eventually, I persuaded Michael," added Beatrice.

"With that in mind, Victoria's miserable." Michael winced. "Properly miserable. Not eating, barely sleeping. Just sort of... existing."

Ash swallowed hard. She knew exactly how that felt. She waited to see what was coming next.

"And I need to confess something," he continued. "It was me who leaked the story to the press. I don't have a decent excuse." He caught Ash's gaze. "I've told Victoria a million times I'm sorry, but I wanted to tell you, too. I think in the recesses of my drunken brain, I thought it might force my parents' hand. It did, but not in the way I imagined."

Ash closed her eyes. Michael. She knew Victoria had hoped it wasn't. She'd be crushed.

"You're both miserable," the Queen Mother observed, her sharp eyes fixed on Ash. "Where's that smile you wore in Balmoral?"

"With all due respect," Ash said, finding her voice, "it's not that simple. Victoria isn't allowed to come out, and I can't go back to hiding or being the 'close friend' in public." Not that anyone would buy that now. "I'm not standing on the sidelines and watching Victoria on some man's arm." She was very clear on that.

"Did you watch my mother's speech yesterday?" Michael asked.

Ash nodded. She'd watched it three times, searching for hidden meanings in every carefully chosen word.

Clare Lydon

"The theme of change wasn't just plucked from the air," the Queen Mother said. "That was about you. Both of you. Victoria spoke to me yesterday, quite forcefully I might add. And I spent the evening speaking with her parents. Times are changing. The monarchy must change with them, or become irrelevant."

"We're working on a plan," Michael added. "A proper one, with the press office involved. No more hiding. No more arranged dates. It won't be easy, but we'll handle it properly this time."

Ash's heart bloomed, and her mind dared to dream. Could it really all be possible? "What do you want me to do?"

"Come with us now," the Queen Mother said. "There's no time like the present. We can drop you in Kensington. Victoria is there."

Ash glanced down at her grey tracksuit. "Now? But I'm not dressed to go anywhere."

"Then get changed," Michael said. "We'll wait."

They weren't taking no for an answer.

Ash looked to her mum, silently asking a question. Her mum seemed to understand.

"You should go, love," her mum said softly. "You've been going through the motions ever since you split up. If there's a chance to make it work, isn't it worth a shot?"

Ash looked at her mum, then at these unexpected visitors who were offering her a way back to Victoria. Back to happiness, maybe, but this time without the shadows.

If not now, then when? She stood up. "Give me ten minutes. I need to find something suitable to wear to surprise a princess."

The Queen Mother's eyes crinkled with approval. "Take 15, dear. Put a brush through your hair. Some occasions deserve proper consideration. While we wait, maybe your mother can divulge her delicious Yorkshire pudding recipe. Victoria has not stopped raving about it."

\* \* \*

Michael led Ash past the kitchen door, and the taste of Victoria's risotto sprang to her lips. Someone had dressed the hallway since she was last here, with garlands wrapped around banisters, and twinkling lights in every window. The house smelled of pine and woodsmoke.

"She's been in there all day," Michael whispered as they approached the lounge. "Just sitting with a book she's probably not reading, and playing that Taylor Swift album on repeat."

Ash knew precisely the one. Something twisted beneath her breastbone.

"Just to let you know, you've got the house to yourself. I'm getting straight back in the car and going to the Palace for an evening with Gran. Apparently, there's a game of monopoly in my future. You wouldn't believe what a tyrant Gran is at that game." He gave her a soft smile, then pressed the door handle. "Ready?"

Ash nodded, though ready wasn't quite the word.

How could she ever be ready for this?

The door opened silently. Victoria was exactly where Ash had imagined, curled into her oversized armchair, firelight playing across her face. She was wearing silk pyjama bottoms and that ridiculously expensive cashmere jumper Ash had worn on a couple of occasions when she'd stayed. Her hair was loose around her shoulders. A book lay open in her lap, but her eyes were fixed on the window, watching the frost patterns forming on the glass. On the speakers, Taylor was singing about her cardigan.

Victoria looked up at the sound of the door, probably expecting Michael. When she saw Ash, she stood quickly, the book slipping from her lap, landing softly on the carpet.

"What are you doing here?" Her voice was barely a whisper, like she thought she might be dreaming.

"Your grandmother and Michael came to my house. They were very persuasive," Ash told her. "Although if they hadn't come, I might have been brave enough in the New Year. They just sped things up a little."

"Gran went to St Albans?" Victoria's hand flew to her mouth.

Ash nodded. "She did. Sat on my parents' sofa. I don't think I've ever seen my mum so shocked."

"She's terrifying when she wants something." Victoria tucked a strand of hair behind her ear.

How Ash had missed seeing that.

"But I'm glad she did. I've been—"

"Miserable?" Ash supplied. "Yeah, me too."

They stood in silence for a moment, the weight of nearly two months apart hanging between them. Then Victoria moved, closing the distance in quick steps, and Ash met her halfway. The kiss was desperate at first, hands clutching at clothes, trying to eliminate any space between them. Then it softened, became something more like coming home.

When they finally broke apart, Victoria pressed her

forehead against Ash's. "I'm so sorry. I should have fought harder."

"Shhh." Ash kissed her forehead. "I was very clear what I wanted. You respected that. But somehow, even after this long apart, things weren't getting better." She kissed her lips again, and Victoria whimpered as she returned it. When Ash pulled back, she swiped her thumb across Victoria's bottom lip, and they both took a huge intake of breath.

"We both made mistakes. But Michael said there's a plan for you to come out?"

Victoria nodded, leading Ash to the leather sofa near the fire. They sat close, fingers intertwined. "The press office are coming over tomorrow to discuss it. Mother and Father have agreed it has to happen, and Gran convinced them there was no time like the present. I wasn't sure they'd really see it through, but did you see her speech?"

"I did. Your grandmother said it was about us." Ash couldn't help her gaze dropping to Victoria's lips. She wanted to kiss them again, feel them on her skin. She would, but not right now.

"It was." Victoria rubbed her ear. "The key thing about that is she recorded that before my gran arrived. Which makes it mean so much more to me."

Ash's mouth formed an 'O'. "Wow."

The Queen was an intimidating woman, but she clearly cared about her daughter's happiness. That was good to know.

"She talked about change, about tradition bending rather than breaking. About the monarchy evolving." Victoria squeezed Ash's hand, then held her gaze. "I think she might mean it this time." She took a deep breath. "I want to try again, Ash.

Properly this time. No hiding, no pretending we're just friends. But only if you want that."

Ash yearned to say yes to it all. But was that wise? She didn't know. All she did know was that what she wanted was sat right in front of her, asking her to try again. If this was football, she'd agree immediately. Try again, learn from what went wrong last time, make this time a success.

Maybe it really was that simple.

"I've missed you so much, too. I've been a mess. But if we do this—"

Victoria squeezed her hand so tight, she almost cut off her circulation.

"—it has to be on our terms. I'm not letting them push some sanitised version of us into the world. We hold hands. We support each other. We're a couple in public."

"Agreed," Victoria said firmly. "We need to control the narrative from the start. Father was talking about a strategic photo opportunity? Something that shows us exactly as we are?"

"I could use my socials, too. Get my team to help. Marianne will love the challenge. Soft launch us in the New Year."

"Talking of the New Year." Victoria stood, stripped off her jumper, unbuttoned her pyjama top, then straddled Ash, her breasts right in front of Ash's face.

Ash cupped Victoria's breast with her hand, and the touch of Victoria's skin sent an arrow of desire right into her centre.

Victoria leaned down, put a finger under Ash's chin and lifted her gaze to meet her own. "New Year," she whispered, her voice a husk. "Focus." A smile ghosted over her lips before she pressed them to Ash's. When she pulled back, it was by mere inches.

"The New Year Ball." Victoria's eyes were dark with want. "I want you to come with me, as my date. That's going to be our first outing as a couple. It was agreed last night. Now we just have to break it to everyone else." She ran a fingertip down Ash's cheek. "What do you think? Will you be my Prince Charming?"

"I would love to be your Prince Charming." Ash cupped the back of Victoria's head, and brought her down into a bruising kiss.

This kiss was different: heated, purposeful. Ash's hands found their way to the soft skin of Victoria's back, and then Victoria stood up and shook off her pyjama bottoms, before pressing her lips back to Ash.

"Fuck me, please," she said, all royal protocols out the window. "It's been two months of wanting you every day, and I can't wait. We can take it slow all night long if you like, but right now." She straddled Ash once more, grabbed her hand, and guided Ash to her very core.

"Just there." Victoria's breath was hot in Ash's ear as her head slumped forward.

"You're so wet," Ash whispered, knowing she was, too, but this wasn't about her. Right now, she had to show Victoria how much she'd missed her.

Ash slid her fingers inside Victoria, and ever so slowly, began to fuck her. As she did, she had a moment of wonder. A big part of her had thought she'd never be in this position again. Making love to the woman she loved. But as Victoria ground her hips into Ash's lap, gratitude rose up high inside Ash. Forces had tried to pull them apart, but this moment showed her they were meant to be together. She was put on this earth to make Victoria tremble against her, to make her eyes blaze with desire. This time, she was going to hold on tight, no matter what life threw at them.

Victoria's hands grasped Ash's shoulders, her nails biting into the fabric of Ash's shirt as she rode her fingers. Ash's mouth watered with the need to taste Victoria's skin, but she focused on the task at hand, her fingers moving in a slow, deliberate rhythm that made Victoria groan and shake.

Ash didn't think she'd ever seen her look more beautiful than right at this moment.

She wasn't the heir to the throne. She was simply, Victoria.

The room around them melted away, leaving only the sensation of their bodies moving in tandem. Ash's fingers curled slightly, finding that spot that made Victoria gasp and arch her back. The sight of her, so open and trusting, sent a thick pulse of yearning through Ash, a reminder of why she was here, why she'd come back.

As the tension built, Victoria's breathing quickened, her body coiling like a spring. Ash's thumb brushed against her clit, and she felt the shiver run through Victoria, the spark that ignited the flame. Victoria's hips jerked, then her body stilled before her orgasm ripped through her. Ash held her close, her fingers still moving, drawing out the pleasure as Victoria's cry echoed through the room. Damn, she'd missed the sound of Victoria in full flow.

As the aftershocks subsided, Ash's fingers slowed, her touch gentle as she stroked Victoria's sensitive skin. Victoria's head fell forward, her forehead pressed against Ash's shoulder, her body vibrating with the aftermath. Ash withdrew her fingers, then wrapped her arms around Victoria, holding her close as they sat there, the only sound the gentle crackling of the fire and Taylor Swift still serenading them.

Victoria eventually righted herself, her cheeks flushed, a satisfied smile on her face. "I will never listen to this song in the same way again."

\* \* \*

Later, tangled in Victoria's cotton sheets after they made it to bed, Victoria traced lazy patterns on Ash's stomach. "These endless weeks have been hell," she said. "I never want to lose you again."

"Agreed. It's going to be a car crash though, isn't it?" But whatever happened, now they both truly knew what they wanted, she could cope. "Do you think we'll be the subject of countless radio phone-ins again, debating the rights of queer people?"

"I don't doubt it." Victoria pressed a kiss to Ash's shoulder. "But we'll be ready. The press office will have a plan, as will your team. Security will be increased for both of us and our families. Plus, this time, nobody's being blindsided. We're leading the story."

Ash put her hand over her eyes. "Dammit, my mum's going to need media training. Ask her a question, and she might divulge all our secrets."

"She can tell the world I love her Yorkshires, and then give everyone the recipe. When you think about it, we're doing a public service." Victoria grinned. "But honestly? Let them talk. Let them write their headlines and make their commentary. We're not the first royal couple to face scrutiny, and we won't be the last."

"Royal couple?" Ash raised an eyebrow. "Am I actually part of a royal couple?" It still sometimes took her by surprise.

Victoria propped herself up on an elbow, suddenly serious. "You are, Ashleigh Woods. I want to build something real with you, something that lasts. Whatever we have to face, I want to face it together. For real this time." She paused, her eyes glassy. "I love you, Ash."

The rush of love she got for Victoria took her breath away. She pulled her in for a soft kiss. "I love you, too. And yes, we'll face it together. But first, can we just stay here for a bit? Just us, before the whole world gets involved? For the next, I don't know, five years?"

"Five years sounds good," Victoria agreed, settling against her. "Just us, and our favourite Deliveroo driver seeing us through." She kissed Ash's breast, before looking up. "Though fair warning: Gran will probably arrive before lunch tomorrow to discuss wardrobe options for the Ball."

"The Queen Mother is coming for lunch?"

"She never misses a chance to meddle in my love life. Speaking of which…" Victoria's hand wandered to Ash's thighs. "We should probably make the most of our privacy while we have it."

Ash rolled them over, pinning Victoria beneath her. "Now that's the kind of royal directive I'm happy to follow."

# Chapter Thirty-Four

The quiet of the dressing room did nothing to calm the riot of butterflies in Victoria's stomach as she prepared for their first public appearance together at the New Year Ball. At least her dress wasn't going to let her down, a masterpiece in midnight blue silk, so deep it appeared black until she moved. It hugged her figure with a sweetheart neckline, while delicate beading traced patterns like scattered stars across the silk. From the fitted waist, the skirt fell in clean, architectural lines. On her wrist, she wore her grandmother's diamond bracelet, donated for the evening.

Victoria popped her head around the door, into the bedroom. "Come help with my zip?"

When Ash stepped into the dressing room, Victoria's breath caught. The tuxedo fitted her girlfriend perfectly, the crisp lines accentuating her slim curves. The way Ash's eyes darkened, then softened as she stared at Victoria made her knees weak. But she didn't have time for anything weak tonight. Strength was the order of the day.

Ash zipped her up, kissed her neck, then they stood side by side, smiling at each other in the full-length mirror. Even though she was nervous, Victoria couldn't remember ever feeling so beautiful, so complete.

Ash linked their fingers softly and smiled. "You look beautiful. You are going to wow the room, like always."

"And you look like Prince Charming," Victoria replied, her voice the definition of swoon. "Luke did a fine job with your tux. But it's the model who makes it."

Ash kissed her hand. "Are you ready for this? It's the big one."

"The night I've been building up to my whole life?" Victoria smoothed invisible wrinkles from Ash's lapel. "I've been ready since I was six." She squeezed her hand. "For the record, there's nobody else I'd rather have by my side."

The walk to the ballroom felt like floating. Victoria's hand trembled in Ash's as they waited for their cue. Michael arrived looking dapper but pensive with Gran on his arm. Her parents joined them, and her father's questioning look – "ready?" – followed by a thumbs-up nearly undid Victoria's composure. But she took a deep breath.

She had to do this.

She *wanted* to do this.

The ballroom doors opened. Hundreds of lights sparkled overhead, faces turned towards them.

For a moment, it was too much.

The enormity of what they were doing, who they were, what this meant crashed over Victoria in a wave. Her stomach lurched, and she thought she might actually be sick. But then Ash's thumb stroked her hand, grounding her.

"Breathe, darling," Gran murmured, squeezing her arm as she passed. "This is all training for the years to come." The knowing look in her grandmother's eyes helped steady her nerves.

Then, just like that, Victoria and Ash walked in together, hand in hand. The world did not collapse, just like Astrid promised, and the Ball carried on around them. With this one step, Victoria had finally stopped apologising for who she was, and it was glorious.

Maybe this wouldn't be so bad, after all.

Marianne appeared with her wife, champagne in hand and mischief in her eyes. "Well, well, if it isn't the happy couple. Finally decided to grace us common folk with your presence?" Victoria had met Marianne before, and liked her instantly. Her familiar teasing made them both smile, breaking some of the tension coiled in her chest.

"How you feeling, woman of the moment?" Marianne asked Ash.

"Like I know what goldfish feel like." She grinned at Victoria. "But also like there's no place I'd rather be."

"I'm beyond proud of you both," Marianne said. "This will make your life easier in the long run. You're also paving the way for so many others."

Ash's parents approached next, elegant and clearly impressed.

Marianne greeted them like old friends: "You fit in like a glove here, Debra. I always said you were destined for greatness."

Ash's mum blushed, smacking Marianne's arm playfully. "You are 99 per cent charm, and I am always here for it." She paused, addressing Victoria. "Compliments to your chef, by the way. Those tiny potatoes with salmon are to die for. And I could so get used to the champagne."

Ash's dad raised his glass. "Here's to a year of possibility."

Behind Victoria's family, Ash's best friend Cam and her now very-much-on girlfriend Hayley appeared. Cam gave Victoria a shy smile as she greeted them. She didn't know them that well yet, but the pair were coming to her place for dinner tomorrow. Victoria was very much looking forward to finally getting to know Ash's friends.

At that moment, her grandmother arrived, still carrying her trusty handbag. She never went anywhere without one. "Debra! You must be Mark." She hugged Ash's mum, then shook her dad's hand. "So lovely to see you again. This time, in far happier circumstances."

Victoria's heart swelled. This was what she'd wanted: her and Ash's worlds merging, acceptance flowing both ways.

They drifted, talking to a variety of guests who all appeared to take her and Ash in their stride. Half an hour later, Dexter and Sidney arrived with Astrid and Sofia, and Victoria struggled to hold it together. Getting on that plane to Marbella six months ago, she'd felt hopeless, lost. She knew Dexter had, too. Now, they were both on the brink of living their best lives.

"Who would have thought this day would come?" Dexter asked, grabbing a fresh flute of champagne from a passing waiter. It truly was his superpower.

Victoria noticed Dexter's parents in the corner, looking less stern than usual. Progress, maybe.

Astrid pulled her close, kissing her cheek. "I hope you know you've got all the support in the room, all the love," she whispered. "I'm so glad you came to your senses and realised she was worth it."

To her right, Ash laughed at something David from the

homeless charity was saying. Victoria loved how naturally she slotted into her world.

Ash was beyond worth it.

When her father asked Victoria to dance, she made sure Ash was okay, then accepted. He'd had his hair cut today, and his Royal Navy uniform always made him look like he was from a fairytale. He kissed Victoria's cheek and pulled her close.

"Holding up okay?"

Victoria nodded. "Nobody's tried to lance me yet." She spied Ash, laughing with Astrid and Sofia. She relaxed a little. Her father followed her line of sight. "I'm sorry for coming on strong with Ash. I could have handled it better. But also, it's better to see if she scares easily. Just like your grandparents did with me. Apparently, she doesn't, which means we have a lot in common."

"If she's half the support you are to Mother, I'm a lucky woman," she told him.

Gran's dance with Victoria was shorter but no less meaningful. "You've got a good one there, so don't scare her away. I'll do my best to make sure your parents behave." Her gran glanced to Ash, who was now dancing with Dexter. Victoria's past and present worlds colliding. "I think she knows you're precious cargo, our future queen."

Victoria squirmed in the way she always did when people talked about a world where her mother was dead. She'd always found it strange, and doubted that would ever change.

Michael's approach made Victoria tense briefly, but his apology was sincere.

"You can stop apologising now," she told him. "It's water under the bridge. Granted, I wanted to push you off said bridge, into the river and hold you down when I found out, but in a weird way, you probably helped." All the obstacles had crystallised what they both truly wanted. Michael definitely sped that process up.

The evening was perfect, but something was missing. Victoria had danced with Michael, her gran, and her father, but not with the one person she wanted most. She crossed the ballroom to where Ash stood with her family, aware of eyes on her, but no longer caring.

This was their moment, their triumph, their love on display for all to see. She held out her hand to Ash, drinking in the smile that was only ever for her. "I'm sorry to interrupt, but may I have this dance?"

Ash's eyes sparkled. "I thought you'd never ask."

\* \* \*

Dexter snapped a series of photos of Victoria and Ash, champagne glasses raised, living their best lives against the backdrop of gilt and crystal. Then he handed Victoria her phone, and kissed her cheek.

"Good luck, ladies. A whole new world awaits."

Victoria took a deep breath, excitement and anxiety swirling within like fireworks lighting up a New Year sky. The vibrant colours of the filter she added heightened the warmth in Ash's eyes. They both knew the significance of this moment. It wasn't just an announcement; it was a declaration of their love, a celebration of their truth. She was in love with a woman, and she was allowed to share it. Everyone else took it for granted, but to her, this was as big as it got.

As her finger hovered over the send button, the world outside faded, leaving just the two of them in their own bubble of happiness. Victoria's heart raced, each beat echoing the weight of their decision. She thought of all the whispered doubts and the nights spent wondering if love was truly enough to conquer the fears that held her back.

"Those kids at the centre." Victoria thought back to their faces. "Seeing them and hearing their stories changed everything for me. It made me realise that hiding who I am was nothing compared to their daily struggles. If I can use my voice to make real change, I will. I owe it to them, and all the kids like them." She took a deep breath. "Are you happy?"

Ash smiled, a reassuring nod that sent a jolt of courage through Victoria. "I couldn't be happier." She peered at the shot again. "The photo's gorgeous because you're in it. Plus, we both look hot, so that's going to piss off the homophobes, too." She pulled back her shoulders and stood up straight. "Send it, and let's get the word out." She grinned. "Let everyone know that princess has officially got a bae."

Victoria pressed send, and her world subtly shifted.

They weren't just stepping into the light; rather, they were dancing in it.

Within minutes, Ash's social team and the Palace's team had it live on both their accounts, using the same simple caption: 'HNY from us both. xxx'. The likes climbed astronomically before Victoria tucked her phone away, her heart stampeding behind her ribs.

The deed was done, there was no turning back. They'd appeared together at the ball. Now, they were officially a couple in the outside world, too. Her smile was as wide as the Palace as she realised what she'd done. Shed years of heartache and worry with the click of a button.

Freedom and joy sashayed through her veins.

"Come with me," she whispered to Ash, taking her hand and fleeing the ballroom. She led her past the red ropes and security, through to the centre room, and finally out the French doors onto the royal balcony. The winter air bit at their skin, but Victoria didn't care. Below them, London sparkled, a carpet of lights stretching to the horizon. There were crowds milling on the mall, ready for the New Year fireworks. Victoria made sure they stuck to the back wall and remained low where they couldn't be seen from the front of the Palace.

"Wow, you could have warned me where we were going." Ash crouched low, taking it all in. "I've seen this on the telly, but being here is something else altogether." She paused. "It reminds me of another balcony," she continued, glancing at Victoria. "Though considerably grander than the one in Marbella."

"That feels like a lifetime ago. Me, terrified of being seen, and you were the opposite. You were fearless. And you gave me beer. Nobody had ever done that before."

"I like to be unique." Ash squeezed her hand. "But I was hardly fearless. I met a princess, I was terrified. Still am, sometimes." She gestured to the view before them. "This might be real one day. Us two, up here. You'll be queen, and I'll be…" she trailed off, colour rising in her cheeks.

"My queen," Victoria finished, turning to face her. "You already are." She desperately wanted to kiss her now. But if she did it on this balcony and it was snapped, her mother would never forgive her. "Shall we go back to the ball? I think it's nearly midnight."

Excitement filled the air as they rejoined the throng in

the ballroom, Victoria grabbing two flutes of champagne. Thankfully, they hadn't been missed.

Moments later, the countdown began.

"Ten! Nine! Eight!"

Victoria looked around at the gathering: her family, the staff, friends old and new. Everyone who had supported them, challenged them, helped them reach this moment.

"Seven! Six! Five!"

She caught her grandmother's eye across the room. The Queen Mother gave her a subtle nod, eyes twinkling.

"Four! Three!"

Ash's fingers found hers, warm and steady.

"Two! One! Happy New Year!"

The room erupted in celebration, couples embracing all around them. Victoria felt the familiar flutter of uncertainty: what were the protocols for this moment? But then she met Ash's eyes, and everything else fell away. The protocols, the fears, the doubts: none of it mattered.

There, in the middle of the dancefloor, Victoria reached for Ash. Their lips met in a dizzying kiss that felt like flying, like freedom, like every New Year's wish coming true at once. Just like two people madly in love.

When she pulled back, happiness lit every inch of her, and Ash's smile was brighter than all the chandeliers combined. "Happy New Year, Victoria Richmond."

Victoria touched her forehead to Ash's, breathing in the moment, wanting to remember every detail: the warmth of Ash's skin, the lingering taste of champagne, the soft music playing in the background, the feeling of absolute rightness settling in her chest.

Clare Lydon

"Happy New Year, Ashleigh Woods," she replied. "I have a feeling it's going to be the most incredible year of our lives."

And standing there, in the arms of the woman she loved, Victoria knew it wasn't just a feeling.

It was a promise.

# Epilogue

*Seven Months Later*

Ash pressed her forehead against the cool glass of the coach window, staring as the roads around Wembley, transformed into a river of red and white. Her headphones provided a barrier between her and the mounting tension in the bus, the constant chatter of her teammates giving way to pre-match nerves.

She needed a distraction, and a football podcast hosted by her old teammate was the perfect solution. Because today wasn't just any match. Today was the World Cup final. England had stuttered through the group stages, exploded through the knockouts, and today was the final that everyone wanted: England versus the USA.

"What a rollercoaster it's been for Ashleigh Woods especially." Dina Thompson's familiar voice crackled through Ash's headphones. She'd retired just as Ash had broken into the senior team, but Ash had always appreciated her help and advice. "That promising start to the season after her injury comeback, then those difficult autumn months when speculation about her personal life overshadowed everything else. The press camped outside her house, following her to training: it clearly affected her game. She wasn't the Woods we know."

Ash nodded. Dina wasn't wrong.

"But since January?" US pundit Sally Chen's voice held a note of admiration. "Since she and Princess Victoria went public at New Year, we've seen a completely different player. Fifteen goals in half a season, leading the Royal Ravens to the league title. Yes, there was heartbreak in the FA Cup final with those penalties, but Woods is playing with freedom again. That weight has lifted."

"That's what happens when you can focus on the football, isn't it?" Dina replied. "When the photographers are actually there to capture your goals rather than trying to catch you meeting your girlfriend in secret."

"And speaking of Princess Victoria: she'll be there today, watching her partner lead out England at Wembley. If the Lionesses win, she'll be presenting the trophy herself. You couldn't write it, could you?"

Dina laughed. "Ash has already lost one cup final at Wembley this season, Sally. I know her well enough to say she won't want to make it two. Ninety thousand people in the stadium, millions watching worldwide: are we about to witness something special?"

"This Lionesses team has unfinished business, Dina. They're ready to write their names into history."

A vice-like grip on Ash's arm yanked her back to the moment. She pulled out her headphones at Cam's insistence, and the wall of noise hit her immediately. Her best mate's eyes glittered with excitement.

"Listen to that!" Cam shouted over the din as the bus turned into the stadium complex. "It's never been like this before. Look at the crowd, the noise!"

Nat Tyler's face appeared over the seat in front, her usual pre-match jitters evident. But Ash knew that once the whistle blew, their flying forward would purr into life.

"Let's give them something to really scream about later, yeah?" Sasha put an arm around Cam, her grin infectious. "Are we ready to win this?"

Ash beamed at her teammates. This was their time.

"One hundred per cent," she replied. "Let's go finish the job we started, shall we?"

\* \* \*

The noise as Ash led the team onto the pitch was honestly deafening. She'd never heard anything like it, not even at the FA Cup Final. The wall of sound hit her like a physical force, making her invincible. Which is exactly how she wanted to feel on World Cup Final day. As her studs sank into the Wembley turf and she squinted up into the afternoon sun, 90,000 voices made every hair on her body stand on end. The training. The sacrifice. The commitment. It was all leading up to this moment.

The national anthems played, and Ash sang every word, her voice strong and clear. She kept her gaze fixed ahead, knowing if she looked for Victoria and the King in the crowd, she might crack. In previous years, she'd sung these words without thinking. Now, she sang them knowing that one day, they'd be about the woman she loved. The woman she wanted to make her wife. Victoria didn't know that yet. There was plenty of time.

Pendants exchanged, handshakes, the coin toss went their way, and the whistle blew.

Ninety minutes to make history. Victoria had messaged earlier.

> Bring that trophy home, darling. Do it in regular time to save my heart, please. I cannot take the stress of penalties. We'll have our own extra time at home later.

She couldn't disappoint her future Queen, could she?

The first half was tense, both sides probing for weaknesses. Cam made two crucial saves, including a spectacular tip onto the crossbar, while Nat nearly broke the deadlock with a thunderous drive that just missed. But Ash hadn't found her moment yet.

At half-time, the dressing room was quiet.

Ash had to show leadership. If they were going to be triumphant, they had to do more. They had to play with passion, and with purpose.

"Listen up!" The group hushed, ready for her words. Ash clenched her calves before she spoke.

"We've got 45 minutes to win this. This crowd deserves it, and we deserve it. Yes, there's pressure, but pressure is a privilege. It means we can affect the outcome of this situation. It means we can make change, and history. Let's get out there and show them why we're the best goddamn team in the world. I'm not leaving here without a winner's medal around my neck."

Roars from the team, and Ash stood by the door, giving every team member a high five and a "Let's fucking go!" as they left for the pitch.

She had to hope they were ready, that she shifted the energy.

The first ten minutes, the Lionesses had a couple of half-chances. One fell to Ash, and she skied it. Groans from the crowd. She calmed her breathing, got up, dusted herself down, and got ready to go again.

The pressure mounted in her head, but she breathed deep. The USA were the favourites, but England were the home team. That evened everything out. One goal could win this, she was well aware. If anybody was going to score it, it was going to be the Lionesses.

Sixty-seven minutes in, the chance appeared. Sasha won the ball in midfield with a crunching tackle – her bread and butter – and Nat was off like lightning down the right. Ash made a run into the centre of the box, losing her marker with a sharp cut inside. Nat's cross was perfect, floating between their centre-backs, one of whom mistimed her jump. That was all Ash needed.

Time seemed to slow as Ash rose, and hung in the air. The ball met her forehead sweetly. The cross had so much whip, it didn't need power. Ash just had to guide it towards goal.

She knew before it left her head this was the moment. That it was in. Sometimes you just do.

When the ball eventually sailed past their keeper and the net rippled, every fibre of Ash's body yelled.

Wembley erupted in a sea of pure joy.

Ash ran before she could think, sliding on her knees towards the corner flag. She pulled up, faced the nearest camera, held out her palm and blew a kiss down its lens. Then she turned, finding that spot in the royal box, and pressed her hand to her heart. Even from this distance, she could see Victoria's arms above her head. Beside her, the King was on his feet, punching the air.

As her teammates reached her to celebrate, Ash threw back her head and roared to the sky.

She'd only gone and done it.

\* \* \*

When the final whistle pierced the air, Ash's legs gave out. She dropped to her knees, hands covering her face, as relief and pride overwhelmed her. Then Cam's familiar weight crashed into her, the goalkeeper's scream of jubilation shrill in her ear, followed by Nat's smaller frame, then Sasha. The sweetest bundle of limbs and tears and joy she'd ever been part of.

"We fucking did it!" Sasha's voice cracked as she spoke. Ash could only grin through her tears. When she was little, and she'd written to her football idol, Heidi Moore, to ask for an autograph. Heidi had written back and told Ash to dream big.

Ash's biggest dream had just come true.

Everything she'd worked for, everything she'd ever dreamed of had finally happened. She'd won the World Cup, and the love of her life was waiting for her pitch side. She didn't think she'd experienced a more perfect moment.

Everything else was just noise.

Sloane Patterson, the US captain, was one of the first to reach her after she'd untangled herself. Her handshake was firm, genuine.

"Helluva game, Woods. You deserved it."

"Thanks," Ash replied, touched by Sloane's sporting actions. "Ella will be unbearable, won't she?"

Sloane laughed through her obvious disappointment. "My wife's going to be impossibly smug about her homeland winning. But at least one of us will be happy tonight."

A TV crew walked towards Ash, and Sloane left her to it.

Dina Thompson in the flesh. She hugged Ash hard before she started the interview.

"Ashleigh Woods, scorer of the winning goal in a very tight World Cup Final. How are you feeling?"

Ash shook her head. "Just incredible," she shouted, hardly able to hear herself over the noise of the crowd. "But we did this for every little girl in the country who's told she can't play football. We did it for the generations before us who struggled to play. We hope we've shown that football is for everyone."

She looked up into the royal box, which was now empty. Which must mean that the trophy presentation was due. Ash glanced to her left, where Victoria and her father were stood beside the presentation platform in the middle of the pitch. Meanwhile, 'Sweet Caroline' played over the sound system, which got the entire stadium singing. Ash shook her head, goosebumps covering her body, and drank it all in.

The USA went first, collecting their medals with speed, looking like they'd rather be anywhere else but here.

Then it was the Lionesses' turn.

How many steps to this medal? It was 20 to collect her MBE, maybe slightly less today.

Ash waited at the side of the presentation platform, her face neutral. She had to keep it together, even though her heart was doing somersaults in her chest. She glanced ahead, where her teammates shook hands with dignitaries and beamed. At the end of the line, Victoria maintained her perfect composure as she started to drape medals around necks, shook hands, offered congratulations.

Fifteen steps. First, Ash shook the hand of the FIFA Women's president, who was a great advocate for the women's game. Ash thanked her for her work.

Twelve steps. Another dignitary. This time, bald. Ahead, Victoria placed a medal around Nat's neck with practised grace, her words of congratulations and smile genuine.

Seven steps. The UEFA president's handshake. Ash nodded at something he said, but he was not the main prize. Along the line, Victoria presented Cam's medal, and whispered something in her ear that made Cam roar with laughter. Ash was a little jealous.

Five steps. Simon from the FA shook her hand with gusto. Ash beamed at him, then took a deep breath. The cameras were on her. She was nearly there.

Three steps. Victoria maintained her perfect poise, the consummate professional even as Sasha bounced excitedly as she received her medal.

Two steps. The King shook her hand. "I never doubted you for a moment. Huge congratulations. I'll give you a proper hug later."

"Thank you, Sir."

One step. Finally, she faced Victoria.

Their eyes met, and for a heartbeat, the princess's composure wavered ever so slightly. Her hands were steady as she draped the medal around Ash's neck, but her whispered words were just for them: "I love pinning medals on you. This one, most of all." She pulled back. "I was right about you the first time, you know."

Ash furrowed her brow. "About what, Ma'am?"

Victoria's eyes sparkled and her mouth curled into a

smile. Then she leaned forward once more. "Extraordinary composure under pressure."

A year ago, their first touch had sparked something neither could have predicted. That nervous footballer meeting a princess and wondering how this could possibly work seemed like a million years ago. With a World Cup winners' medal around her neck, Ash had come full circle.

Now, the roar of 90,000 voices wrapped around them like a blanket, with banners of support for them both, and their love. The football community had embraced them, and slowly but surely, so was the wider world. This was more than just a medal ceremony. This was every dream Ash ever had crystallising into one perfect moment: sporting glory, personal joy, and the love of her life all intertwined beneath the Wembley arch.

Later, there would be celebrations and champagne, headlines and history books. There would be quiet moments in palace gardens and loud family dinners, royal protocols and football practice. There would be a different ceremony, with different goals and promises.

But right now, with confetti falling like snow and her team's jubilant screams filling the air, Ash Woods stood at the pinnacle of her professional career, received her greatest honour from the woman who held her heart, and knew with absolute certainty that some dreams really did come true. The little girl who'd kicked a ball against her garden wall would never have believed this happy ending.

Then again, this wasn't really an ending at all.

It was just the beginning.

THE END

*Want more from me? Sign up to join my VIP Readers'*
*Group and get a FREE lesbian romance,*
**It Had To Be You!** *Claim your free book here:*
*www.clarelydon.co.uk/it-had-to-be-you*

# Would You Leave Me A Review?

 I hope you enjoyed this royal romance that proves we all deserve a queen! If the answer's yes, I wonder if you'd consider leaving me a review wherever you bought it. Just a line or two is fine, and could really make the difference for someone else when they're wondering whether or not to take a chance on me and my writing. If you enjoyed the book and tell them why, it's possible your words will make them click the buy button, too! Just hop on over to wherever you bought this book – Amazon, Apple Books, Kobo, Bella Books, Barnes & Noble or any of the other digital outlets – and say what's in your heart. I always appreciate honest reviews.

Thank you, you're the best.

Love,
Clare x

# Also By Clare Lydon

## Other Novels
A Taste Of Love
Before You Say I Do
Change Of Heart
Christmas In Mistletoe
Don't Marry Me At Christmas
Hotshot
It Started With A Kiss
Just Kiss Her
Nothing To Lose: A Lesbian Romance
Once Upon A Princess
One Golden Summer
The Christmas Catch
The Long Weekend
Twice In A Lifetime
You're My Kind

## London Romance Series
London Calling (Book One)
This London Love (Book Two)
A Girl Called London (Book Three)
The London Of Us (Book Four)
London, Actually (Book Five)
Made In London (Book Six)
Hot London Nights (Book Seven)
Big London Dreams (Book Eight)
London Ever After (Book Nine)

## All I Want Series
Two novels and four novellas chart the course
of one relationship over two years.

Get great bundle deals and other offers when you
buy direct at clarelydon.shop!

Made in the USA
Middletown, DE
27 May 2025